FRANKLIN PARK PUBLIC LIBRARY

3 1316 00460 5260

W9-AYA-517

FRANKLIN PARK PUBLIC LIBRARY
FRANKLIN PARK, IL.

Each borrower is held responsible for all library
material drawn on his card and for fines accruing on
the same. No material will be issued until such fine
has been paid.

All injuries to library material beyond reasonable
wear and all losses shall be made good to the
satisfaction of the Librarian.

Replacement costs will be
billed after 42 days overdue.

NORTH CAROLINA
STATE LIBRARY
RALEIGH

MY BEIJING

Four Stories of Everyday Wonder

NIE JUN

Translated by **EDWARD GAUVIN**

**FRANKLIN PARK
PUBLIC LIBRARY DISTRICT**
10311 GRAND AVENUE
FRANKLIN PARK, IL 60131

Graphic Universe™ • Minneapolis

THANKS TO MR. WANGNING, MANAGING DIRECTOR OF BEIJING
TOTAL VISION, NICOLAS GRIVEL, AND MY WIFE, GE JING
—NIE JUN

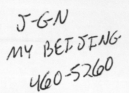

Story and illustrations by Nie Jun
Translation by Edward Gauvin

First American edition published in 2018 by Graphic Universe™

Copyright © 2016 by Nie Jun and Gallimard Jeunesse. Published by arrangement with Sylvain
Coissard Agency.

Graphic Universe™ is a trademark of Lerner Publishing Group, Inc.

All US rights reserved. No part of this book may be reproduced, stored in a retrieval system, or
transmitted in any form or by any means—electronic, mechanical, photocopying, recording, or
otherwise—without the prior written permission of Lerner Publishing Group, Inc., except for the
inclusion of brief quotations in an acknowledged review.

Graphic Universe™
A division of Lerner Publishing Group, Inc.
241 First Avenue North
Minneapolis, MN 55401 USA

For reading levels and more information, look up this title at www.lernerbooks.com.

Photo on page 123: Rolf_52/Getty Images.
Title font: Anastasia Sergeeva/Shutterstock.com.

Main body text set in Andy Std 11/11.5. Typeface provided by Monotype Typography.

Library of Congress Cataloging-in-Publication Data

The Cataloging-in-Publication Data for My Beijing: Four Stories of Everyday Wonder is on file at the
Library of Congress.
ISBN 978-1-5124-4590-9 (lib. bdg.)
ISBN 978-1-5415-2642-6 (pbk.)
ISBN 978-1-5124-9859-2 (eb pdf)

LC record available at https://lccn.loc.gov/2017055276

Manufactured in the United States of America
1-42520-26196-2/6/2018

YU'ER'S DREAM

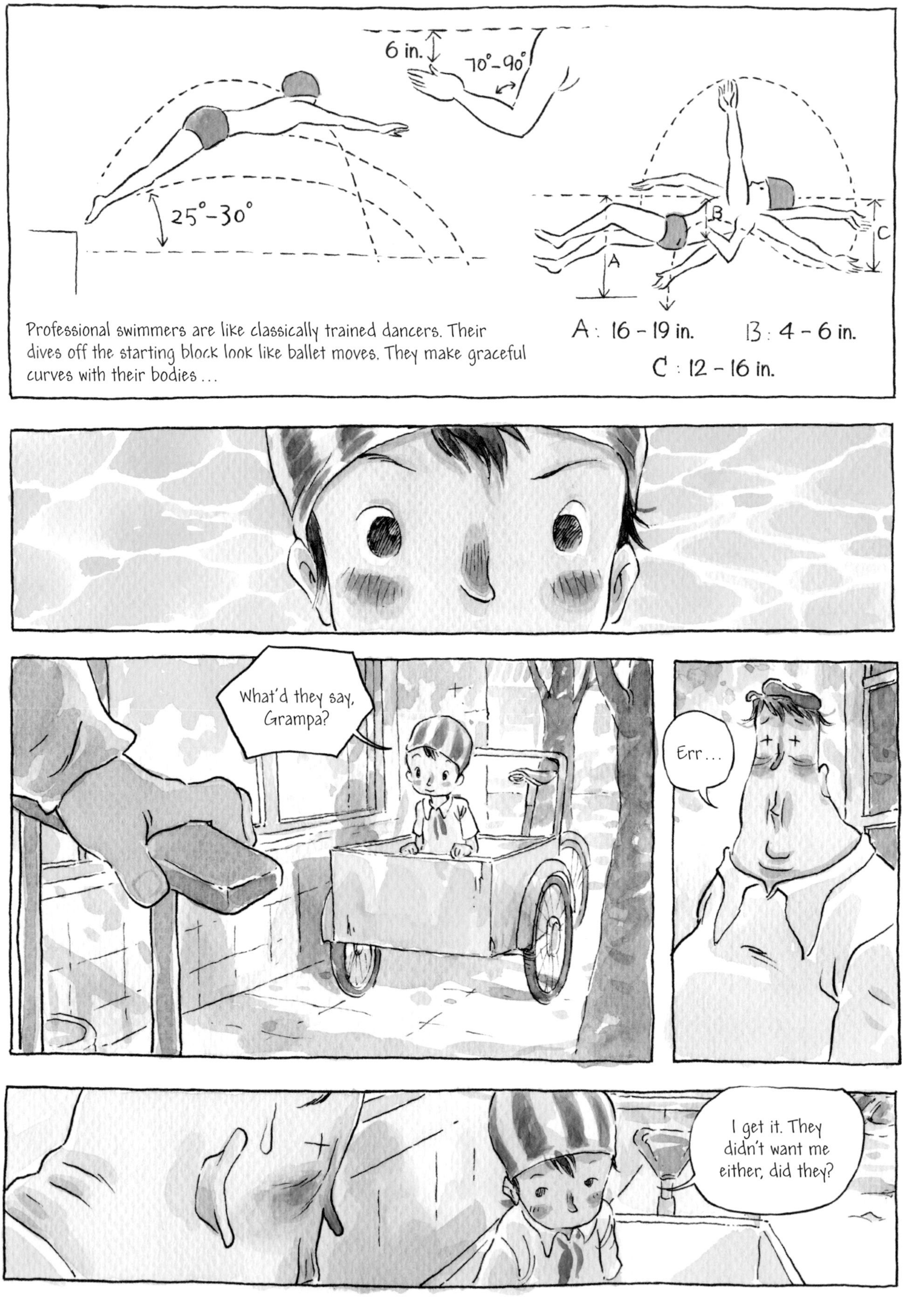
6 in.
70°–90°
25°–30°
Professional swimmers are like classically trained dancers. Their dives off the starting block look like ballet moves. They make graceful curves with their bodies …
A
B
C
A : 16 – 19 in.
B : 4 – 6 in.
C : 12 – 16 in.
What'd they say, Grampa?
Err…
I get it. They didn't want me either, did they?

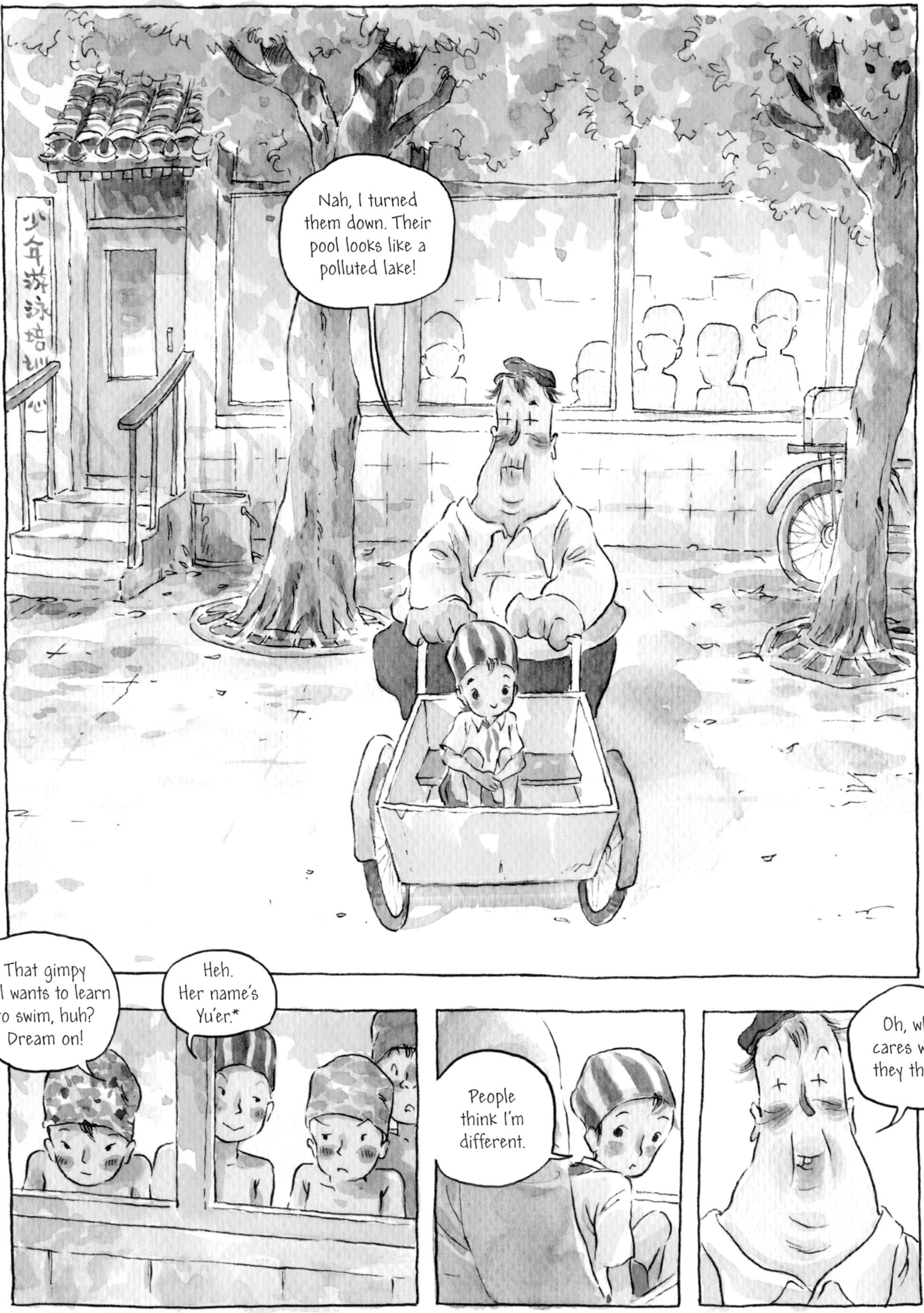
少年游泳培训
Nah, I turned them down. Their pool looks like a polluted lake!
That gimpy girl wants to learn to swim, huh? Dream on!
Heh. Her name's Yu'er.*
People think I'm different.
Oh, who cares what they think!

* *Yu*: fish; *er*: child

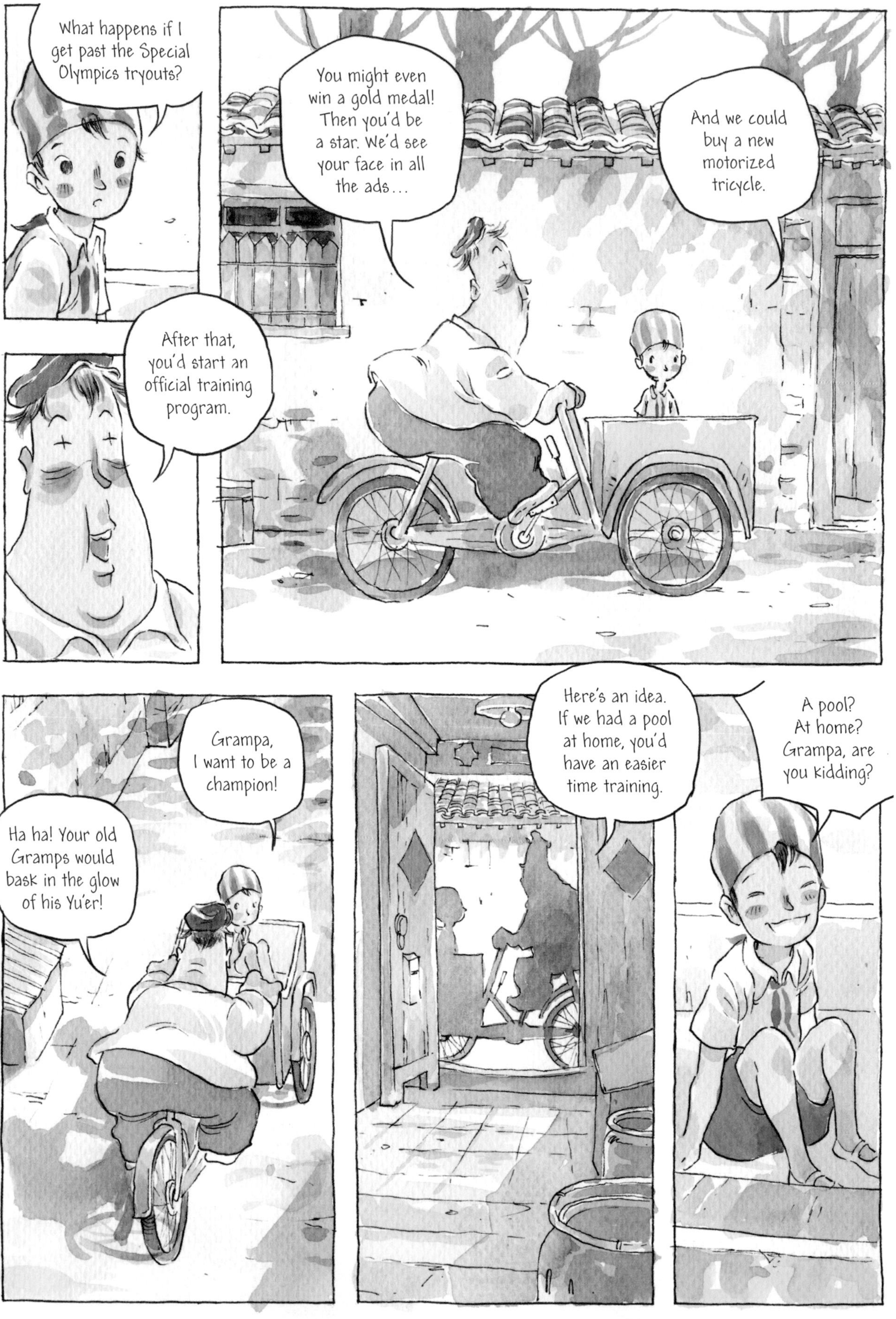
What happens if I get past the Special Olympics tryouts?
You might even win a gold medal! Then you'd be a star. We'd see your face in all the ads…
And we could buy a new motorized tricycle.
After that, you'd start an official training program.
Grampa, I want to be a champion!
Ha ha! Your old Gramps would bask in the glow of his Yu'er!
Here's an idea. If we had a pool at home, you'd have an easier time training.
A pool? At home? Grampa, are you kidding?

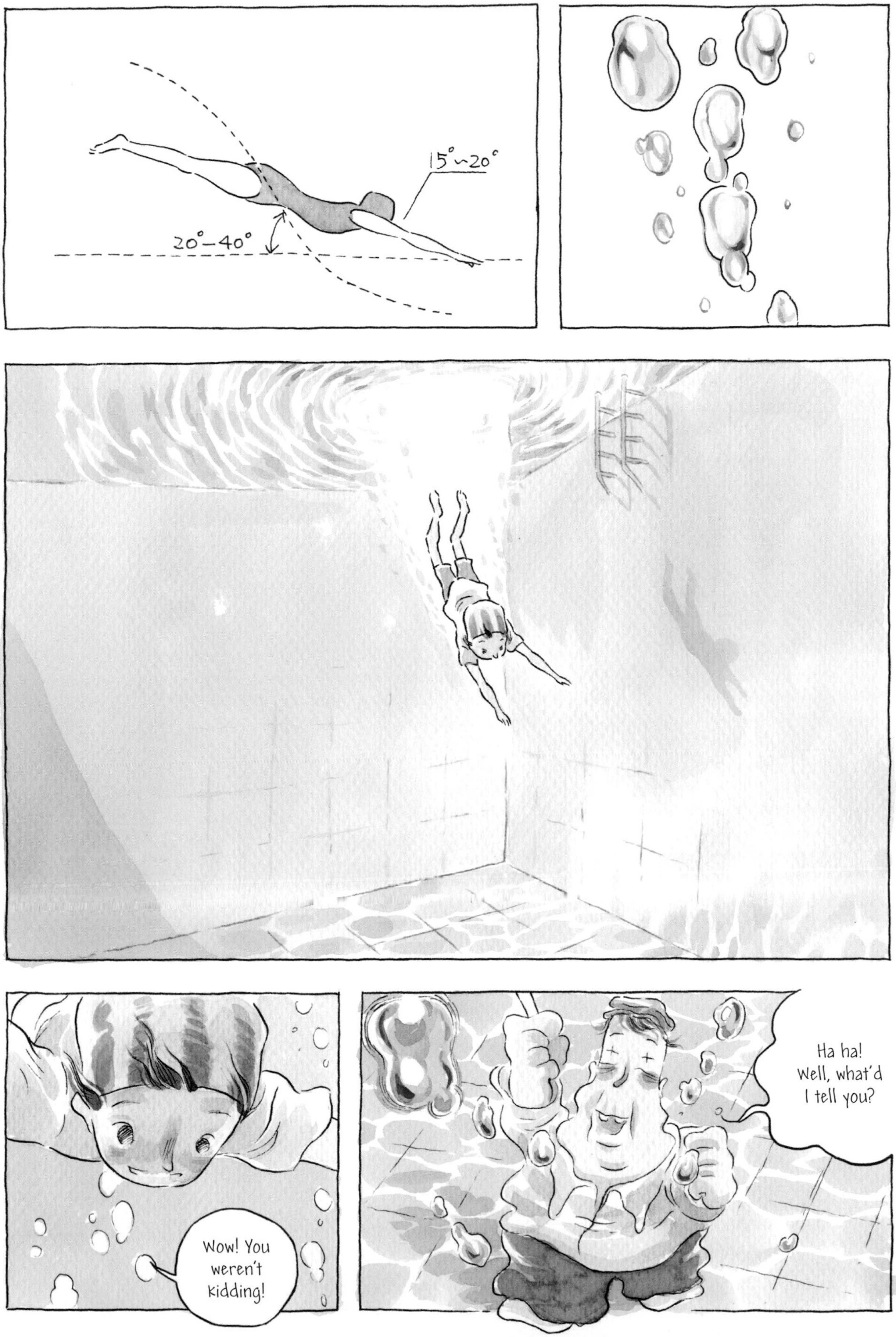
15°~20°
20°–40°
Wow! You weren't kidding!
Ha ha! Well, what'd I tell you?

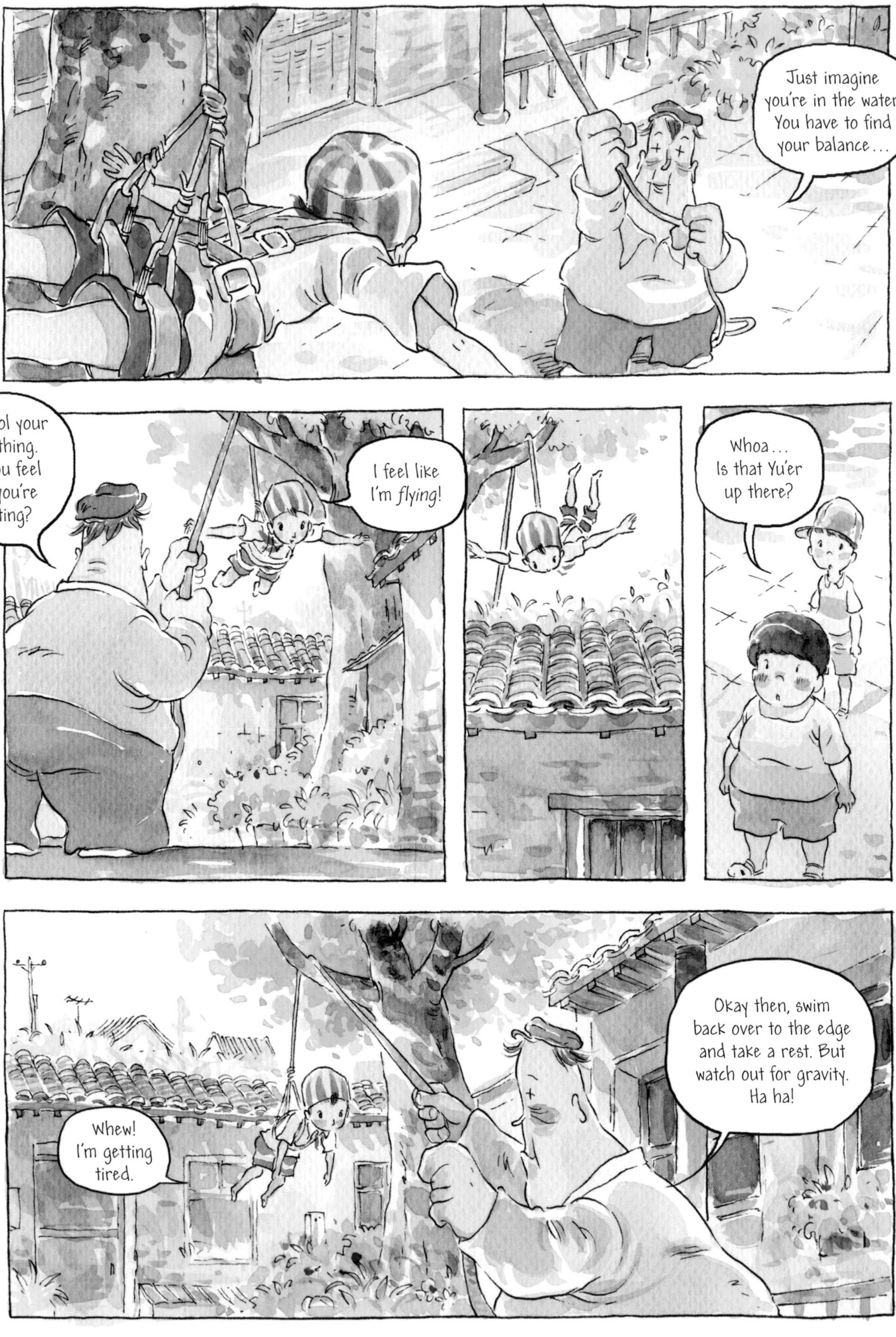
Just imagine you're in the water. You have to find your balance . . .
Control your breathing. Do you feel like you're floating?
I feel like I'm *flying*!
Whoa . . . Is that Yu'er up there?
Okay then, swim back over to the edge and take a rest. But watch out for gravity. Ha ha!
Whew! I'm getting tired.

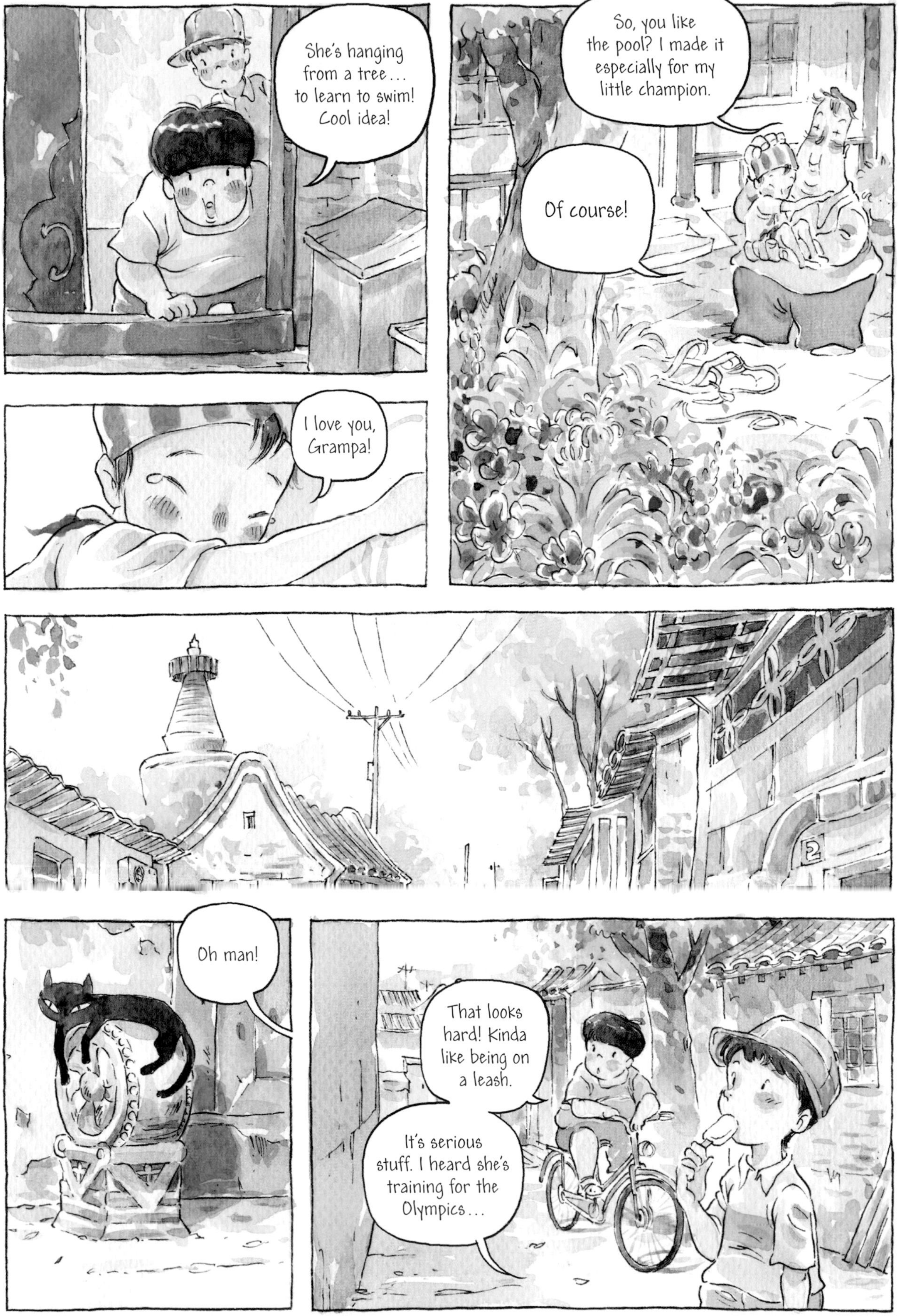
She's hanging from a tree... to learn to swim! Cool idea!
So, you like the pool? I made it especially for my little champion.
Of course!
I love you, Grampa!
Oh man!
That looks hard! Kinda like being on a leash.
It's serious stuff. I heard she's training for the Olympics...

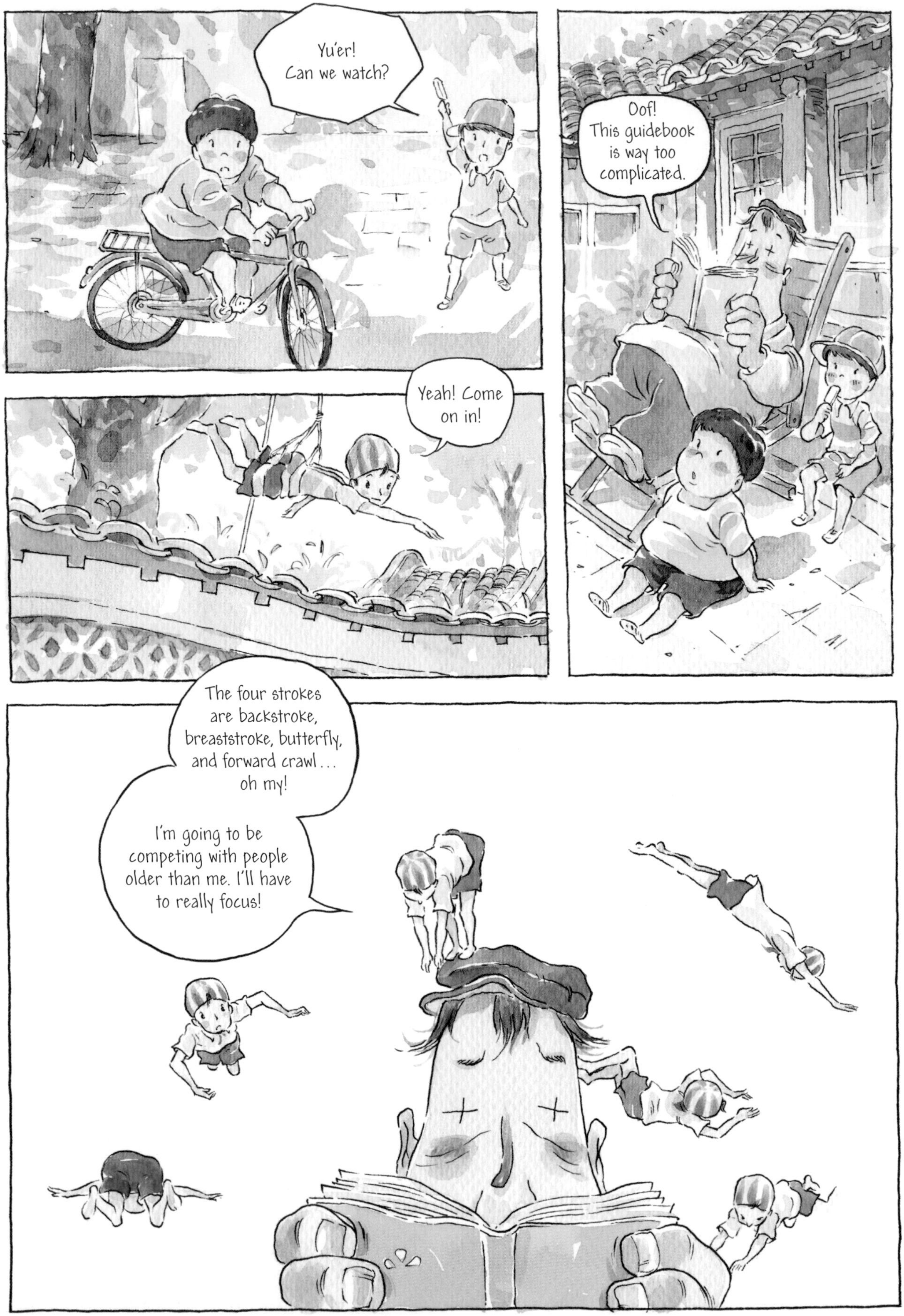
Yu'er! Can we watch?
Oof! This guidebook is way too complicated.
Yeah! Come on in!
The four strokes are backstroke, breaststroke, butterfly, and forward crawl... oh my!
I'm going to be competing with people older than me. I'll have to really focus!

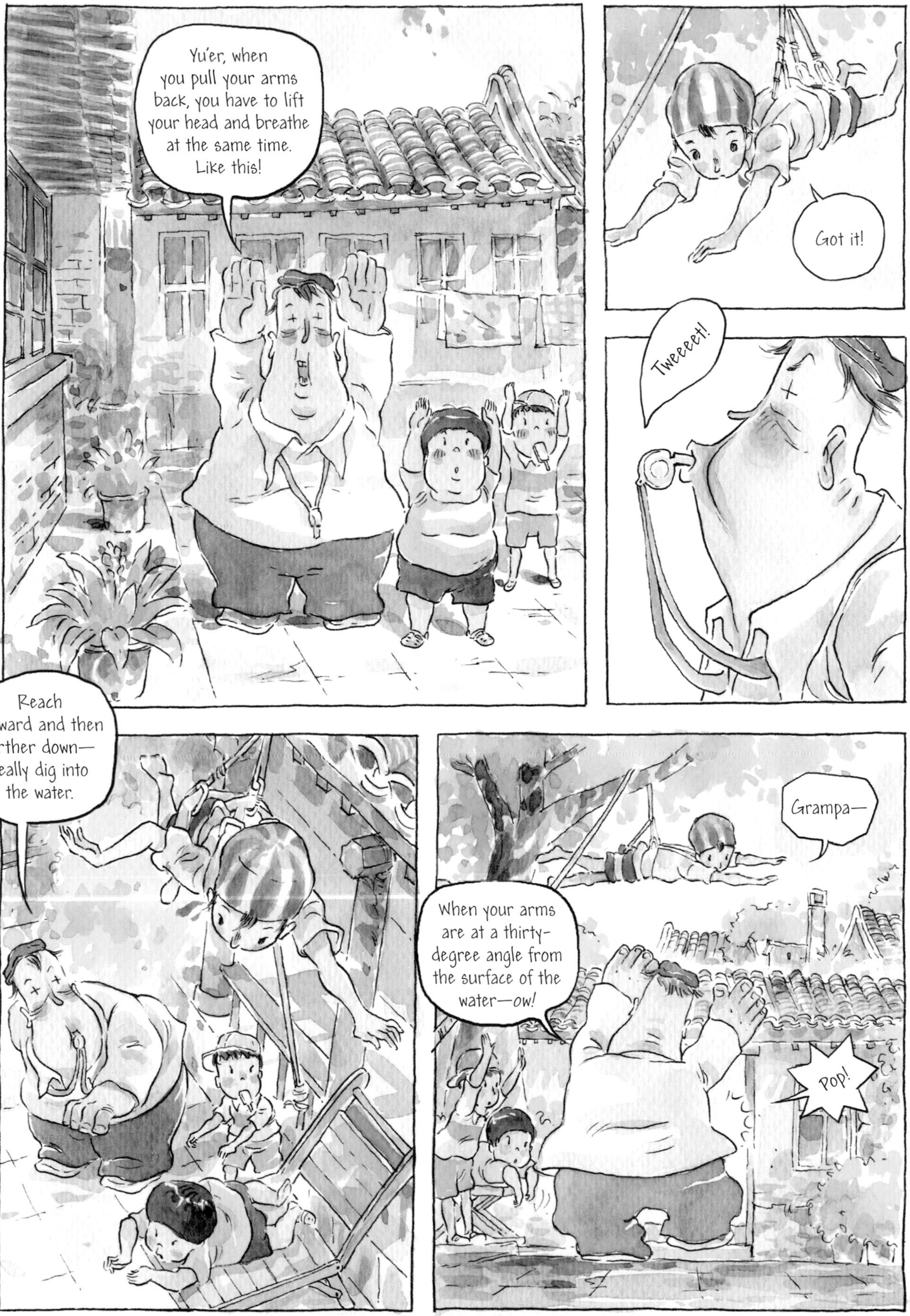
Yu'er, when you pull your arms back, you have to lift your head and breathe at the same time. Like this!
Got it!
Tweeeet!
Reach forward and then farther down—really dig into the water.
Grampa—
When your arms are at a thirty-degree angle from the surface of the water—ow!
Pop!

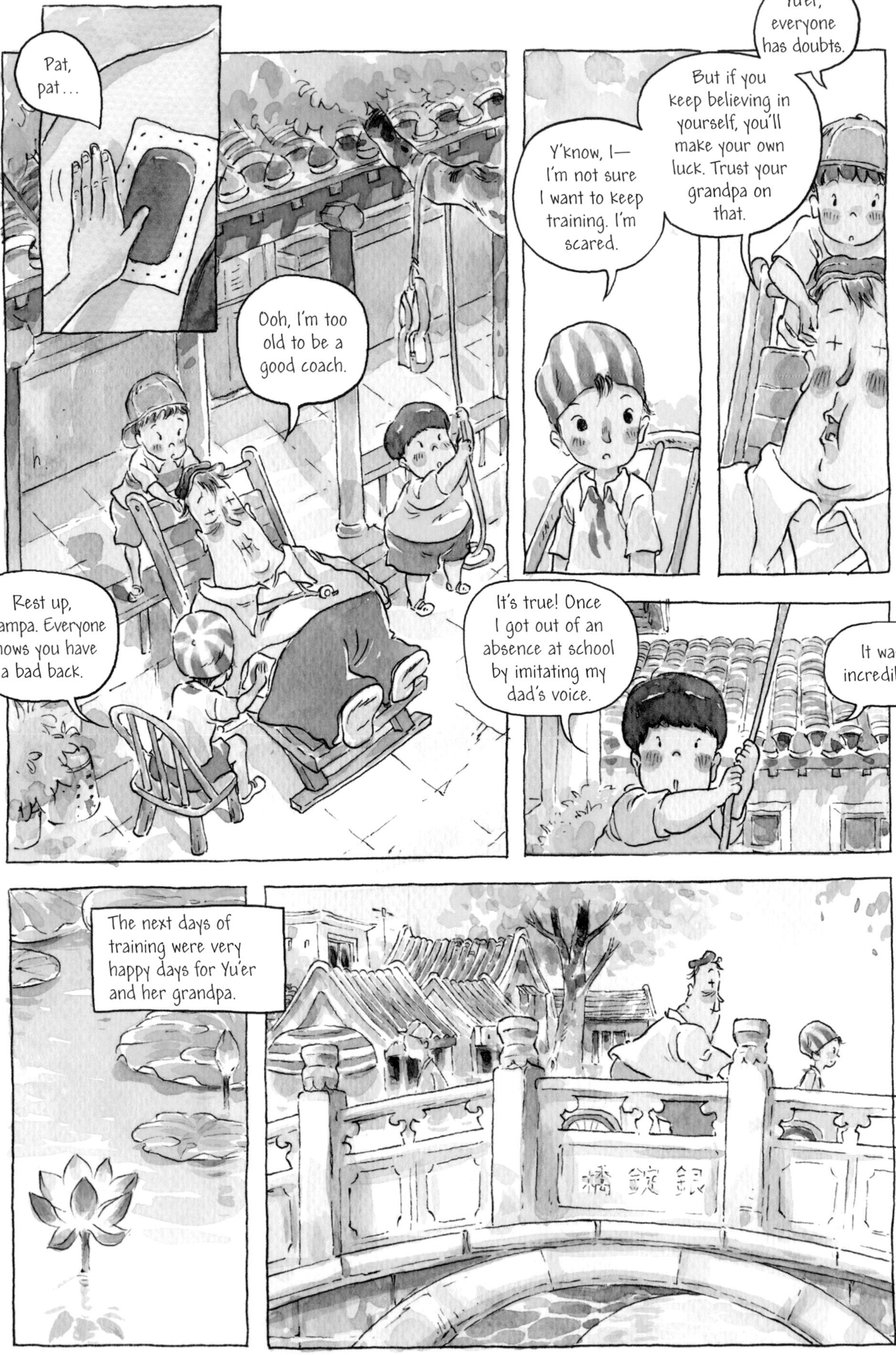
Pat, pat…
Ooh, I'm too old to be a good coach.
Rest up, Grampa. Everyone knows you have a bad back.
Y'know, I— I'm not sure I want to keep training. I'm scared.
Yu'er, everyone has doubts.
But if you keep believing in yourself, you'll make your own luck. Trust your grandpa on that.
It's true! Once I got out of an absence at school by imitating my dad's voice.
It was incredible!
The next days of training were very happy days for Yu'er and her grandpa.
銀錠橋

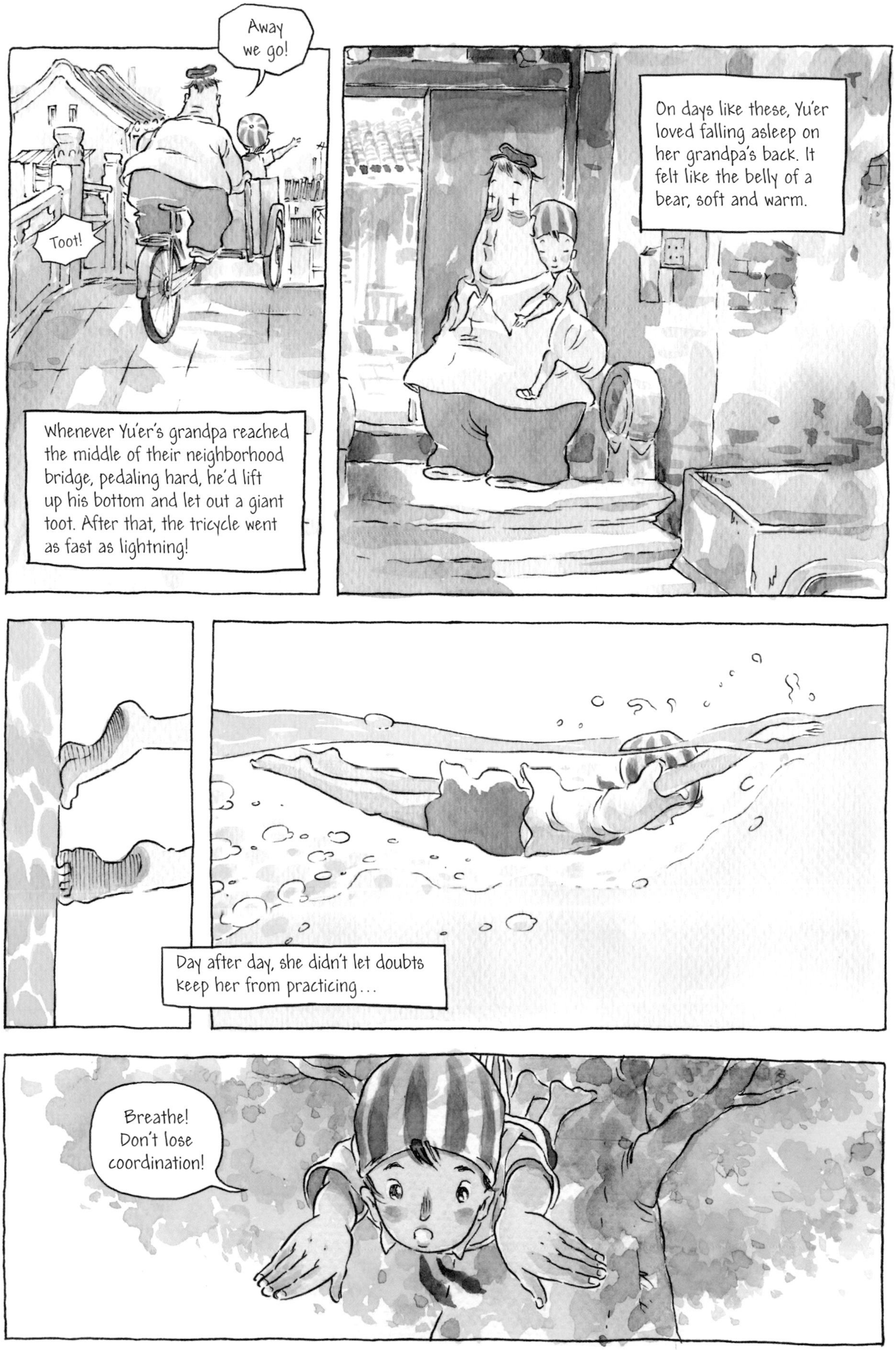
Away we go!
Toot!
Whenever Yu'er's grandpa reached the middle of their neighborhood bridge, pedaling hard, he'd lift up his bottom and let out a giant toot. After that, the tricycle went as fast as lightning!
On days like these, Yu'er loved falling asleep on her grandpa's back. It felt like the belly of a bear, soft and warm.
Day after day, she didn't let doubts keep her from practicing…
Breathe! Don't lose coordination!

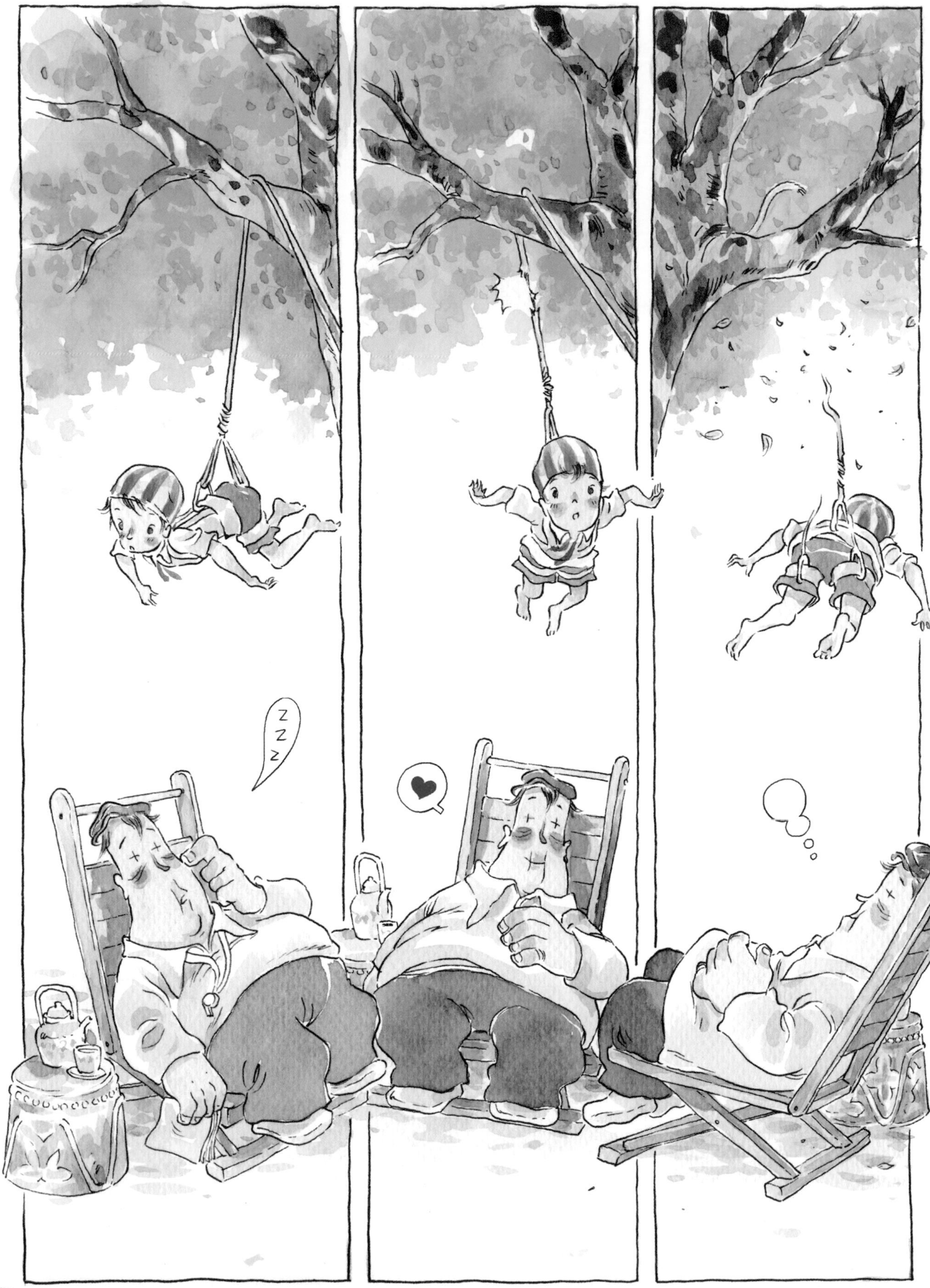
Z Z Z

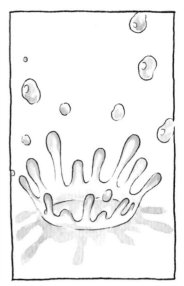

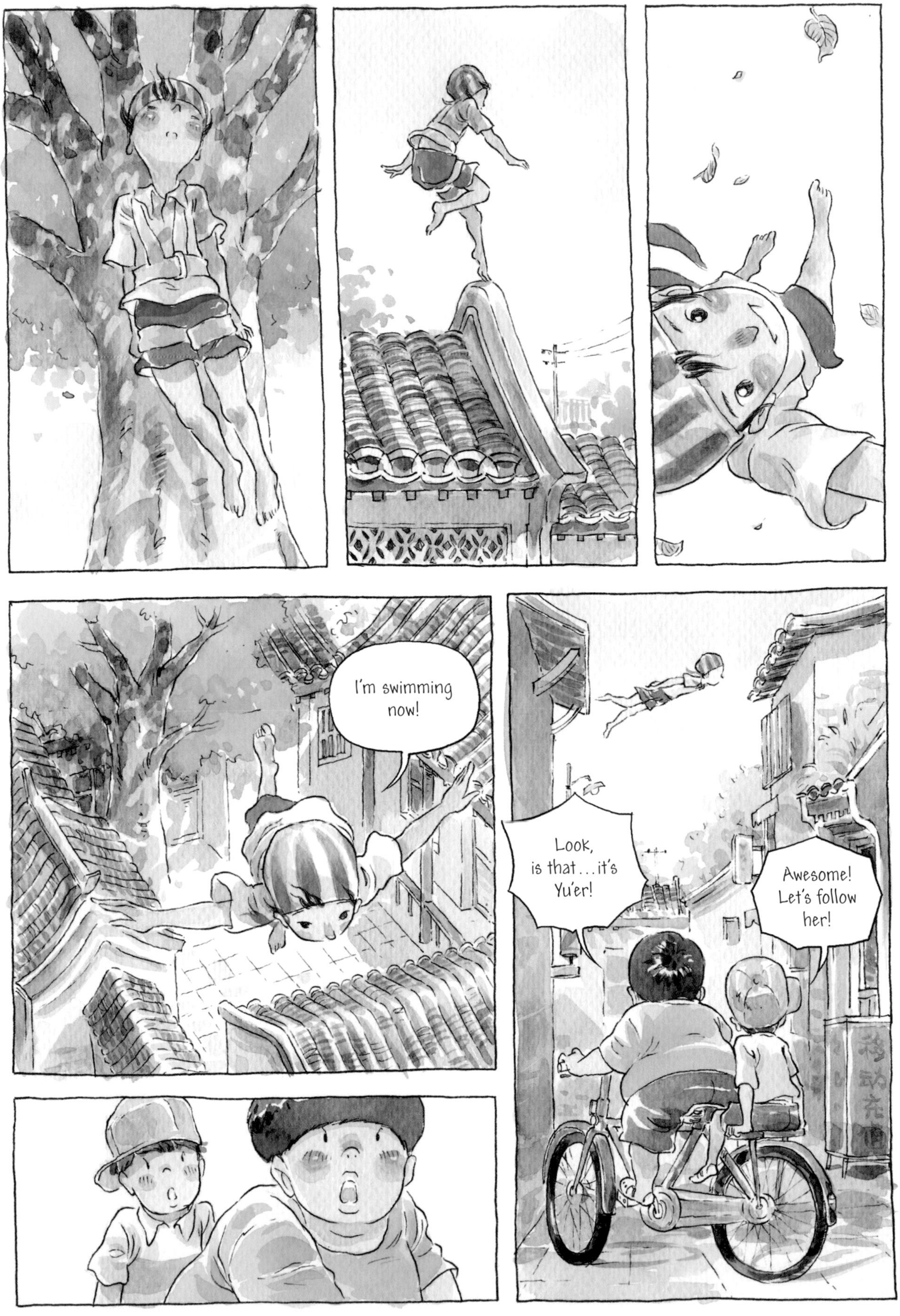
I'm swimming now!
Look, is that…it's Yu'er!
Awesome! Let's follow her!

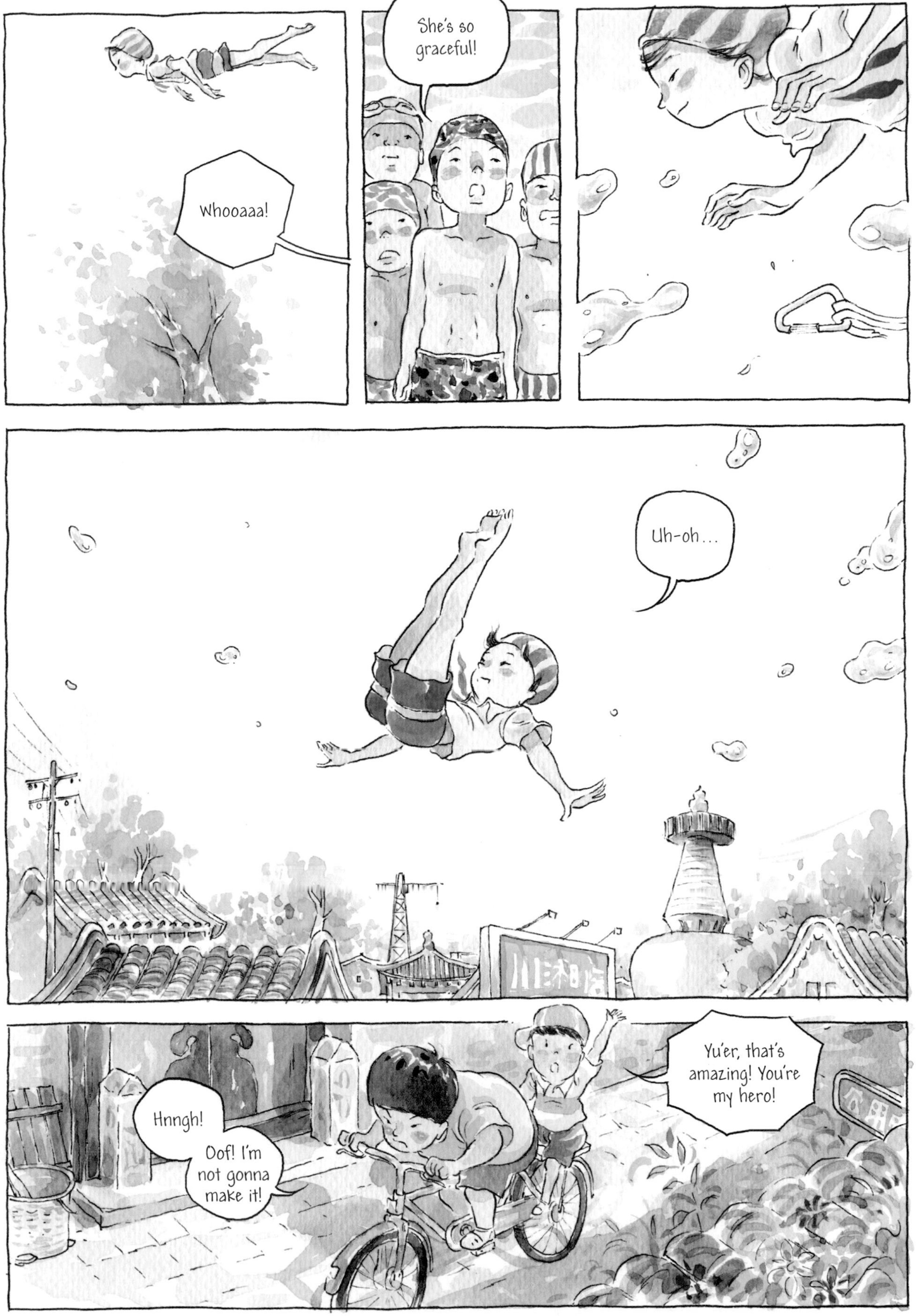
Whooaaa!
She's so graceful!
Uh-oh...
Hnngh!
Oof! I'm not gonna make it!
Yu'er, that's amazing! You're my hero!

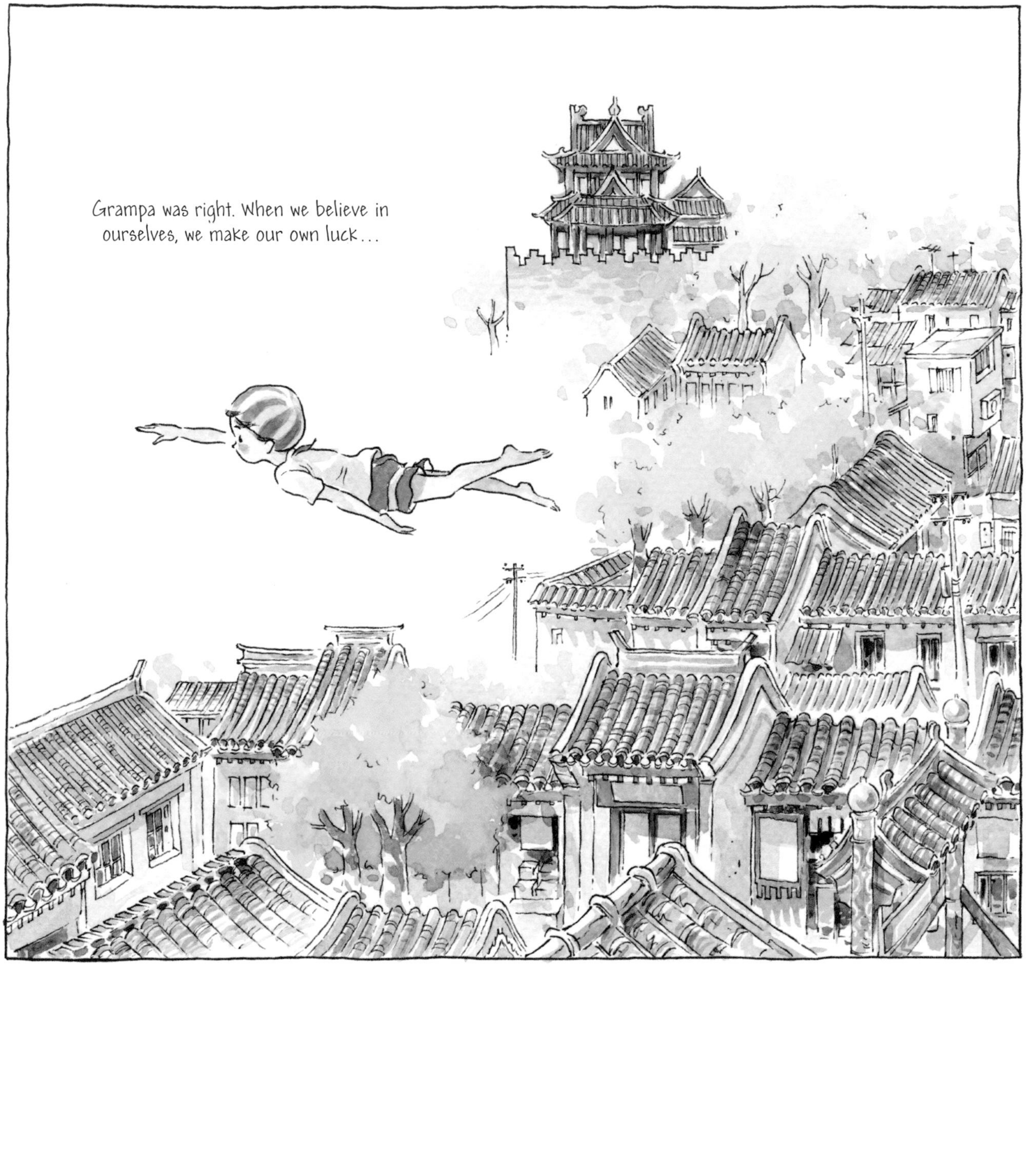
Grampa was right. When we believe in ourselves, we make our own luck...

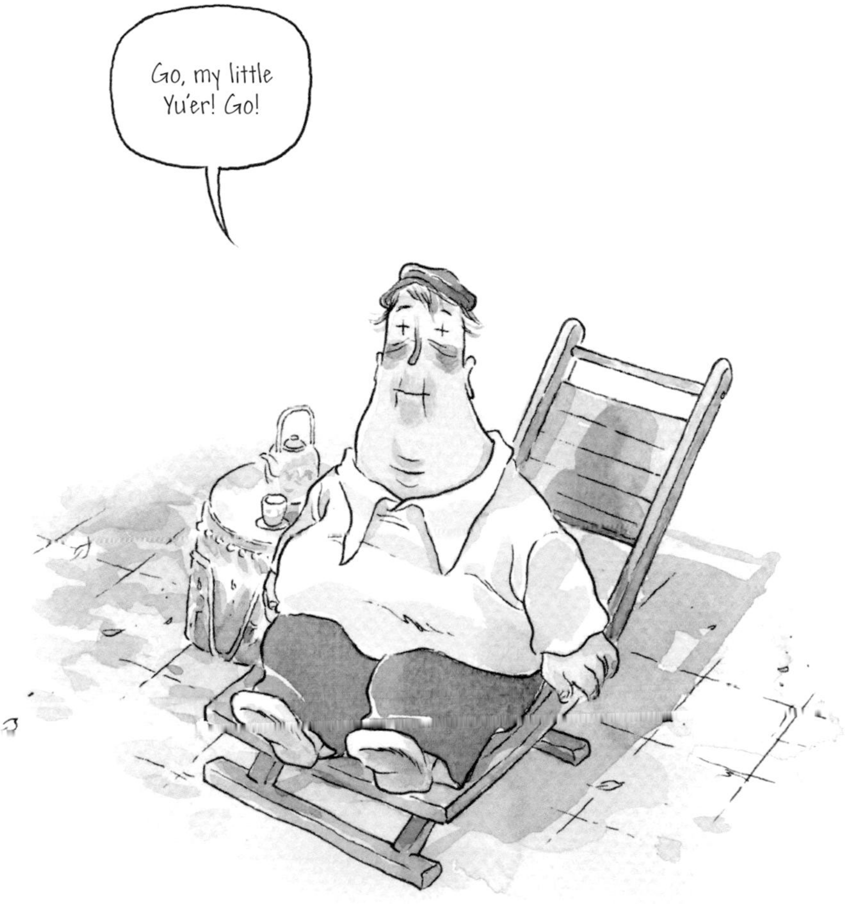
Go, my little Yu'er! Go!

THE END

BUG PARADISE

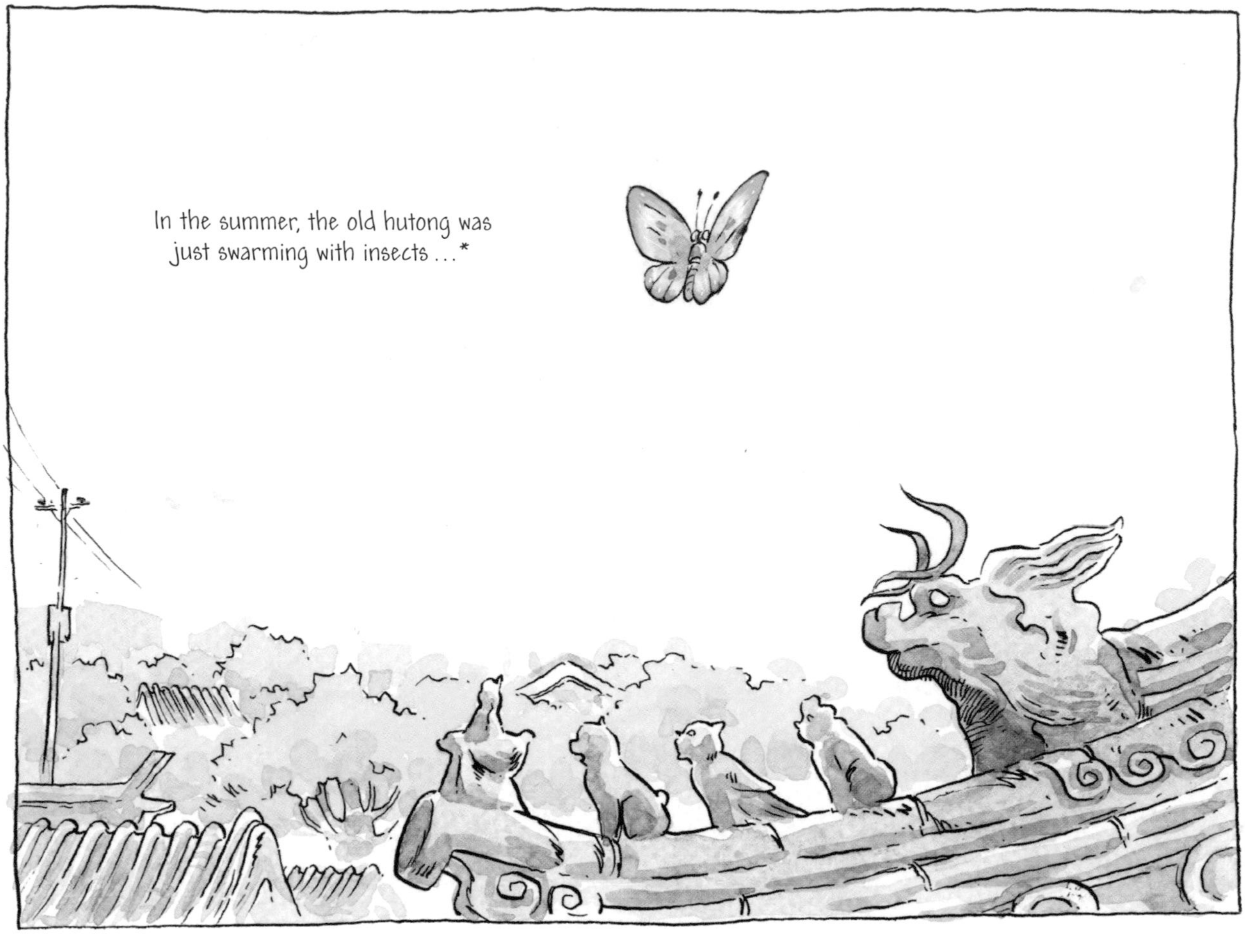
In the summer, the old hutong was just swarming with insects . . .*

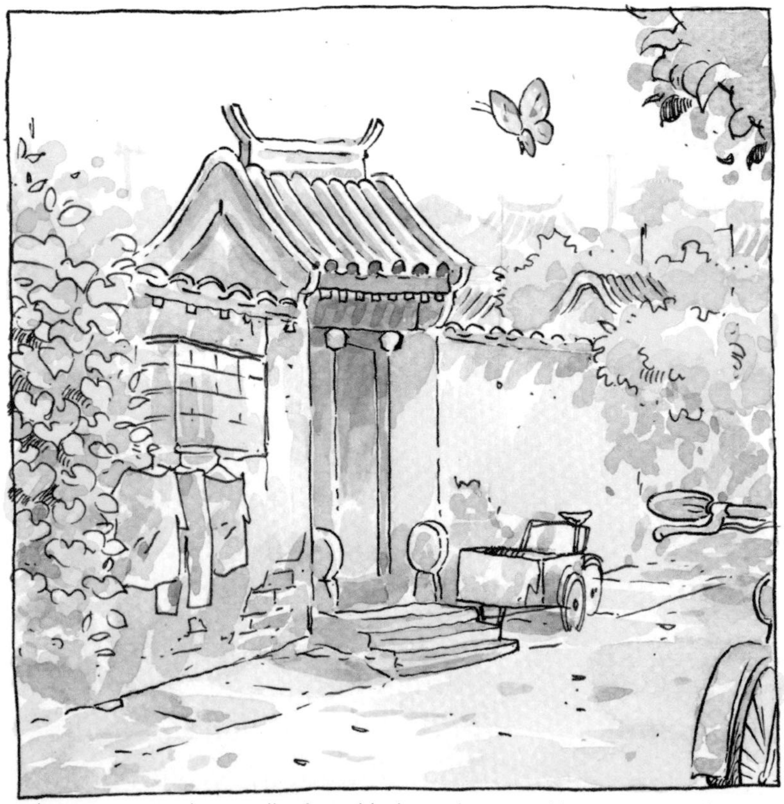

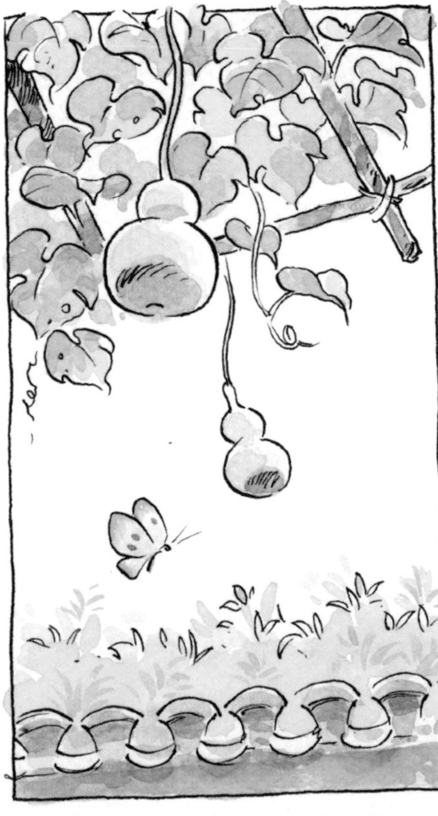

* *hutong*: a narrow lane or alley formed by lines of courtyard homes. Among the many cities in China, Beijing is best known for its hutongs.

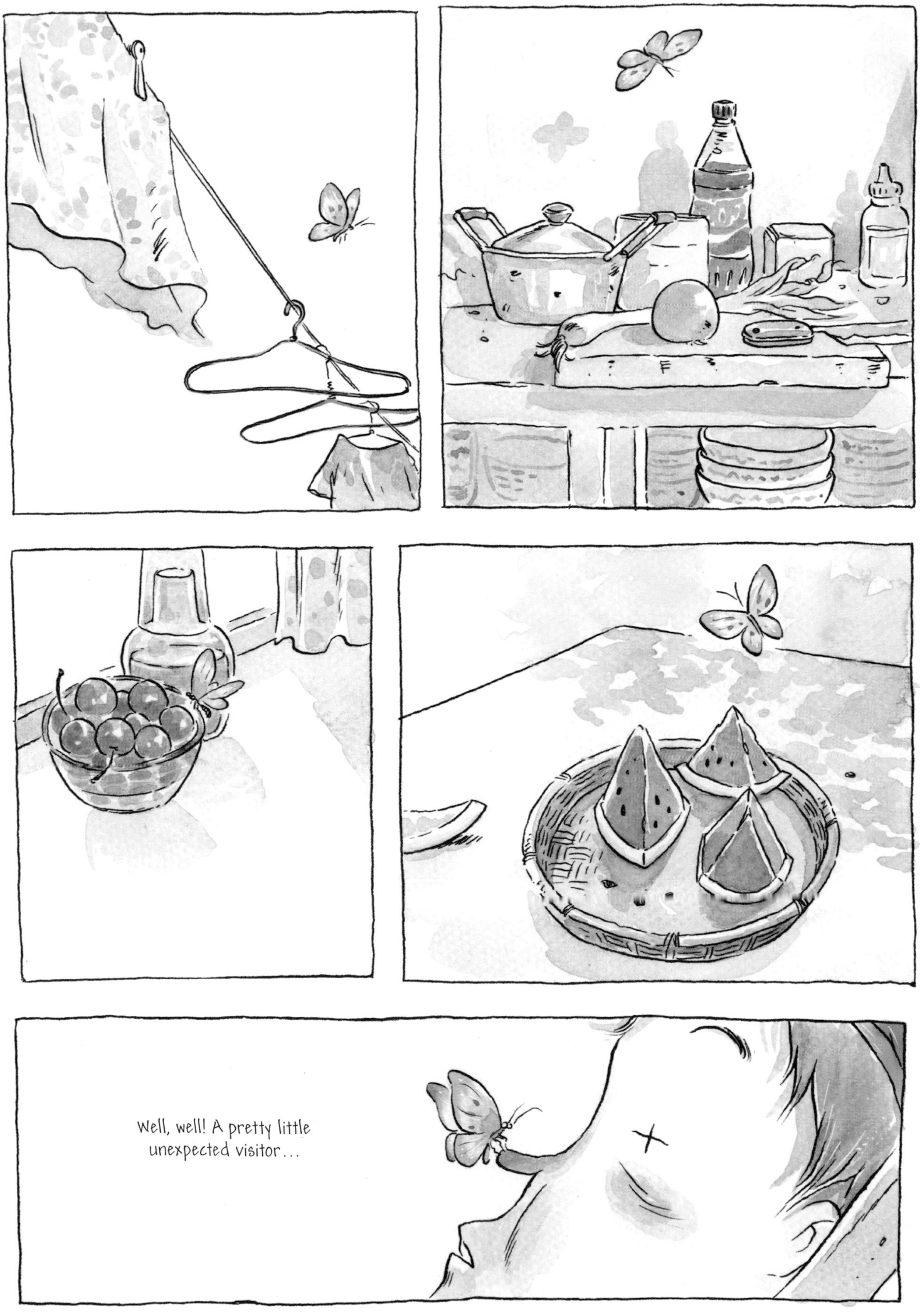
Well, well! A pretty little unexpected visitor...

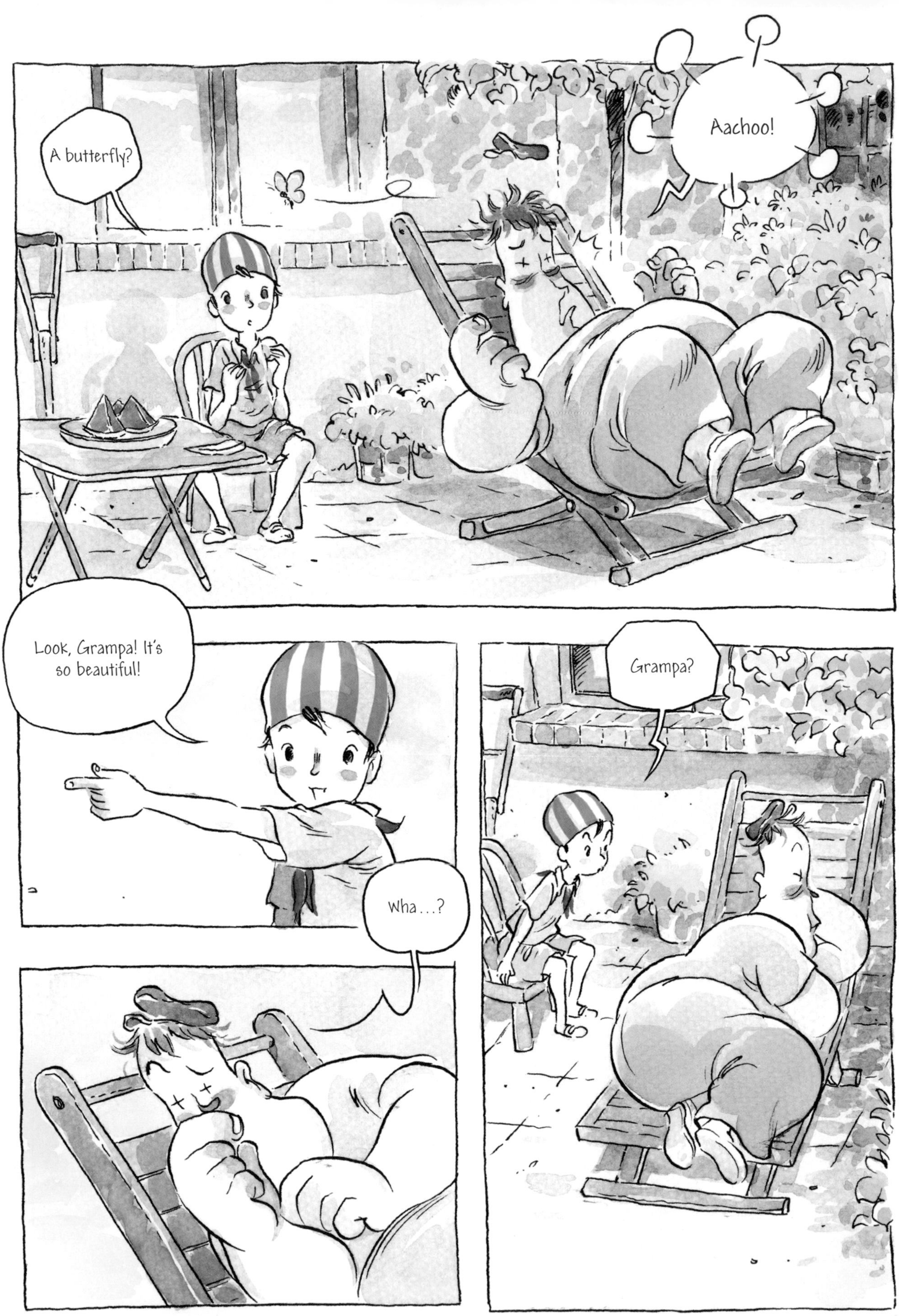
A butterfly?
Aachoo!
Look, Grampa! It's so beautiful!
Wha...?
Grampa?

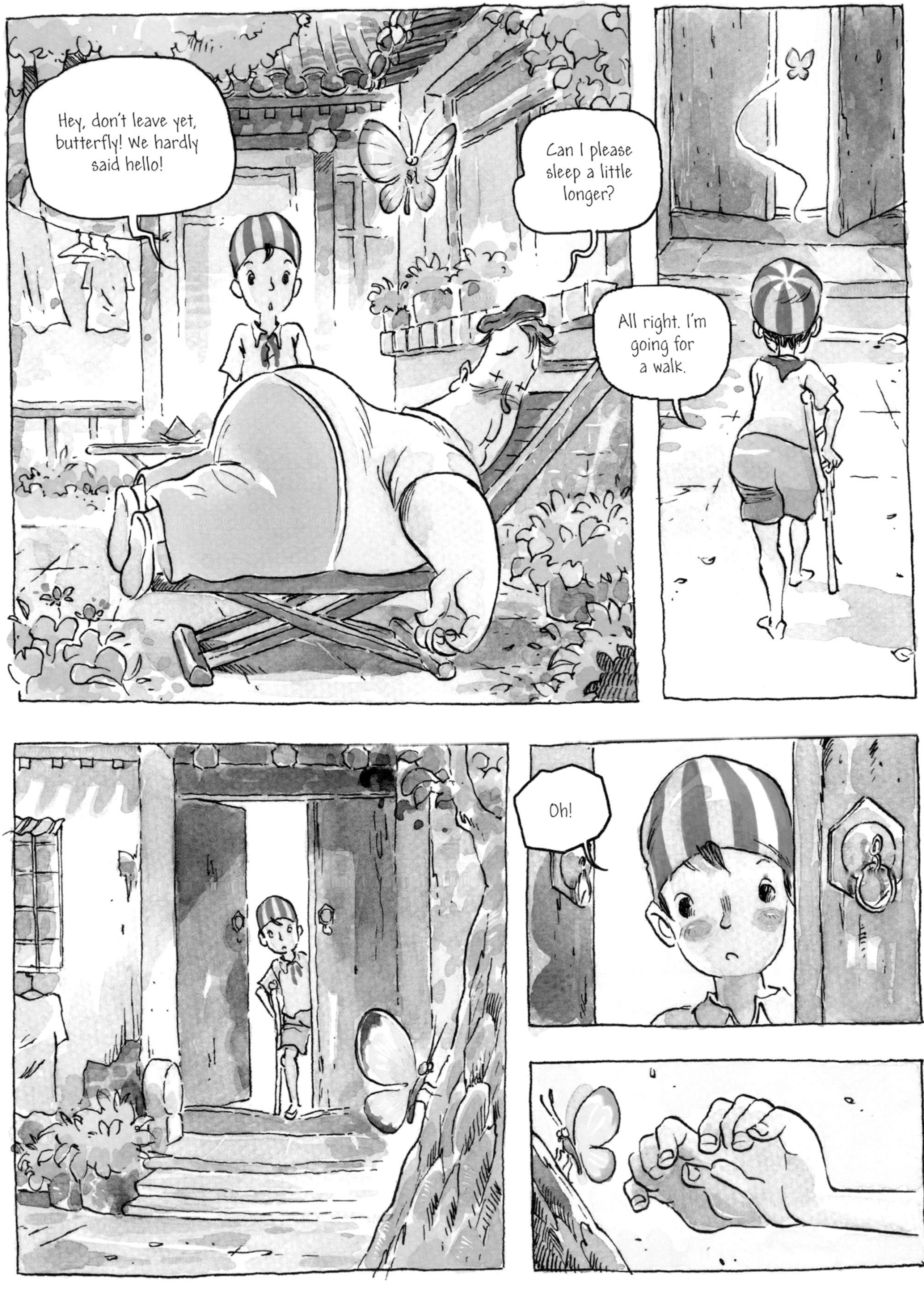
Hey, don't leave yet, butterfly! We hardly said hello!
Can I please sleep a little longer?
All right. I'm going for a walk.
Oh!

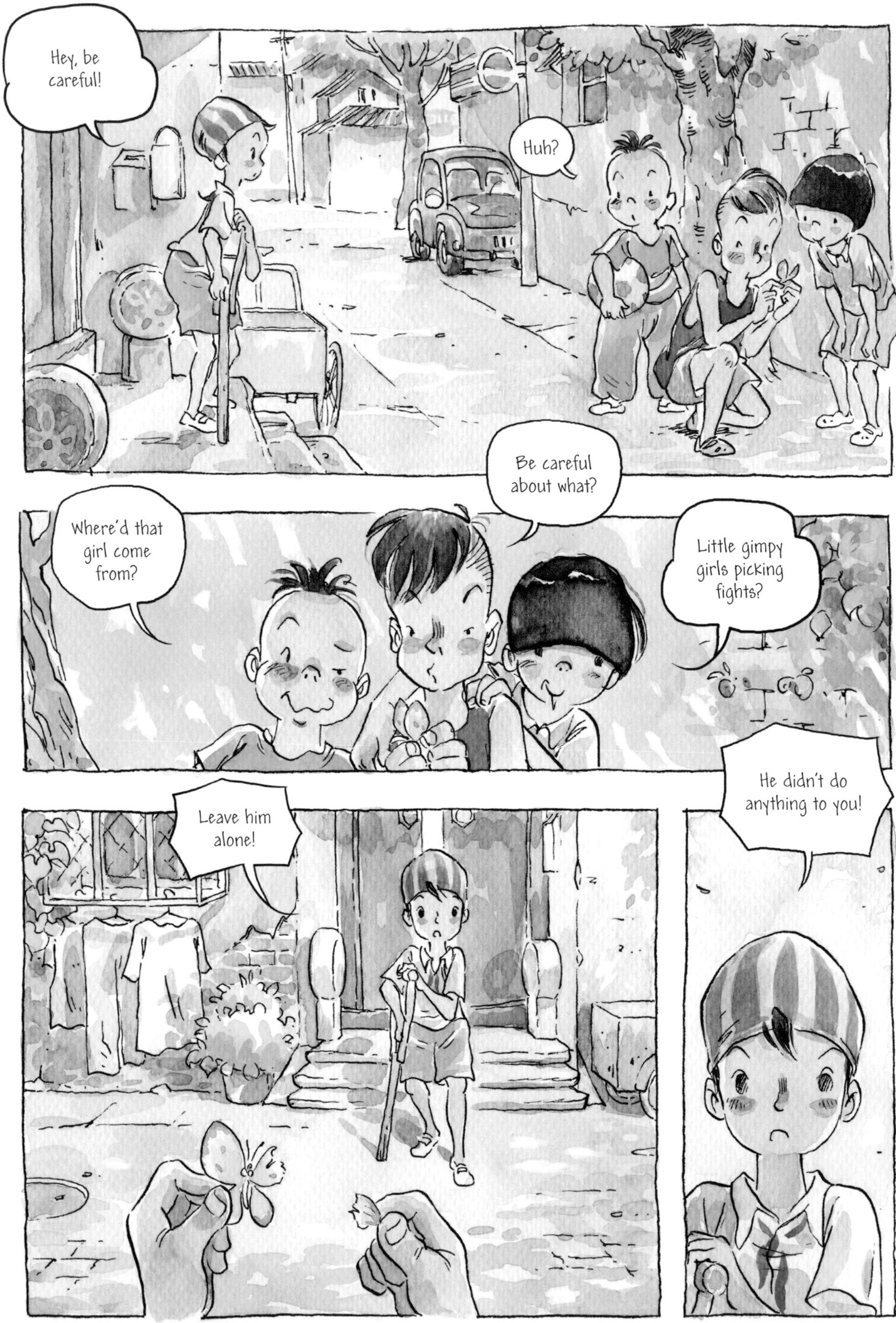
Hey, be careful!
Huh?
Be careful about what?
Where'd that girl come from?
Little gimpy girls picking fights?
Leave him alone!
He didn't do anything to you!

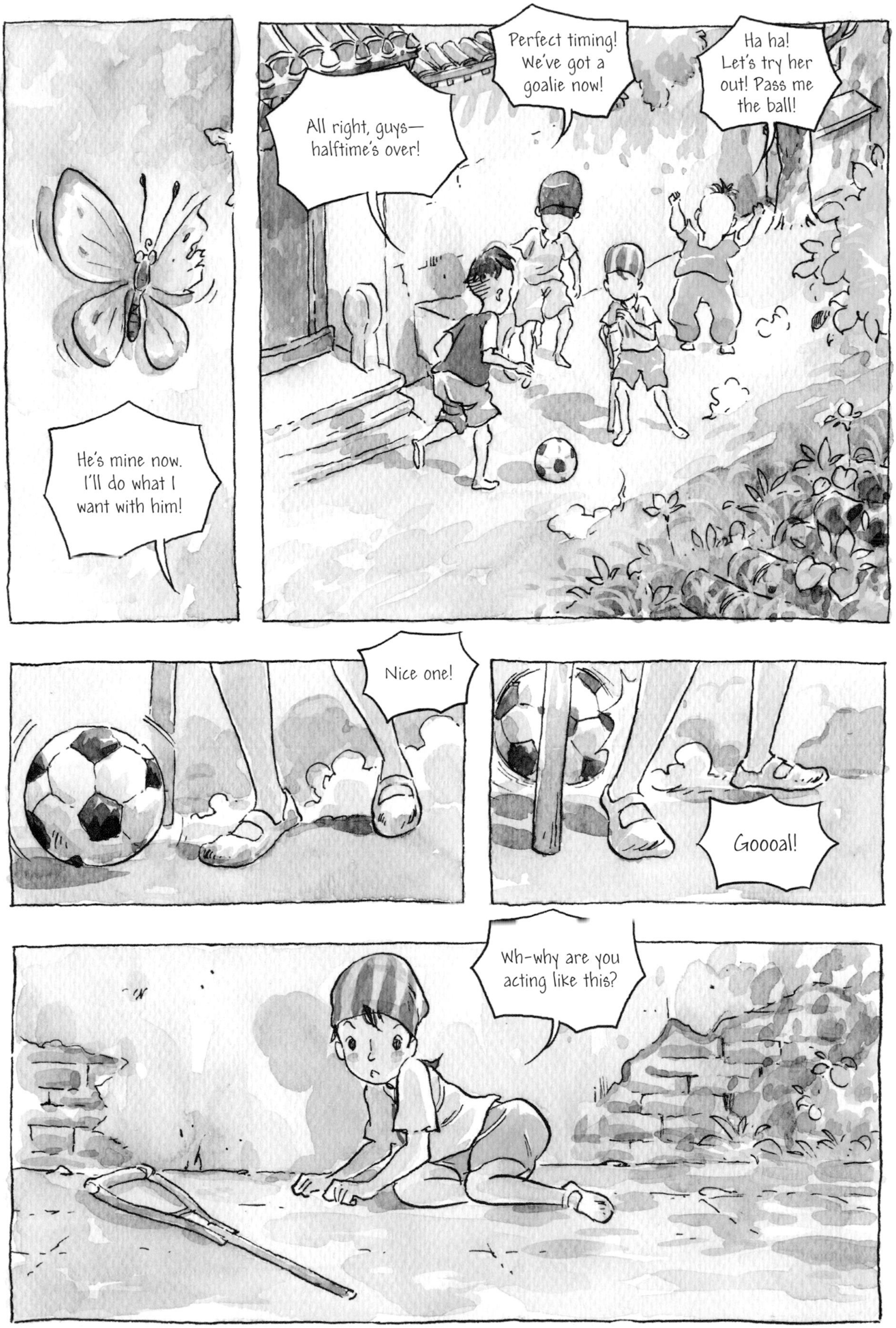
He's mine now. I'll do what I want with him!
All right, guys—halftime's over!
Perfect timing! We've got a goalie now!
Ha ha! Let's try her out! Pass me the ball!
Nice one!
Goooal!
Wh-why are you acting like this?

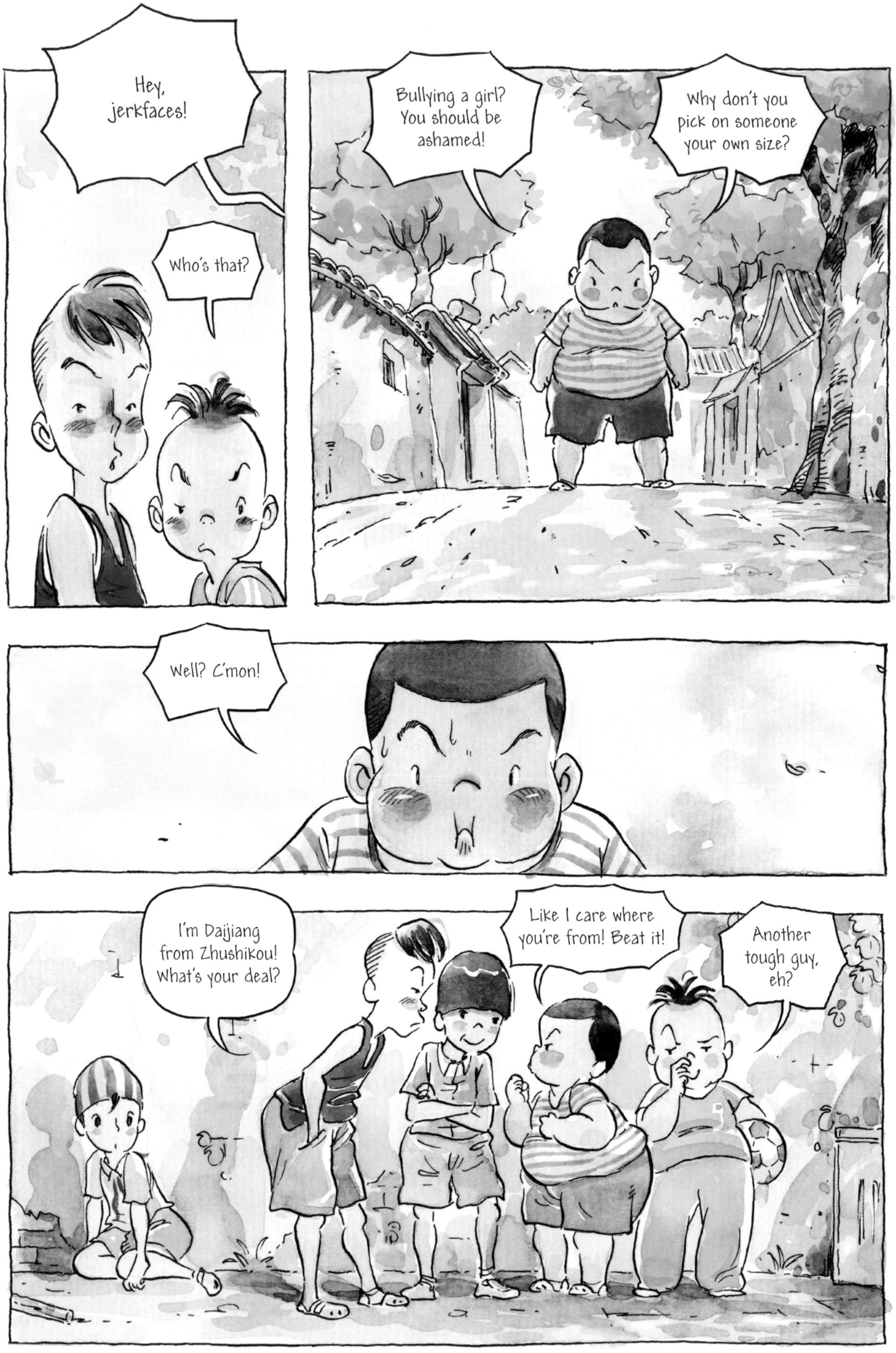
Hey, jerkfaces!
Who's that?
Bullying a girl? You should be ashamed!
Why don't you pick on someone your own size?
Well? C'mon!
I'm Daijiang from Zhushikou! What's your deal?
Like I care where you're from! Beat it!
Another tough guy, eh?

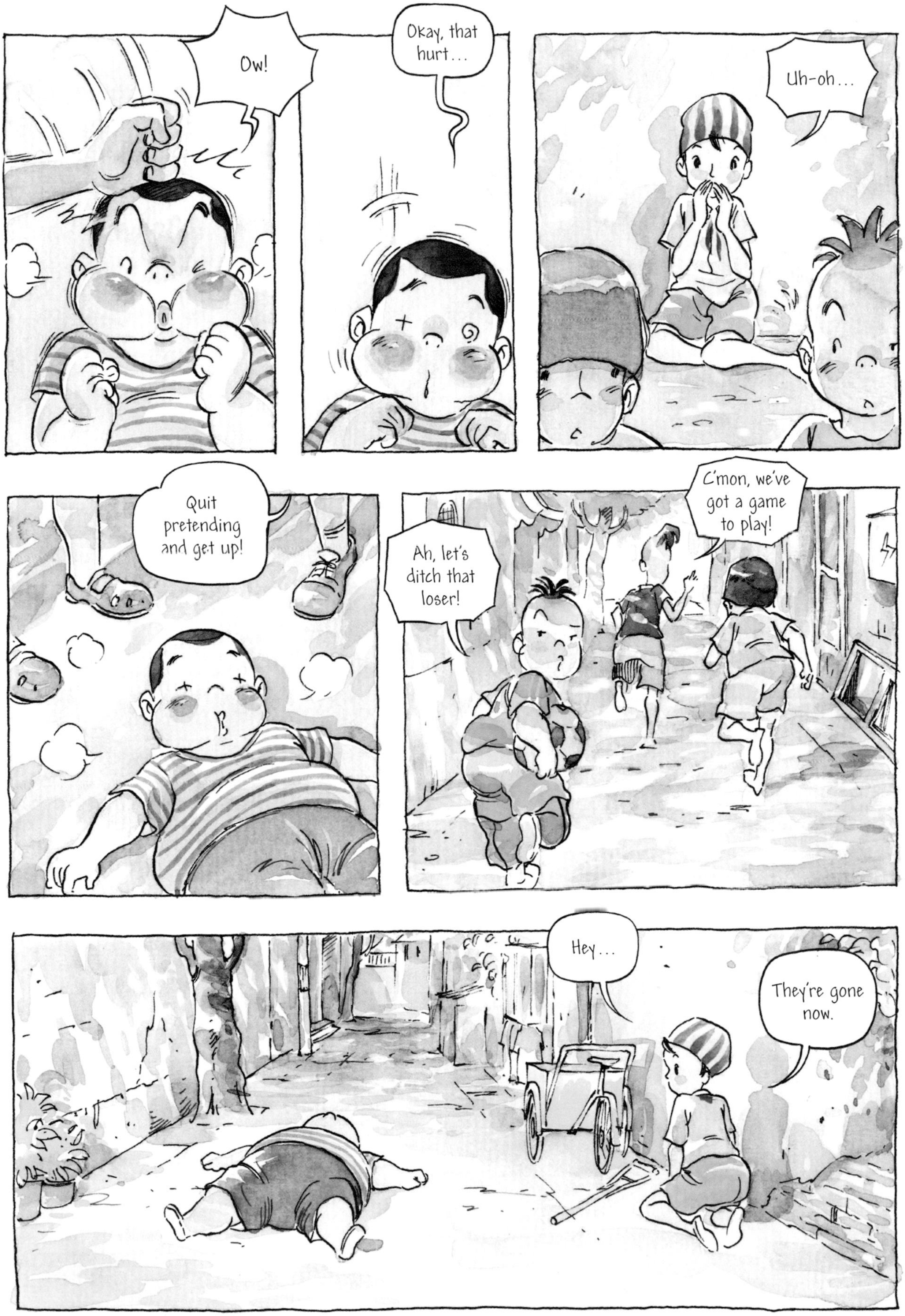
Ow!
Okay, that hurt...
Uh-oh...
Quit pretending and get up!
Ah, let's ditch that loser!
C'mon, we've got a game to play!
Hey...
They're gone now.

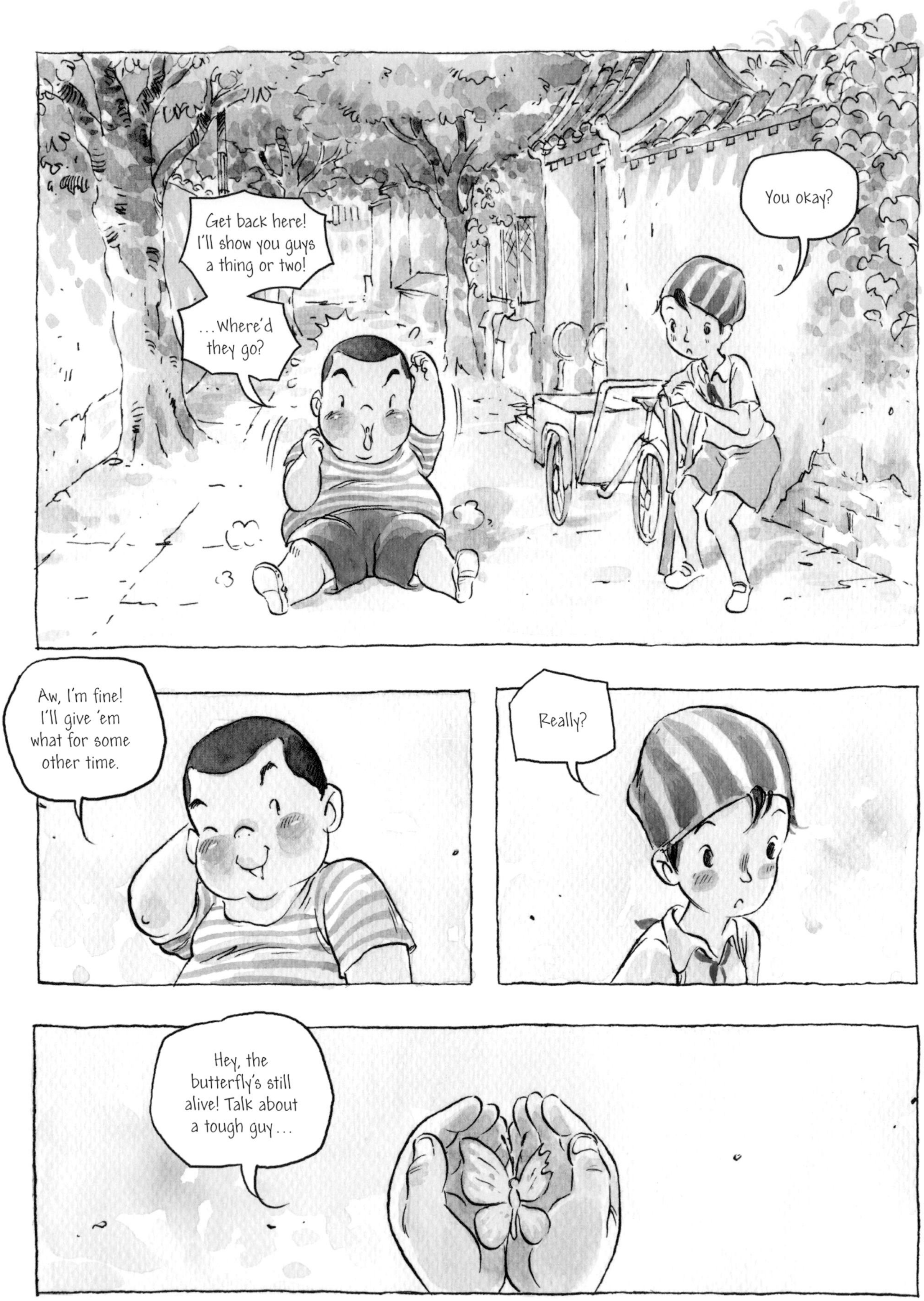
Get back here! I'll show you guys a thing or two!
...Where'd they go?
You okay?
Aw, I'm fine! I'll give 'em what for some other time.
Really?
Hey, the butterfly's still alive! Talk about a tough guy...

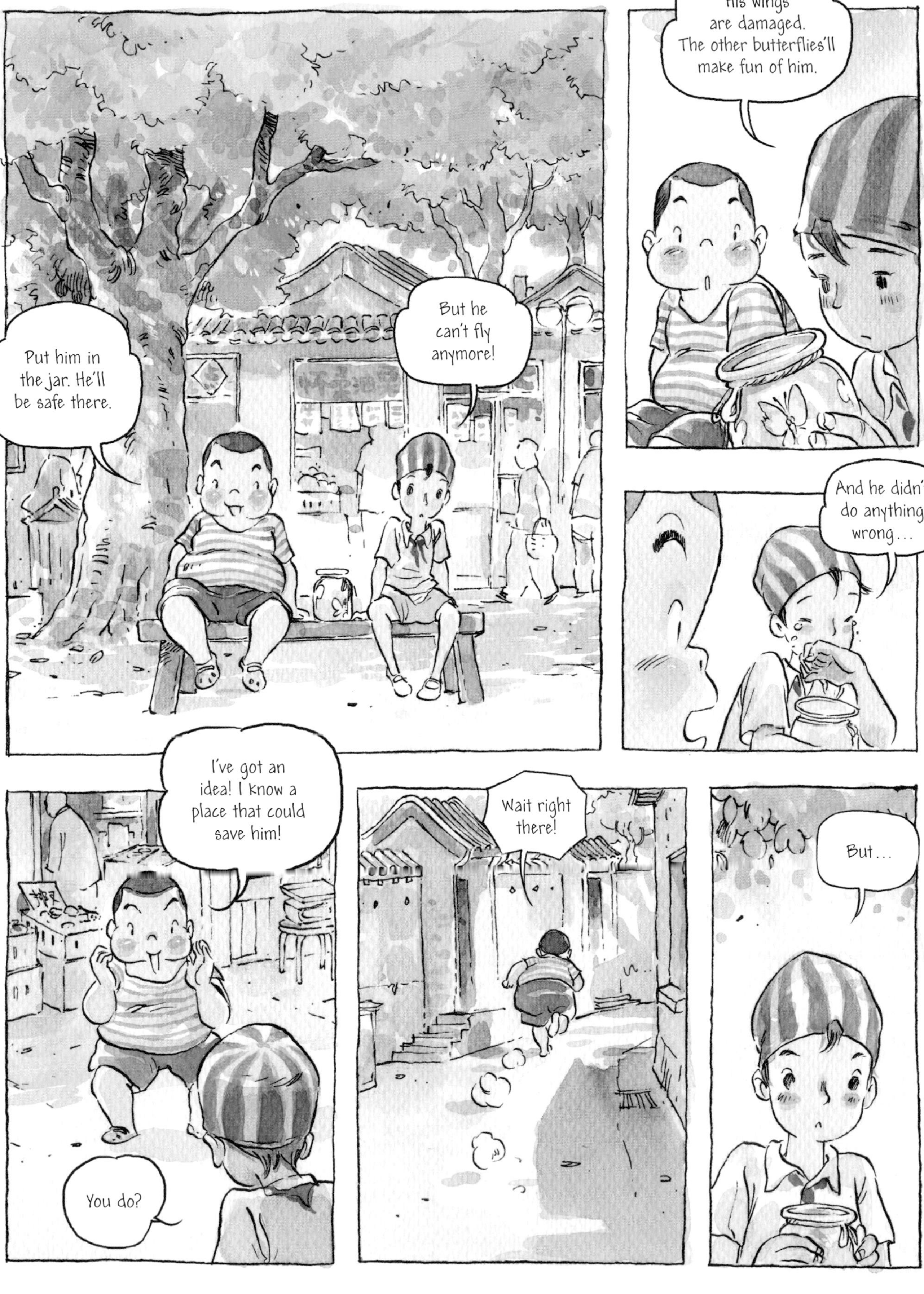
Put him in the jar. He'll be safe there.
But he can't fly anymore!
His wings are damaged. The other butterflies'll make fun of him.
And he didn't do anything wrong...
I've got an idea! I know a place that could save him!
You do?
Wait right there!
But...

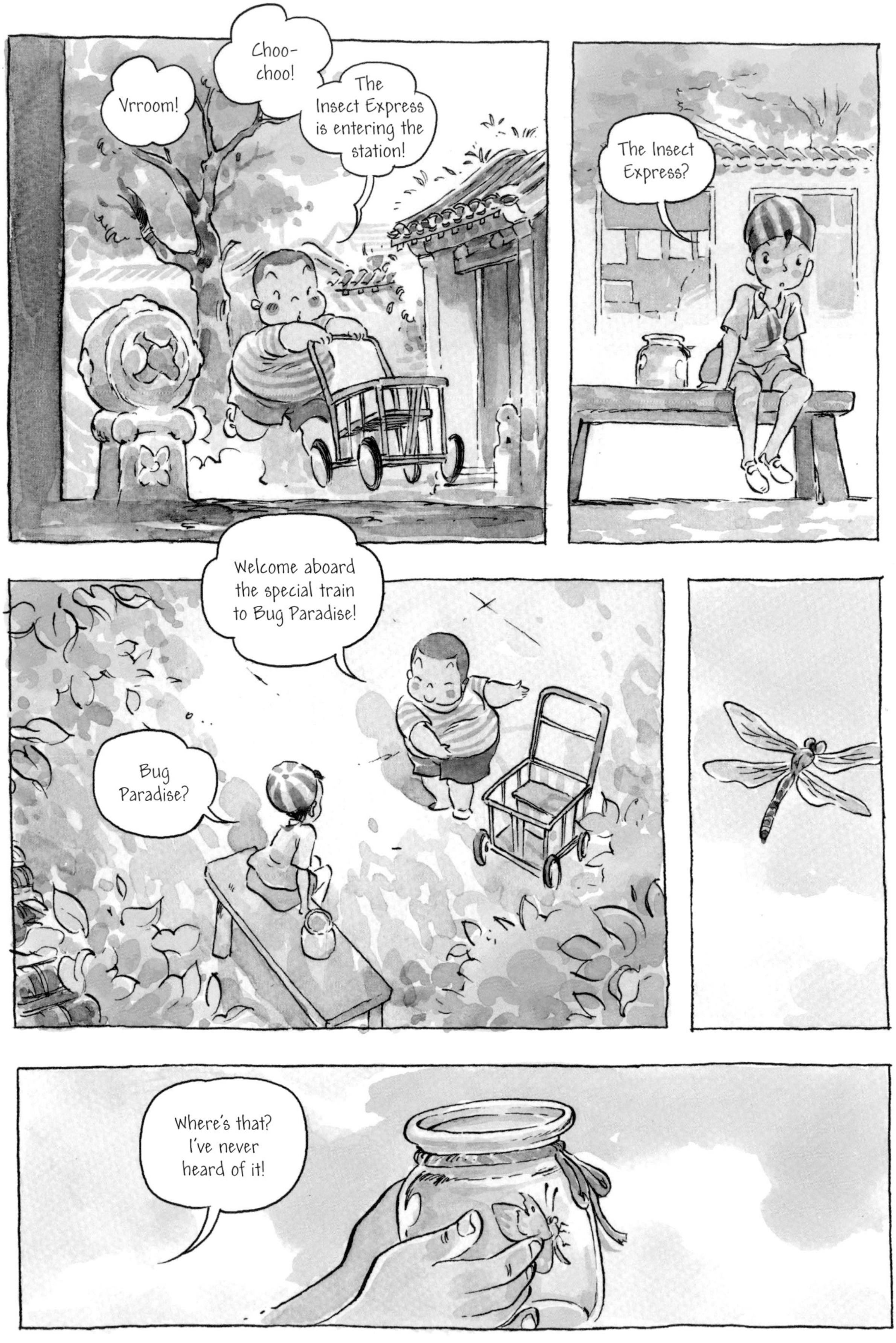
Vrroom!
Choo-choo!
The Insect Express is entering the station!
The Insect Express?
Welcome aboard the special train to Bug Paradise!
Bug Paradise?
Where's that? I've never heard of it!

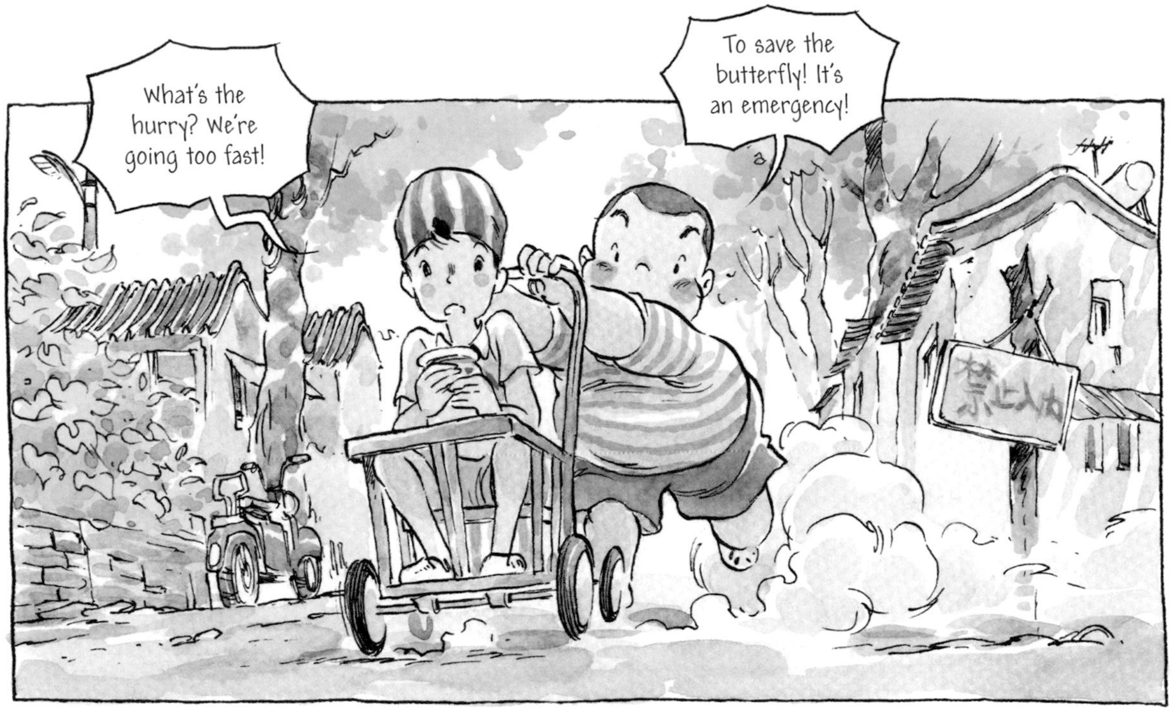
What's the hurry? We're going too fast!
To save the butterfly! It's an emergency!

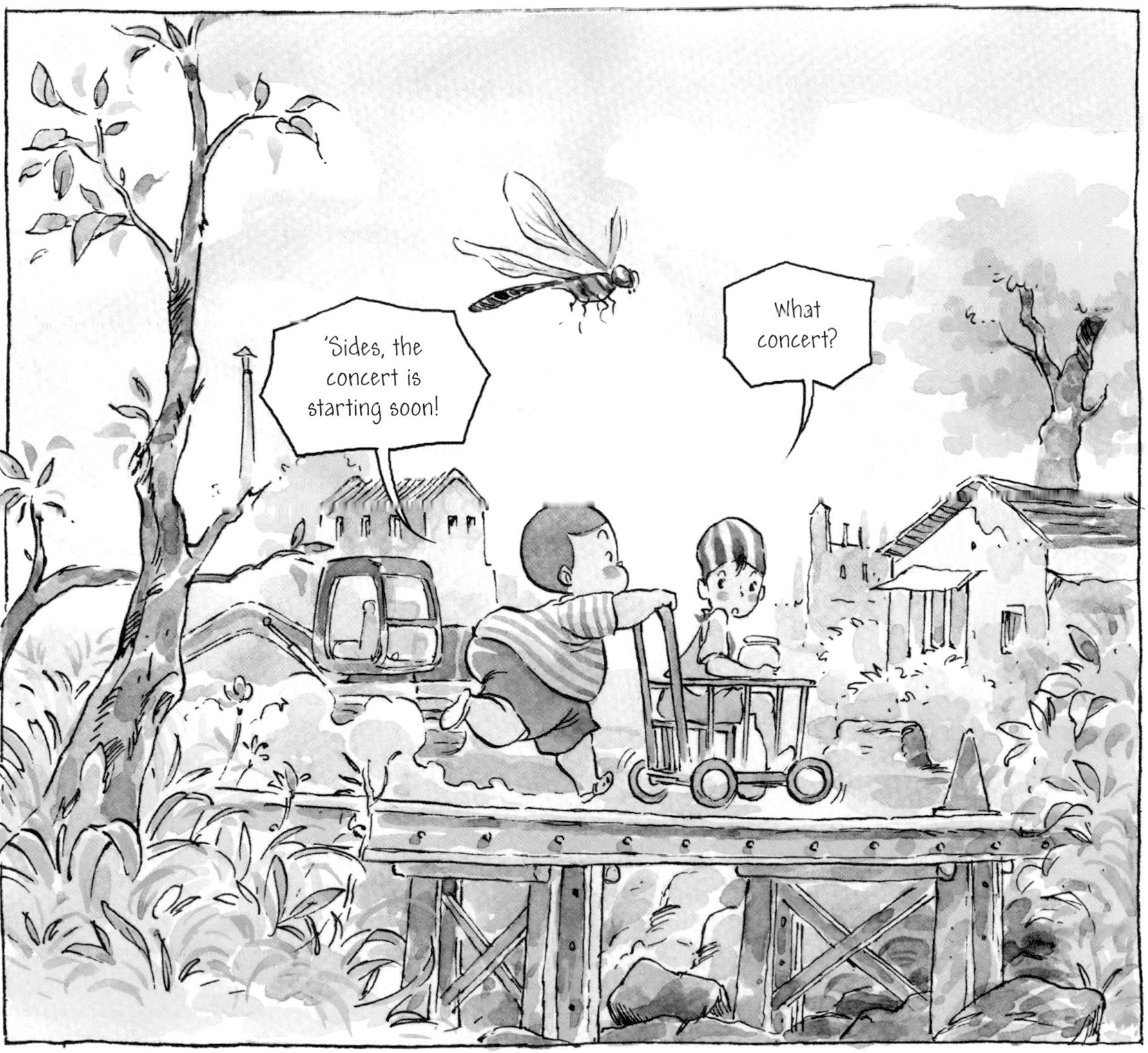
'Sides, the concert is starting soon!
What concert?

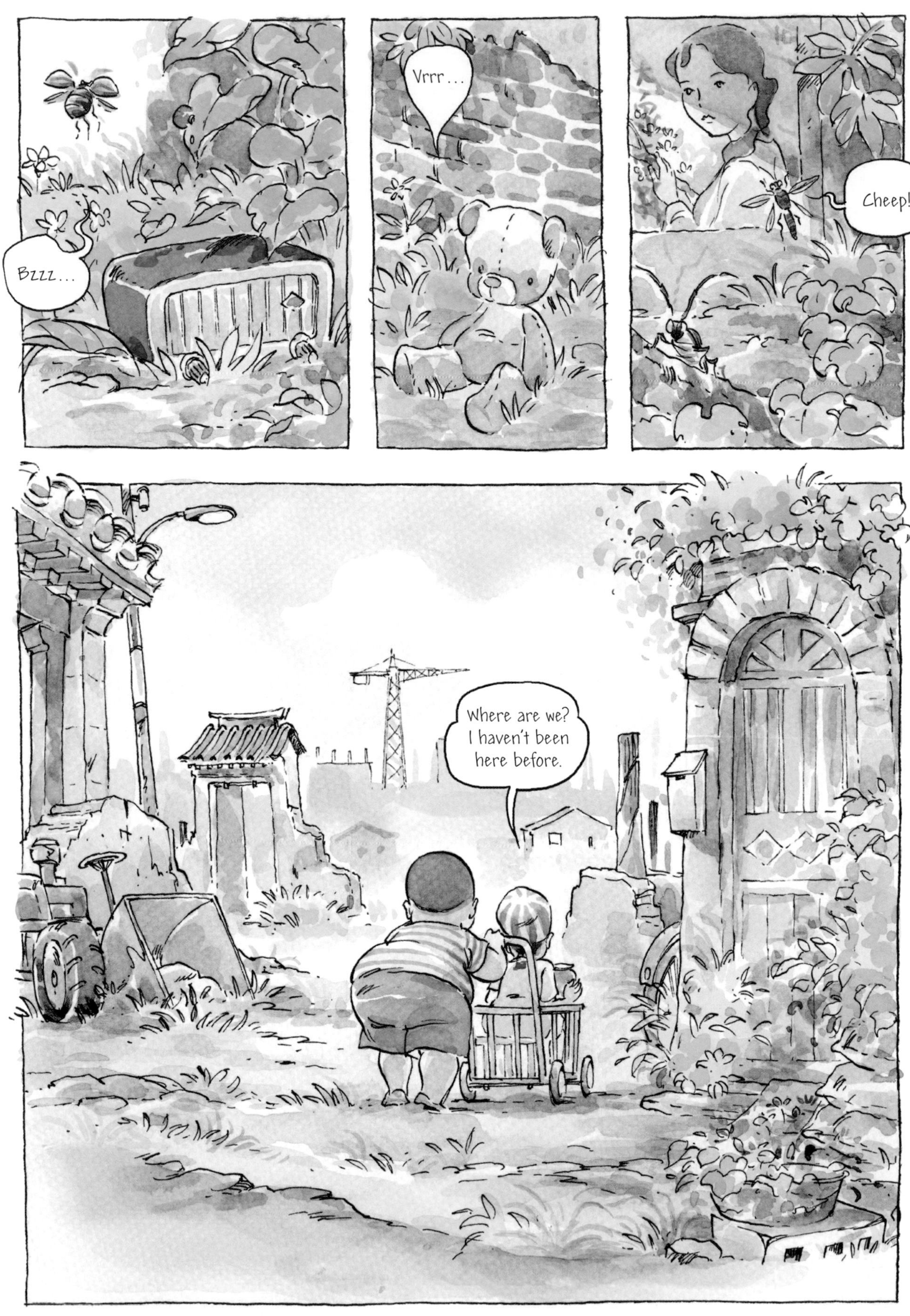
Bzzz...
Vrrr...
Cheep!
Where are we? I haven't been here before.

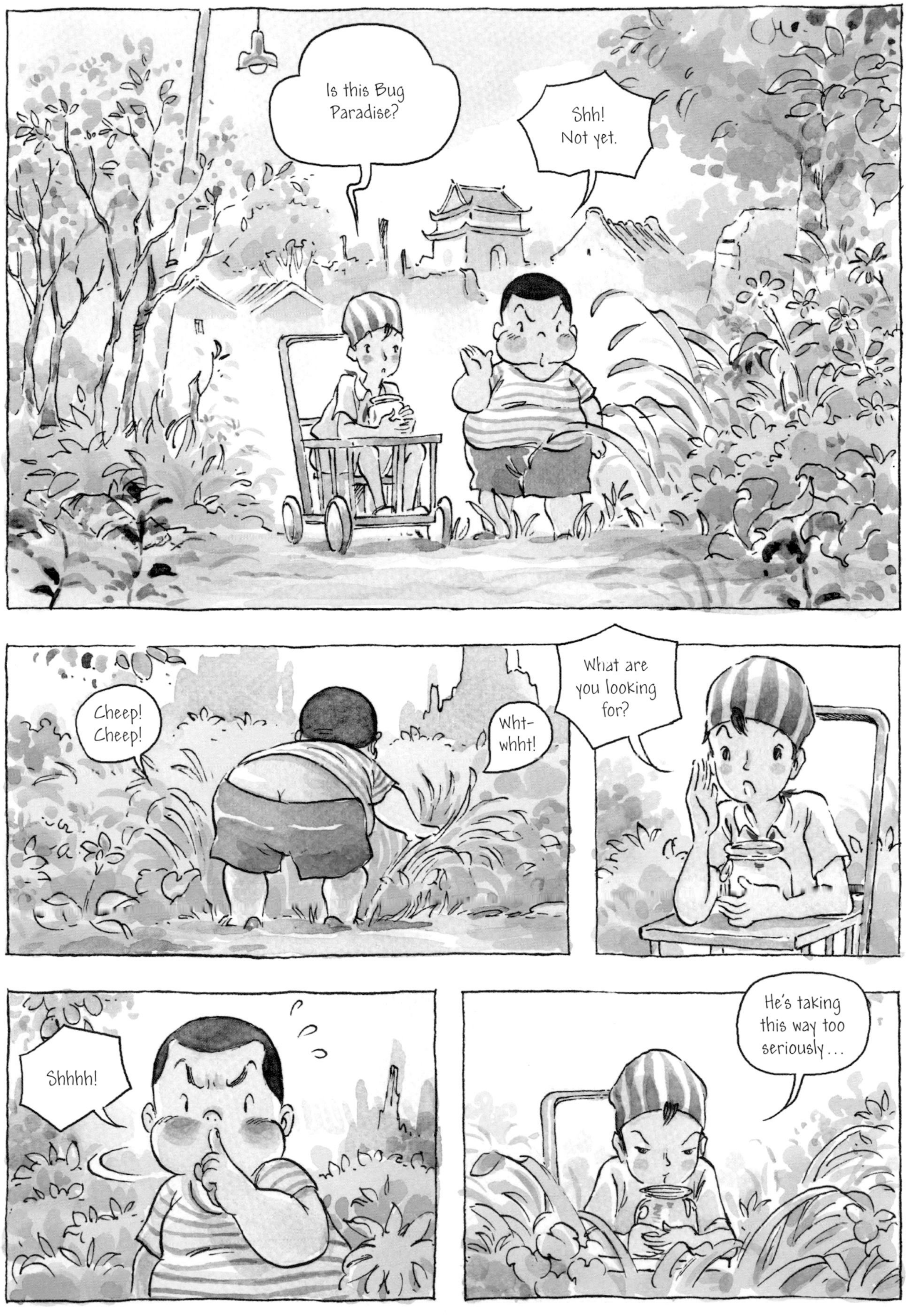

Is this Bug Paradise?
Shh! Not yet.
Cheep! Cheep!
Wht-whht!
What are you looking for?
Shhhh!
He's taking this way too seriously...

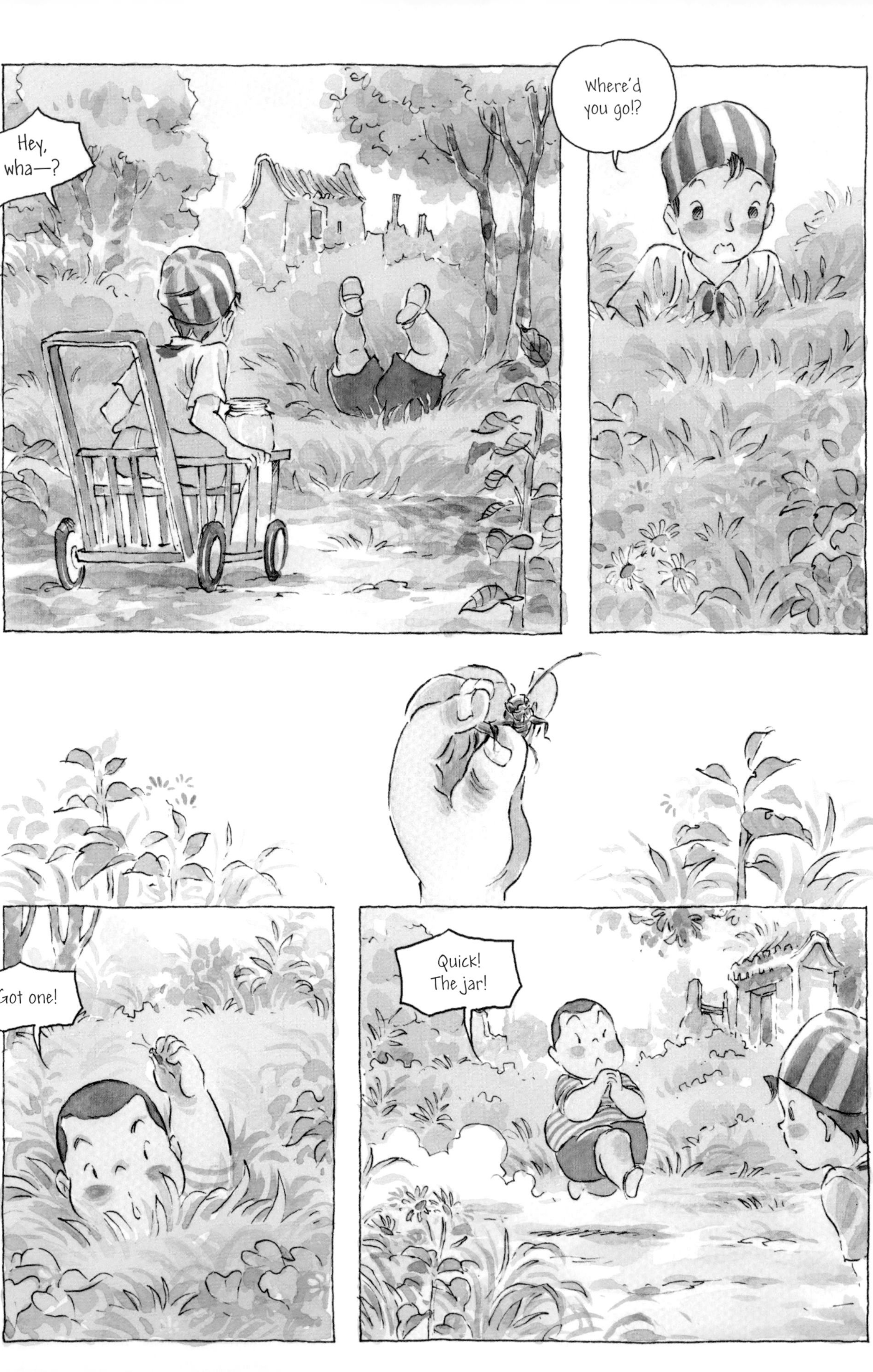
Hey, wha—?
Where'd you go!?
Got one!
Quick! The jar!

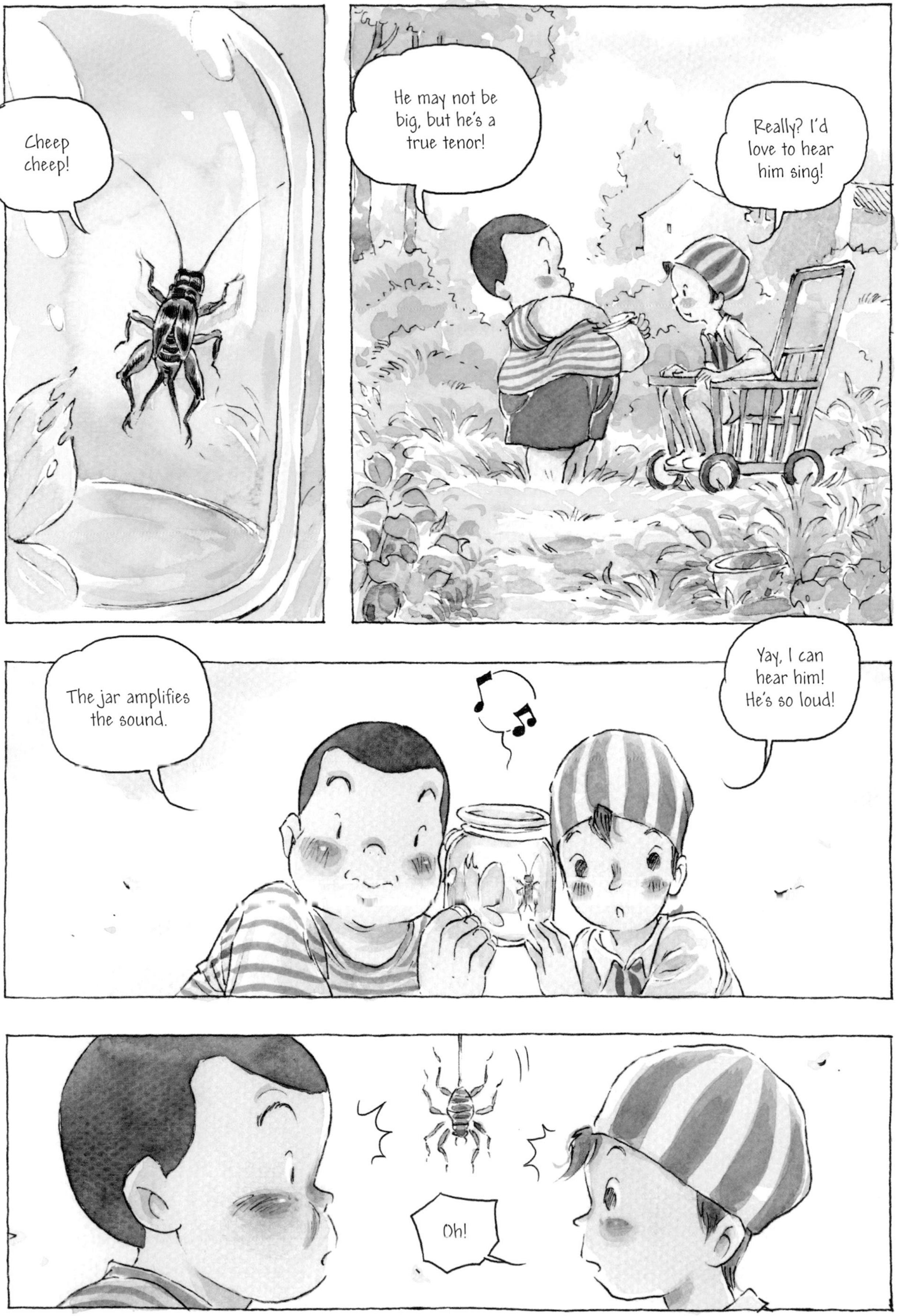
Cheep cheep!
He may not be big, but he's a true tenor!
Really? I'd love to hear him sing!
The jar amplifies the sound.
Yay, I can hear him! He's so loud!
Oh!

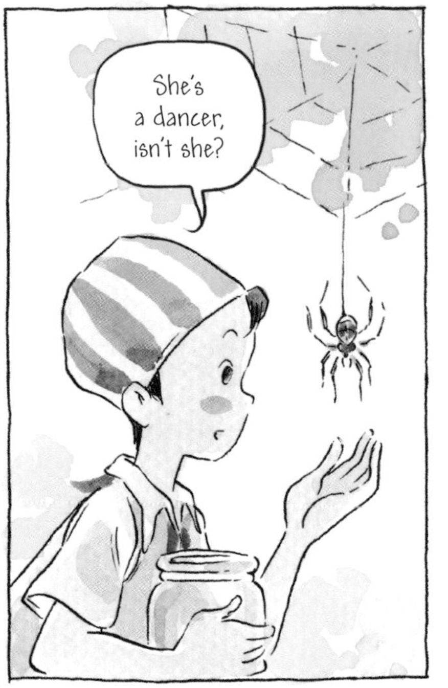
She's a dancer, isn't she?
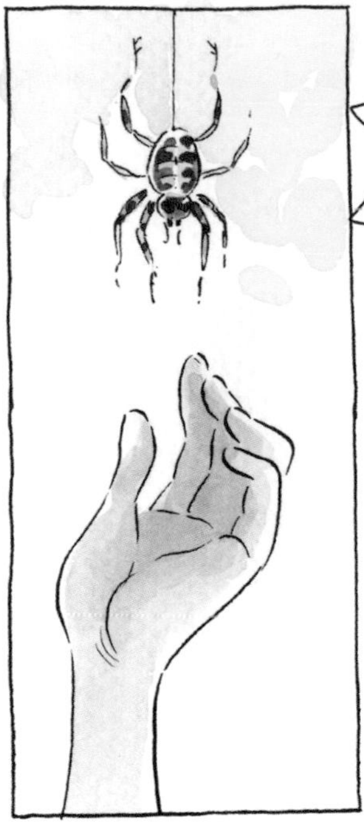
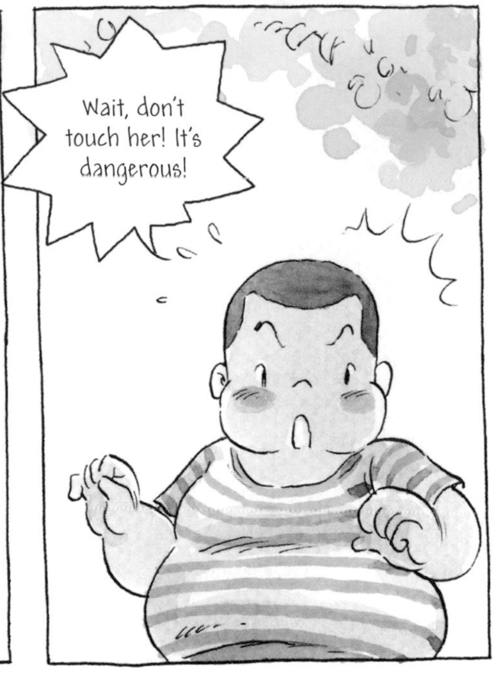
Wait, don't touch her! It's dangerous!
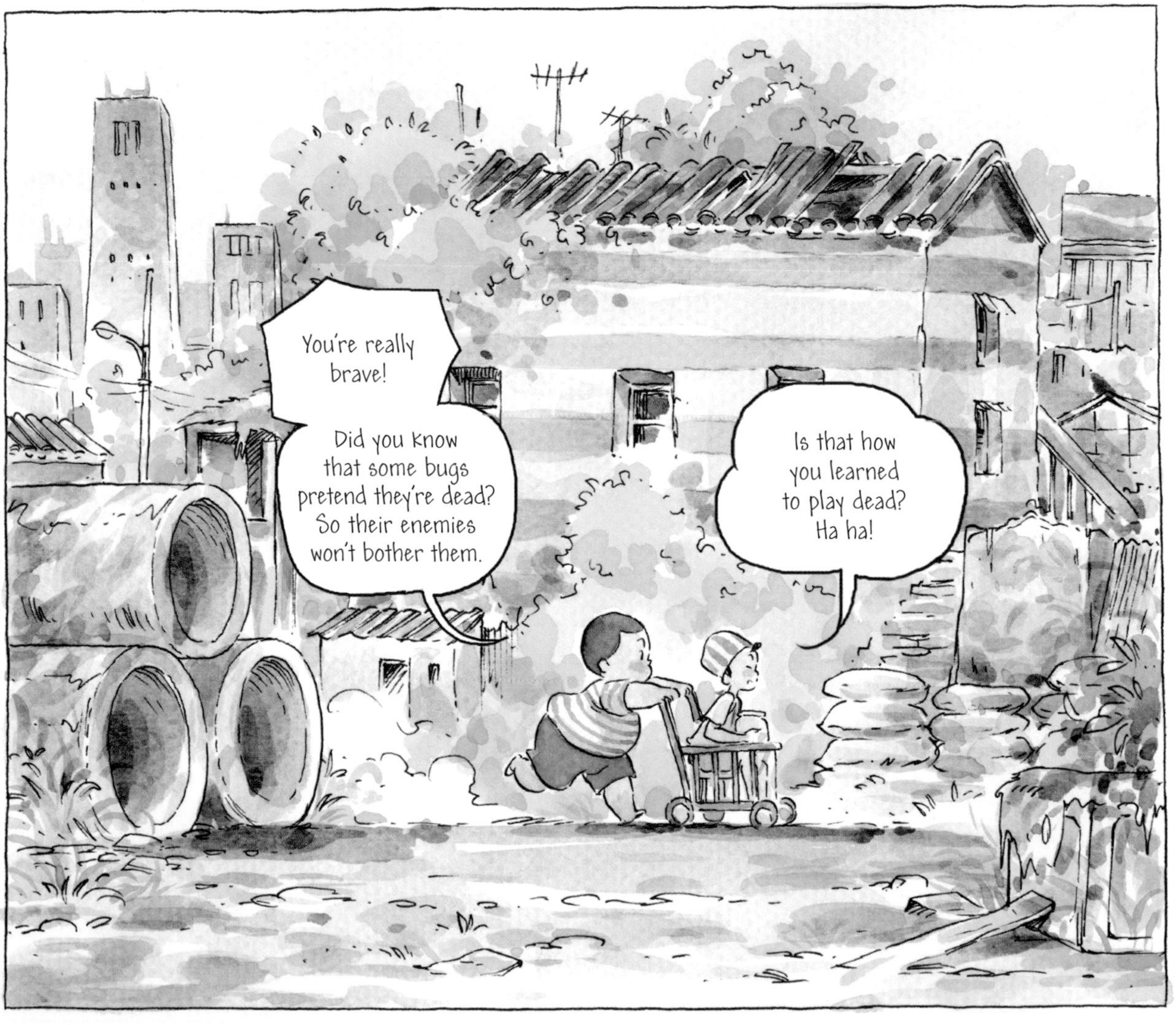
You're really brave!
Did you know that some bugs pretend they're dead? So their enemies won't bother them.
Is that how you learned to play dead? Ha ha!

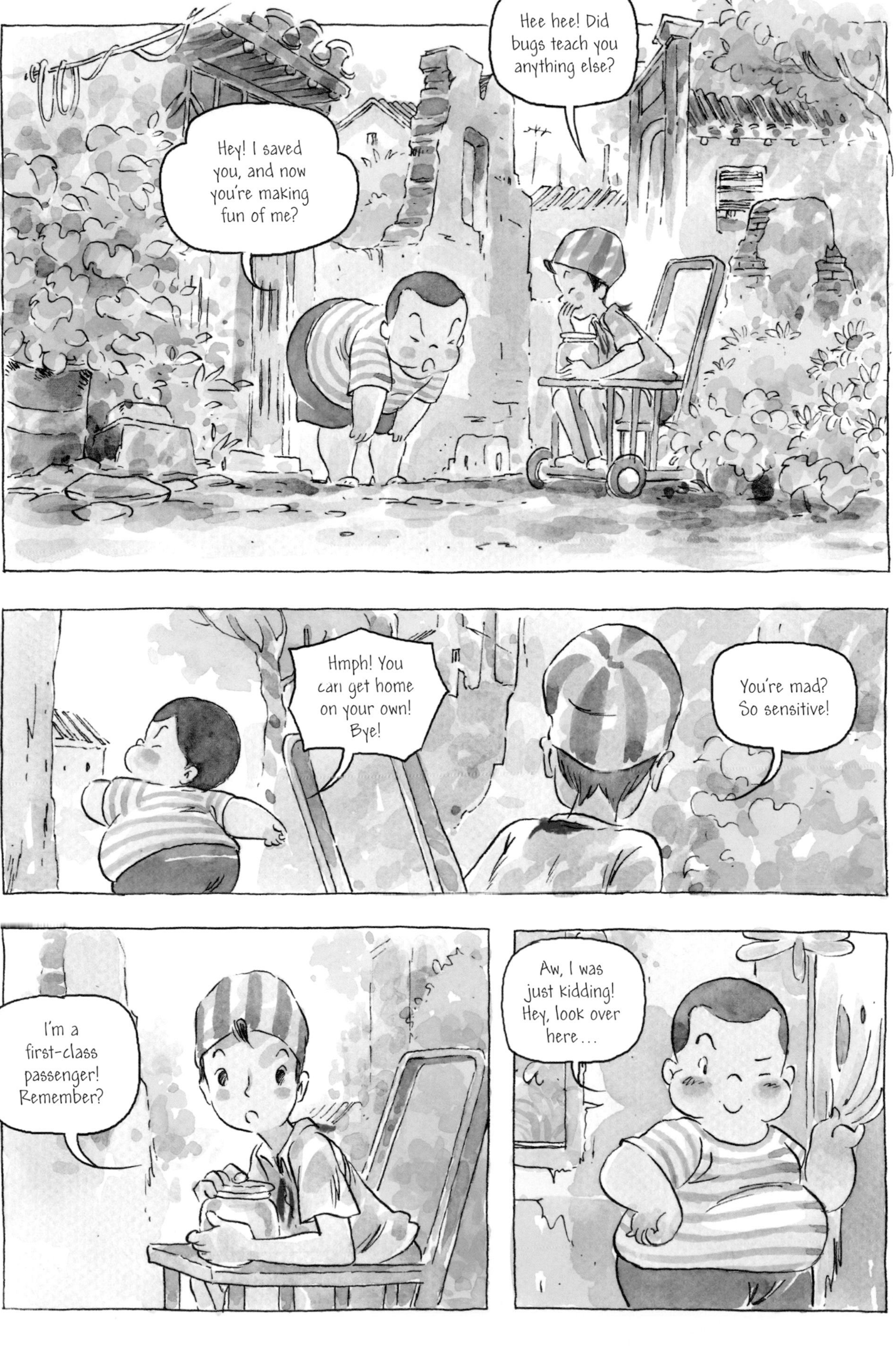
Hee hee! Did bugs teach you anything else?
Hey! I saved you, and now you're making fun of me?
Hmph! You can get home on your own! Bye!
You're mad? So sensitive!
I'm a first-class passenger! Remember?
Aw, I was just kidding! Hey, look over here...

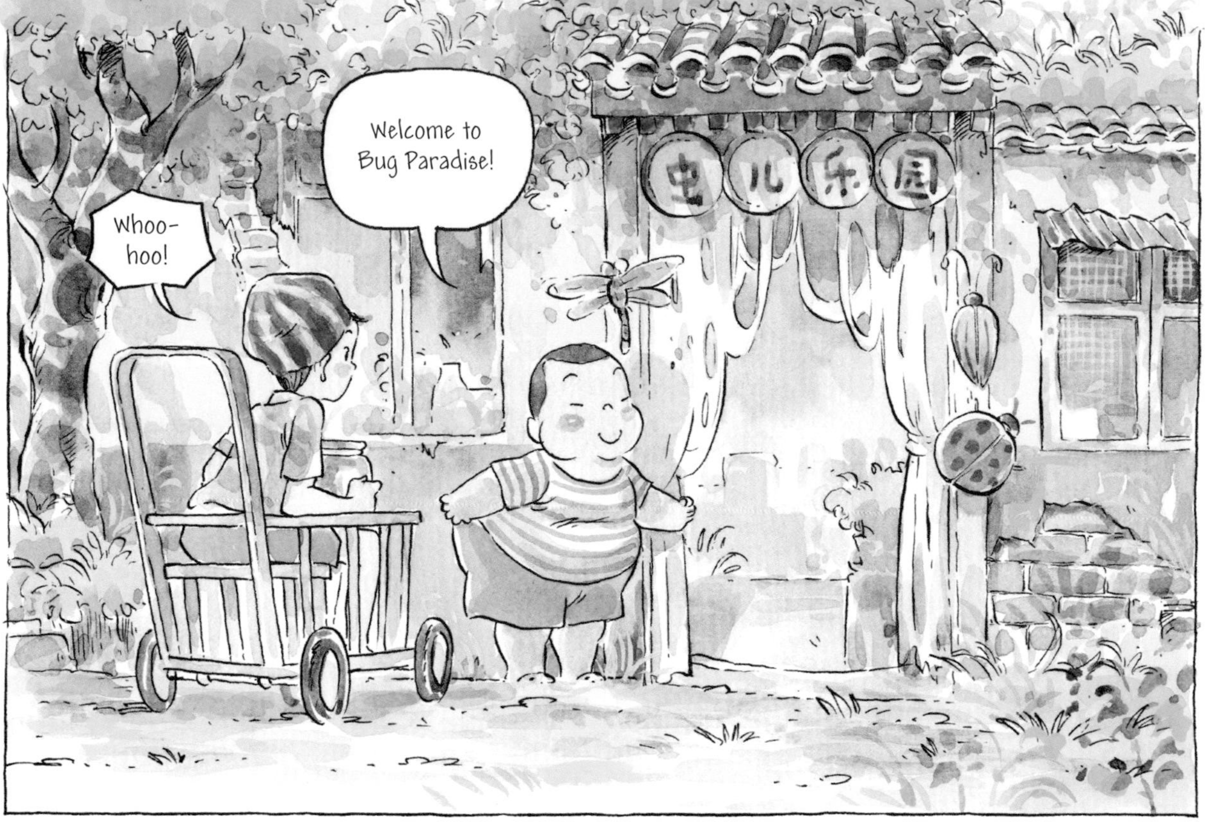
Welcome to Bug Paradise!
Whooo-hoo!
虫儿乐园

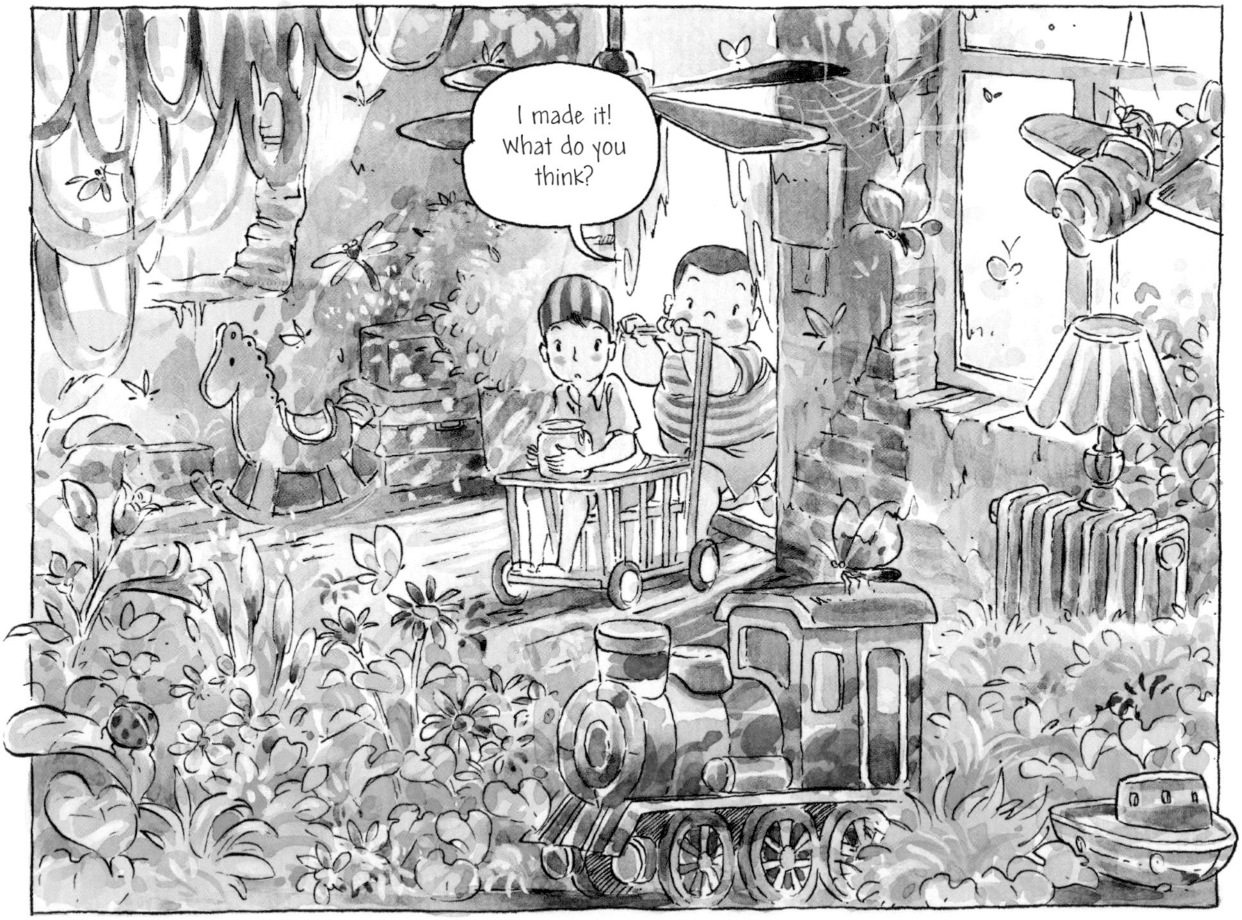
I made it! What do you think?

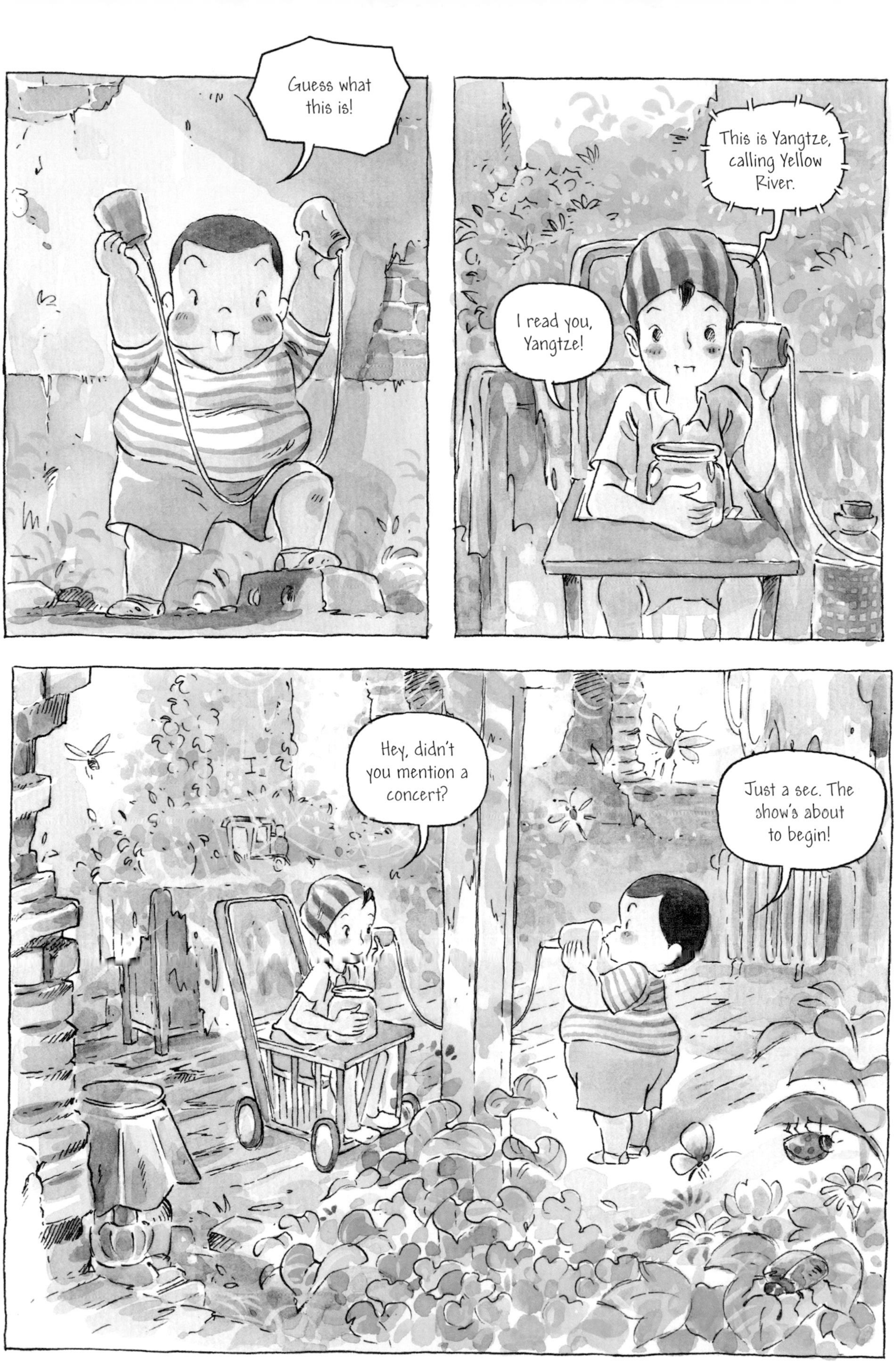
Guess what this is!
This is Yangtze, calling Yellow River.
I read you, Yangtze!
Hey, didn't you mention a concert?
Just a sec. The show's about to begin!

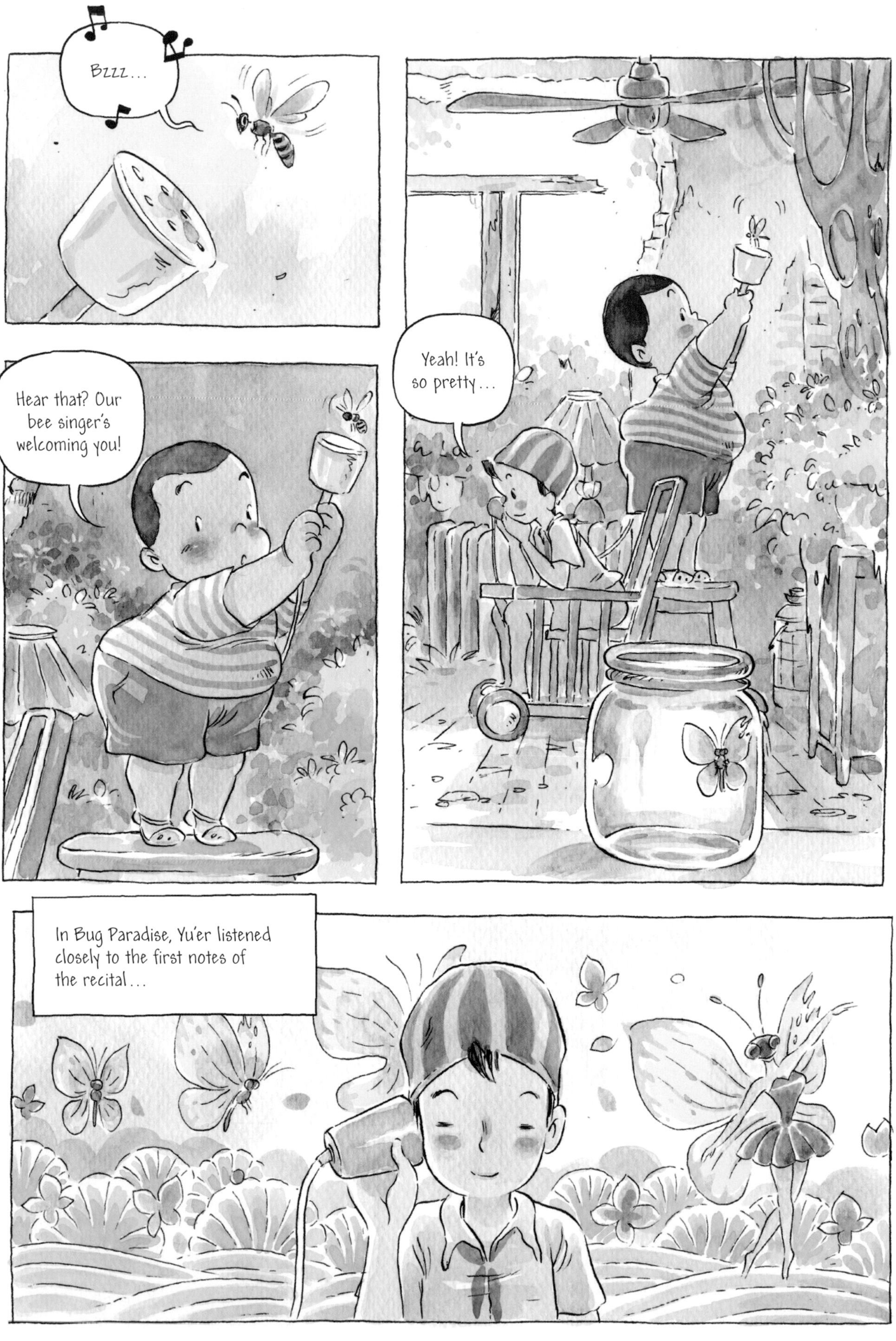
Bzzz...
Hear that? Our bee singer's welcoming you!
Yeah! It's so pretty...
In Bug Paradise, Yu'er listened closely to the first notes of the recital...

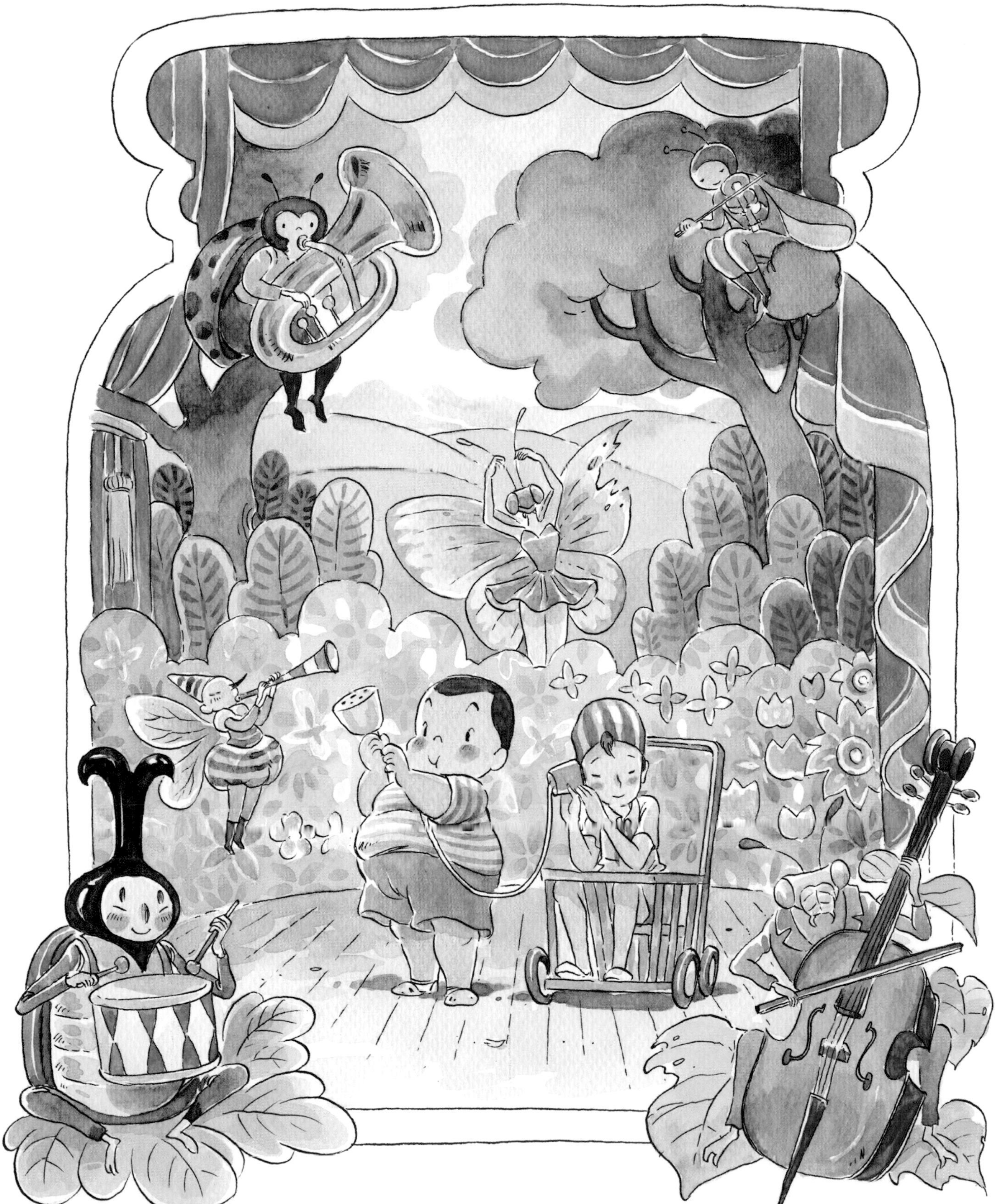

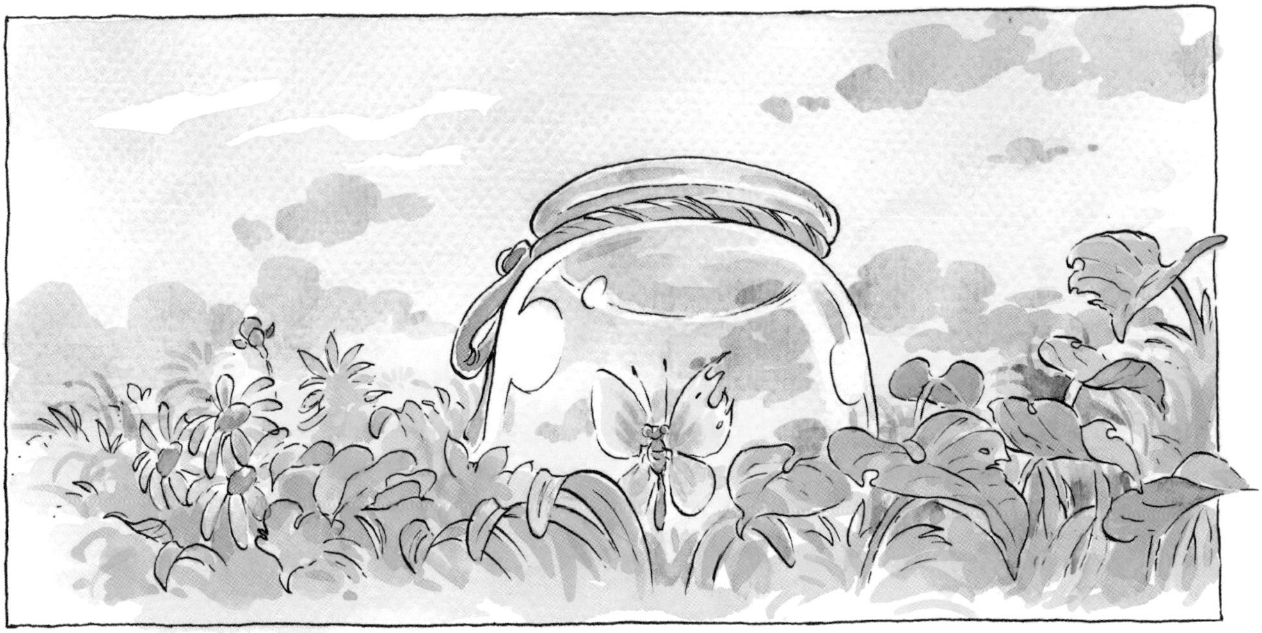

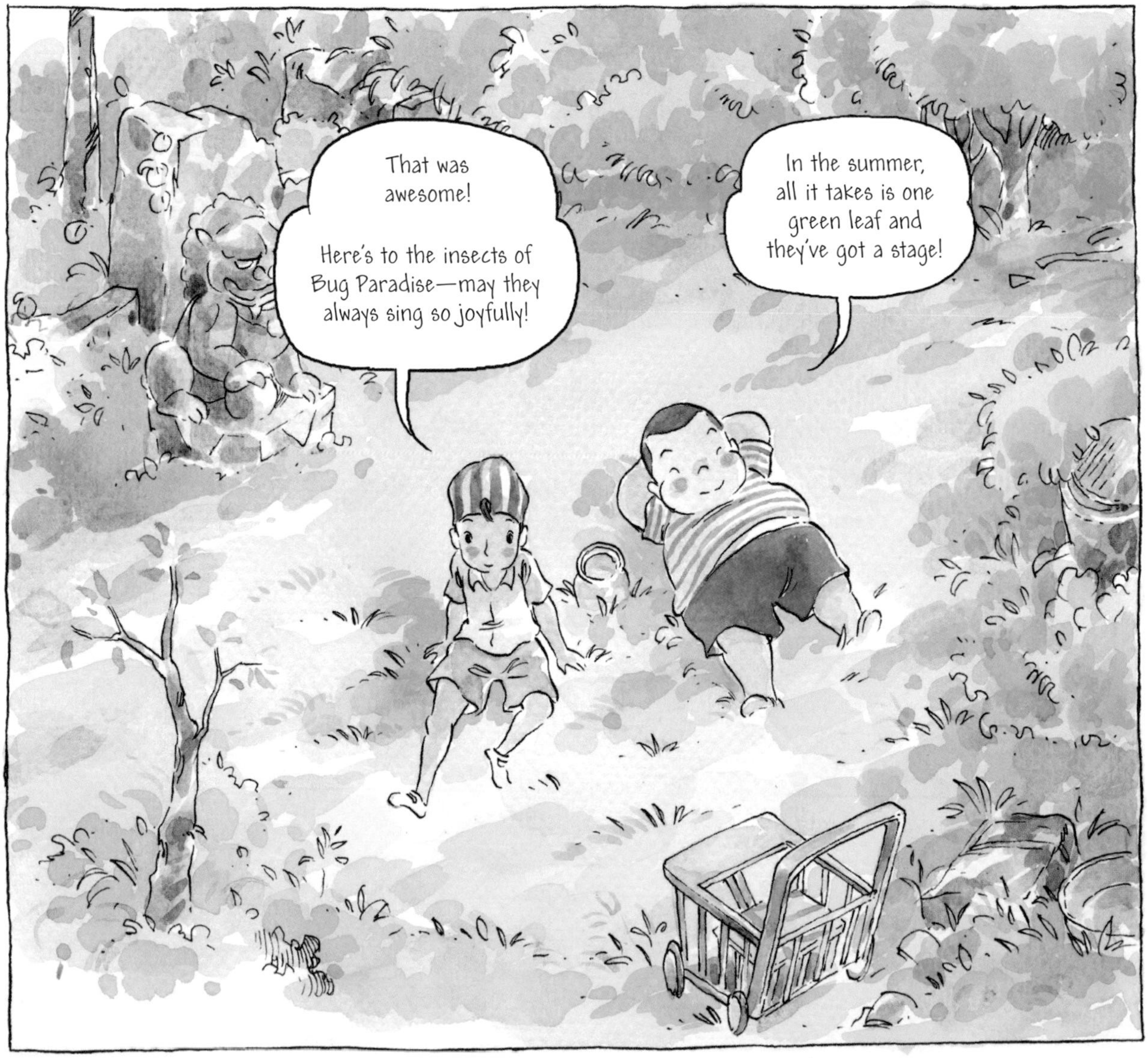

That was awesome!
Here's to the insects of Bug Paradise—may they always sing so joyfully!
In the summer, all it takes is one green leaf and they've got a stage!

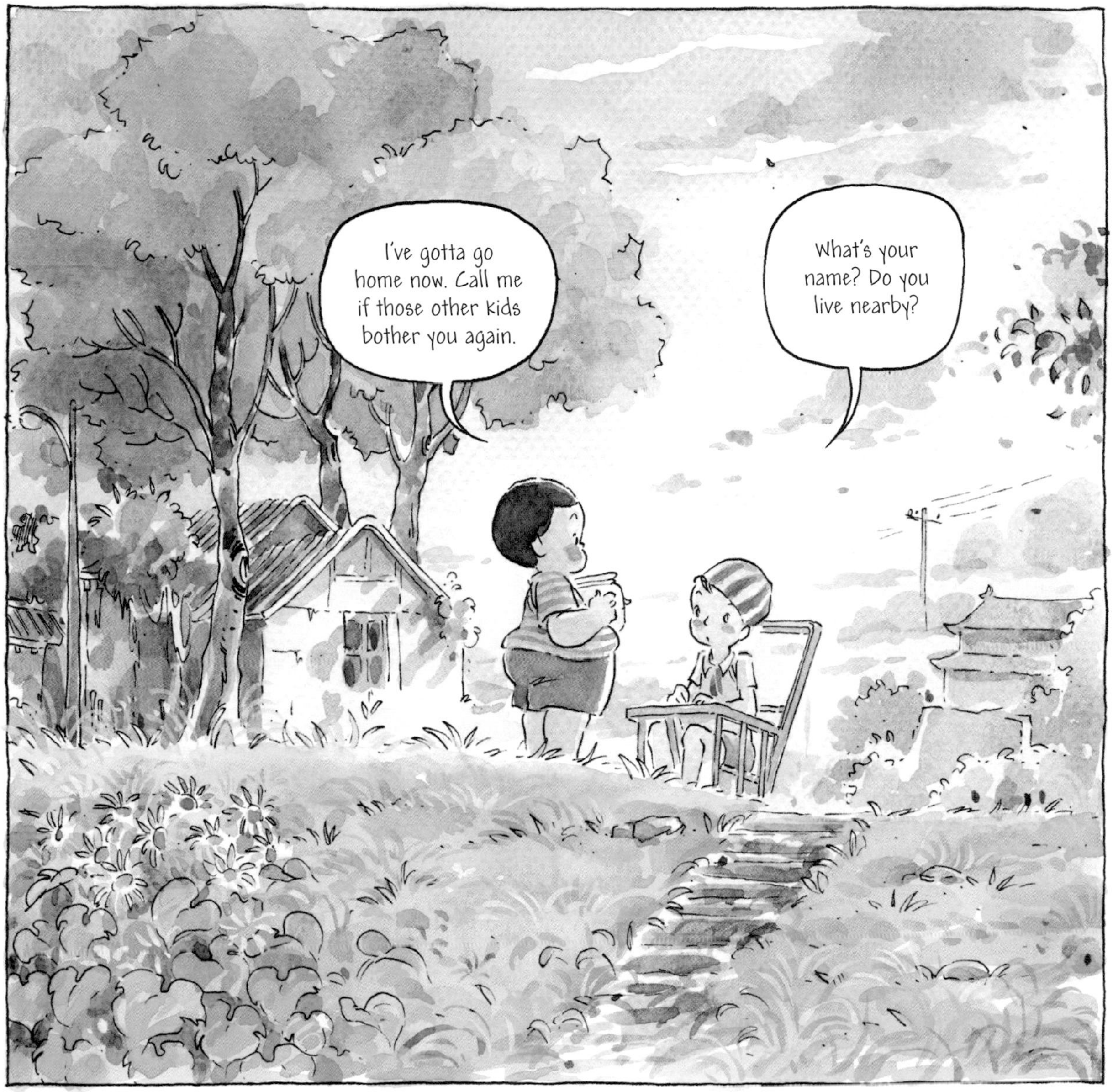
I've gotta go home now. Call me if those other kids bother you again.
What's your name? Do you live nearby?

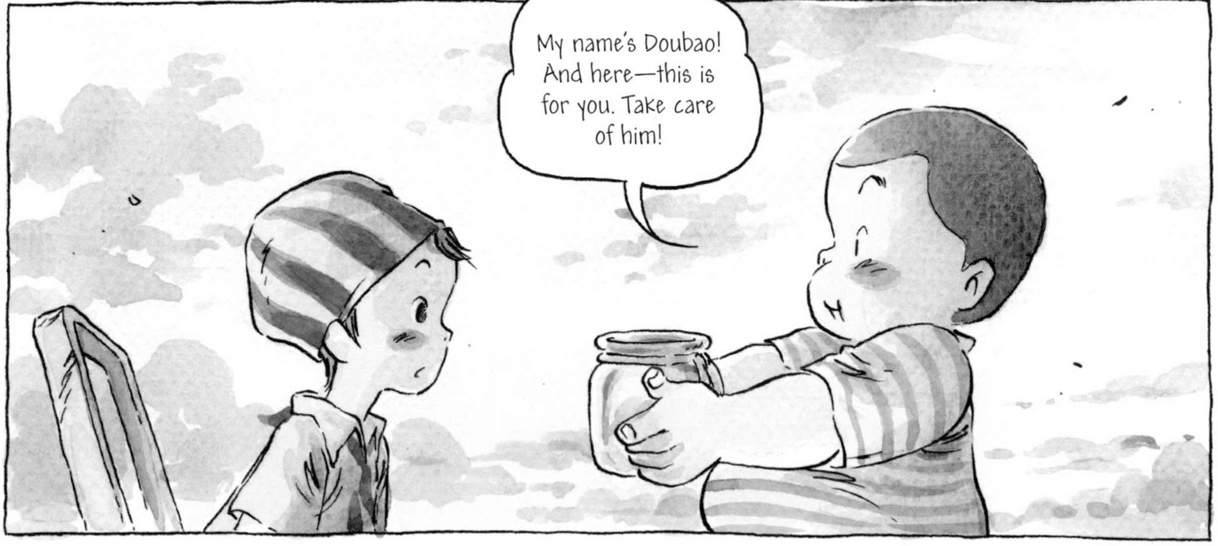
My name's Doubao! And here—this is for you. Take care of him!

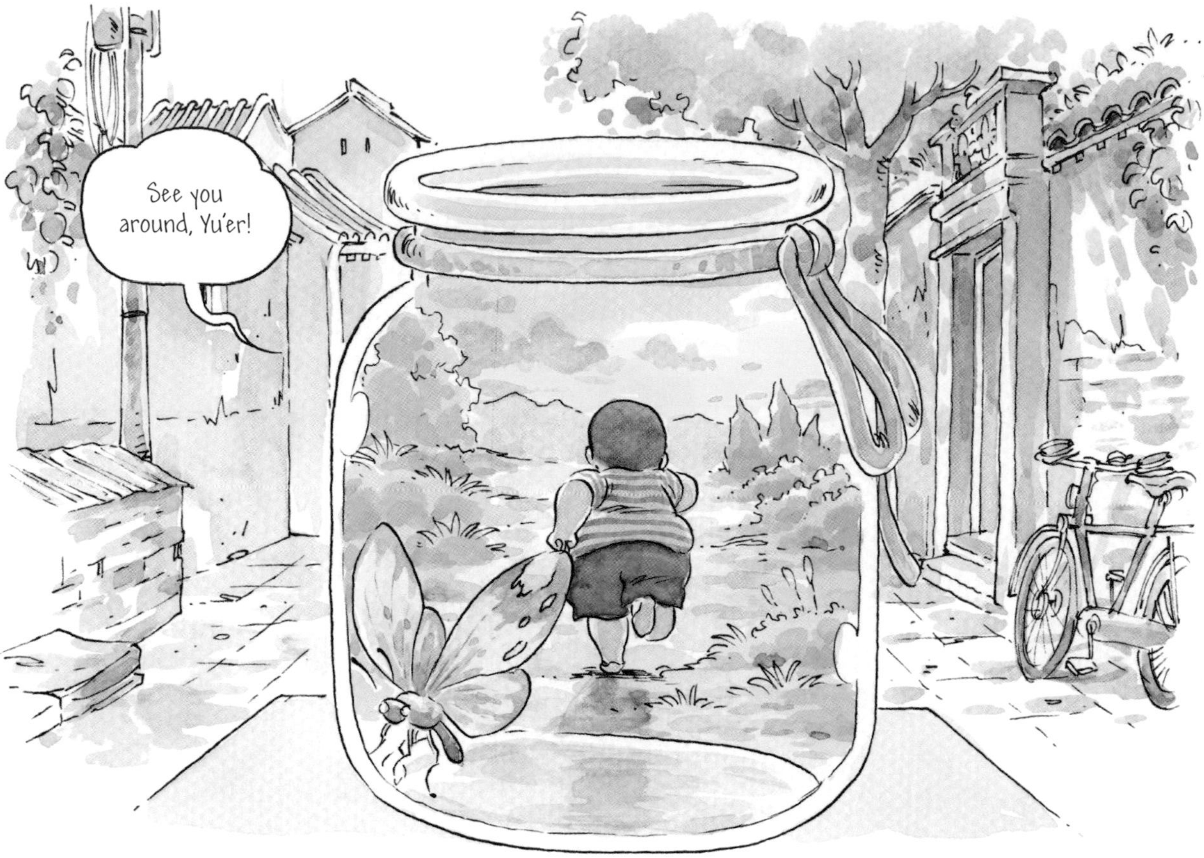
See you around, Yu'er!

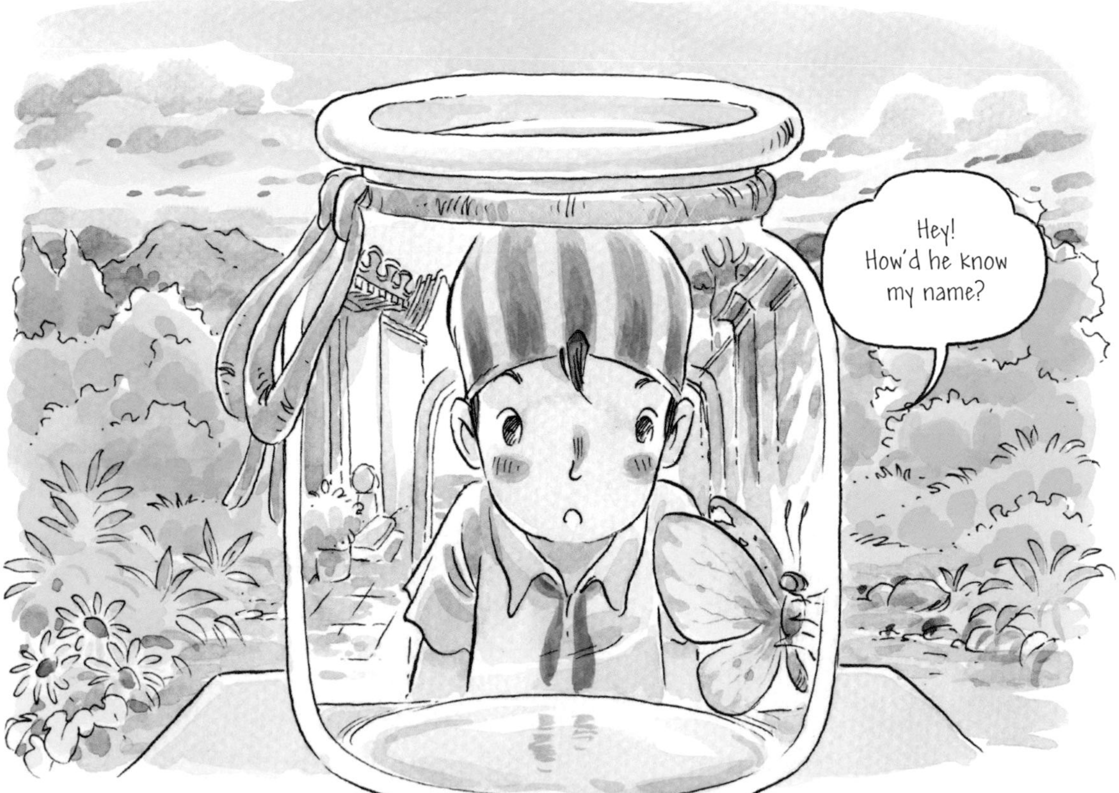
Hey! How'd he know my name?

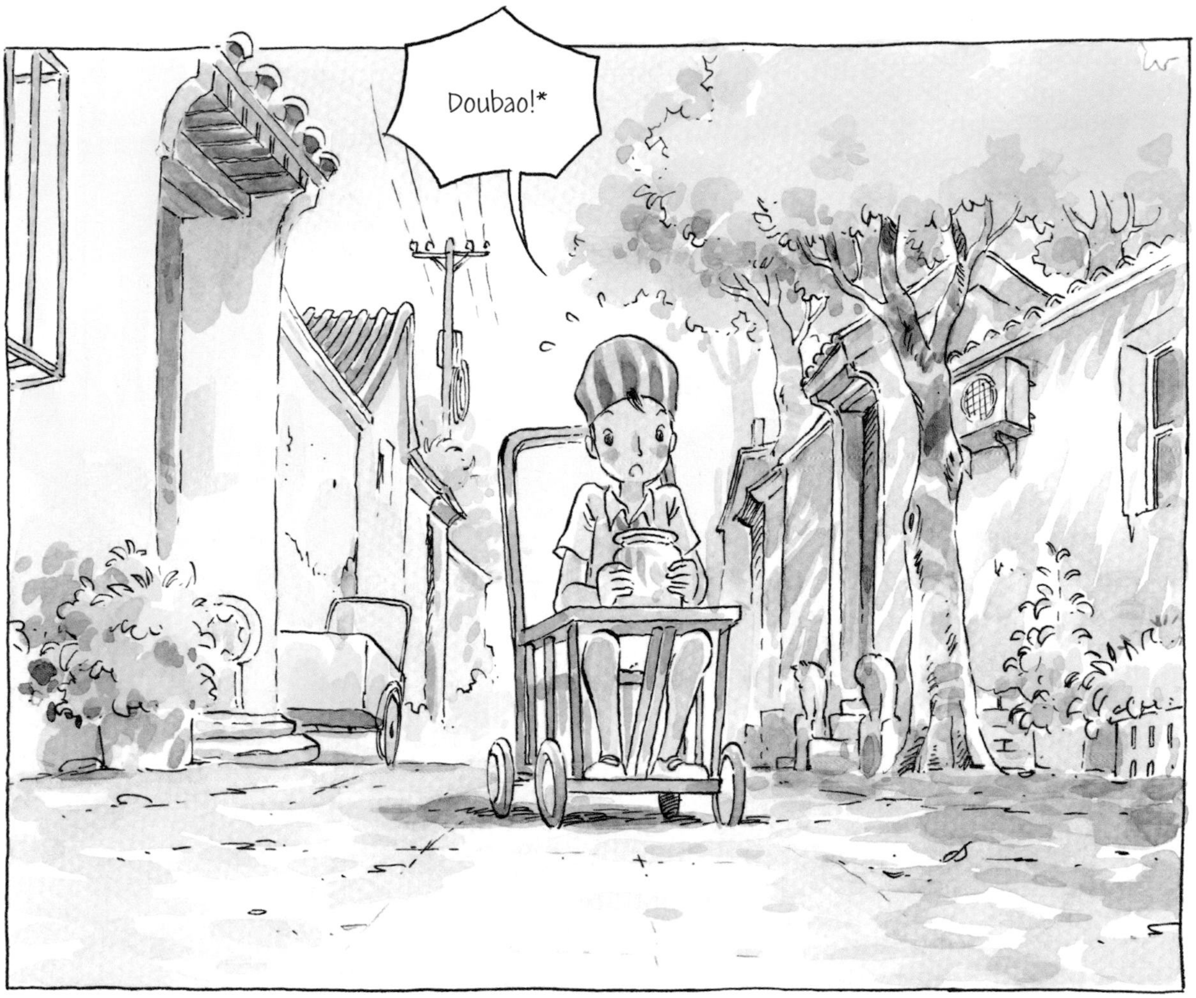
Doubao!*

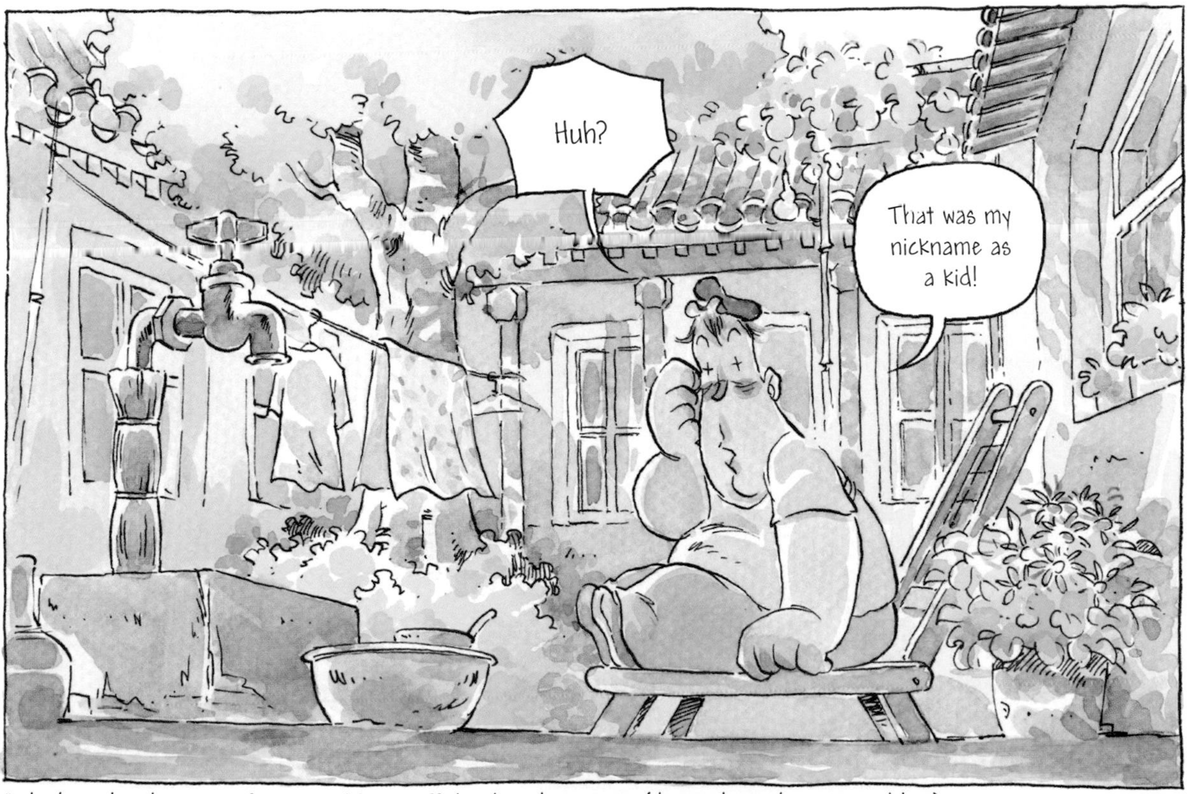
Huh?
That was my nickname as a kid!

* *doubao*: also the name of a steamed bun stuffed with soybean paste (*dou*: soybean; *bao*: steamed bun)

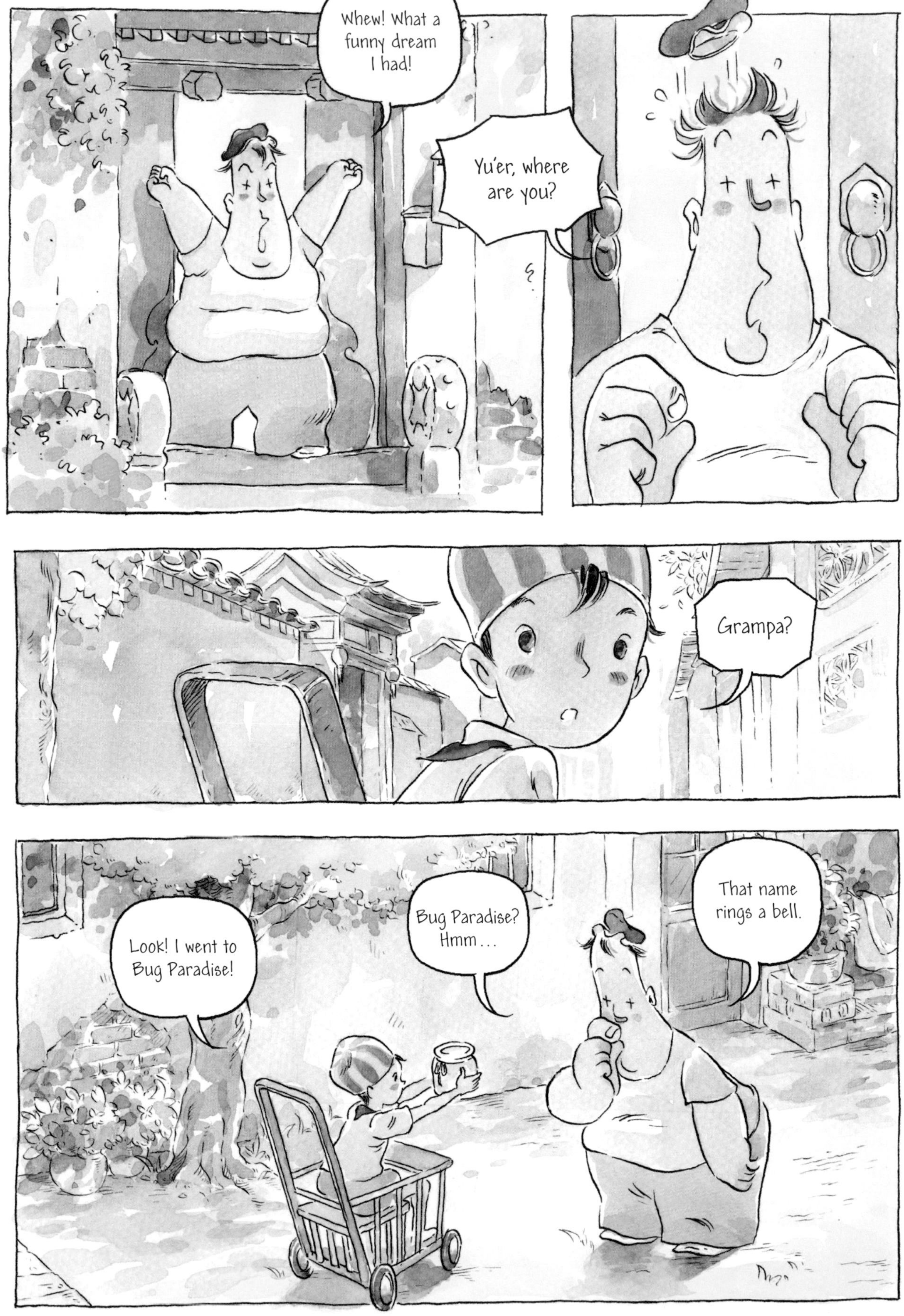
Whew! What a funny dream I had!
Yu'er, where are you?
Grampa?
Look! I went to Bug Paradise!
Bug Paradise? Hmm...
That name rings a bell.

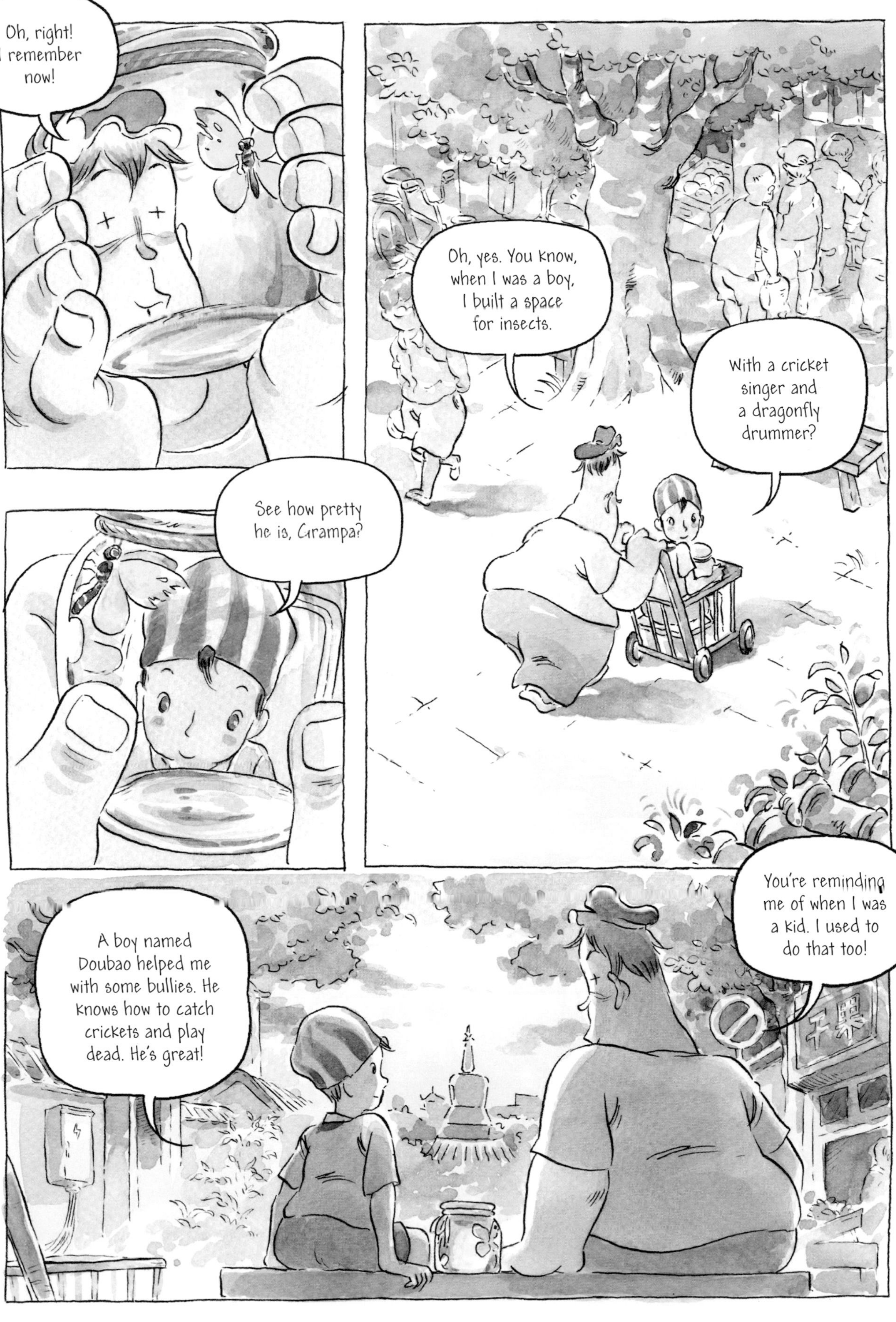
Oh, right! I remember now!
Oh, yes. You know, when I was a boy, I built a space for insects.
With a cricket singer and a dragonfly drummer?
See how pretty he is, Grampa?
A boy named Doubao helped me with some bullies. He knows how to catch crickets and play dead. He's great!
You're reminding me of when I was a kid. I used to do that too!

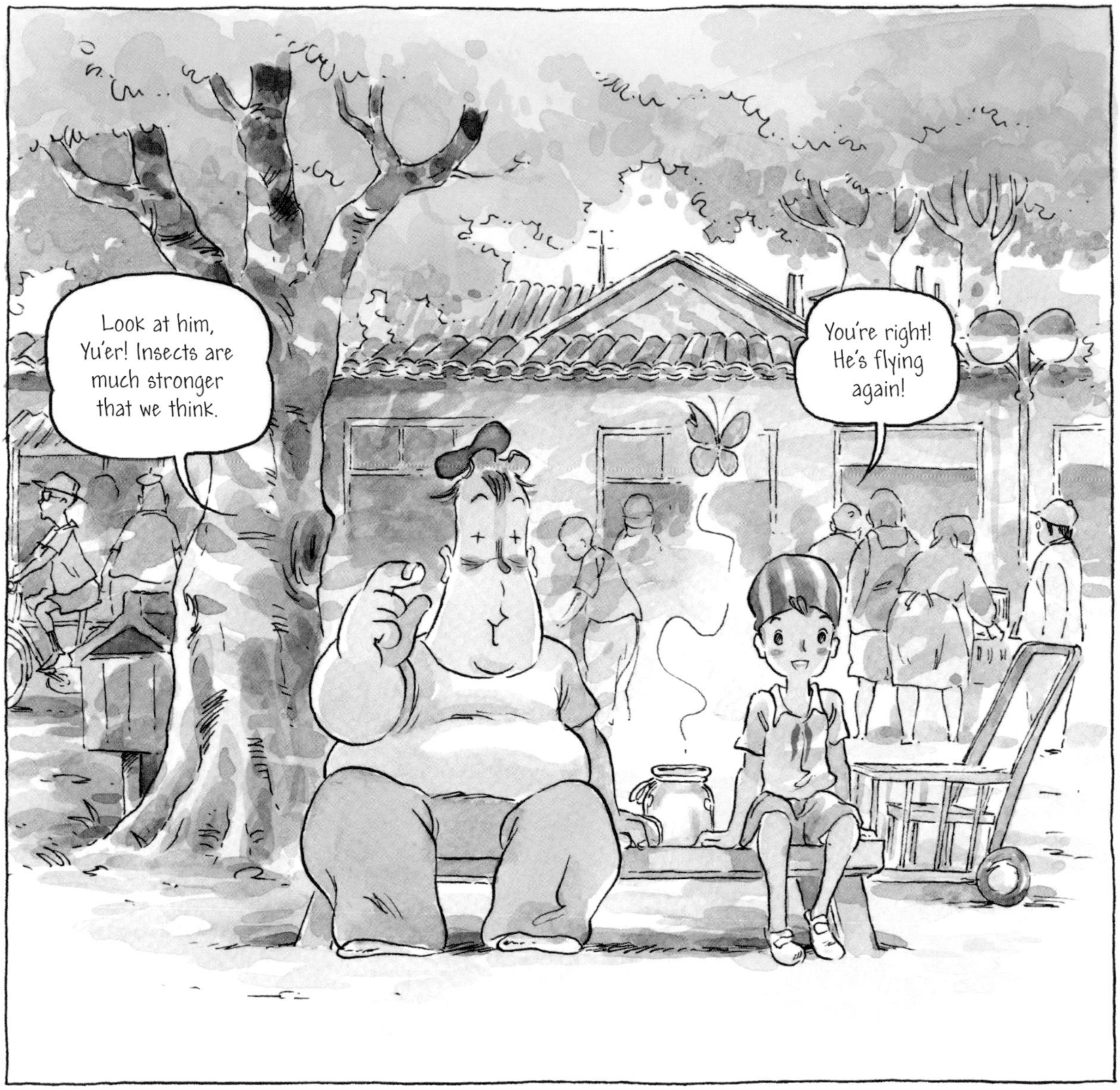
Look at him, Yu'er! Insects are much stronger that we think.
You're right! He's flying again!

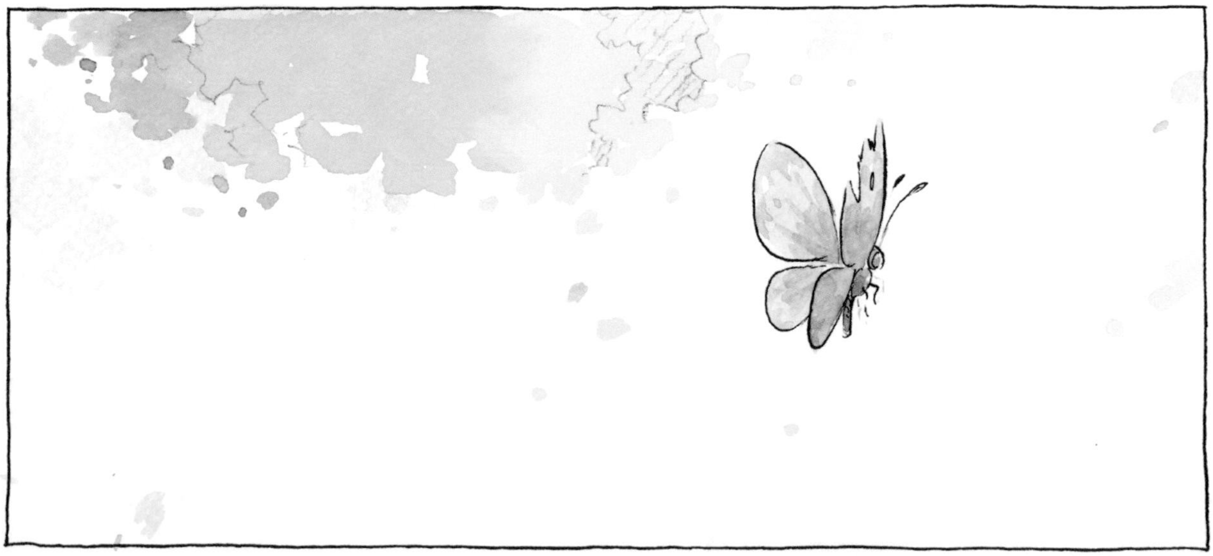

Yu'er never saw the boy named Doubao
again. But one day, she found an old photo
of her grandpa from many years ago...

THE END

THE LETTER

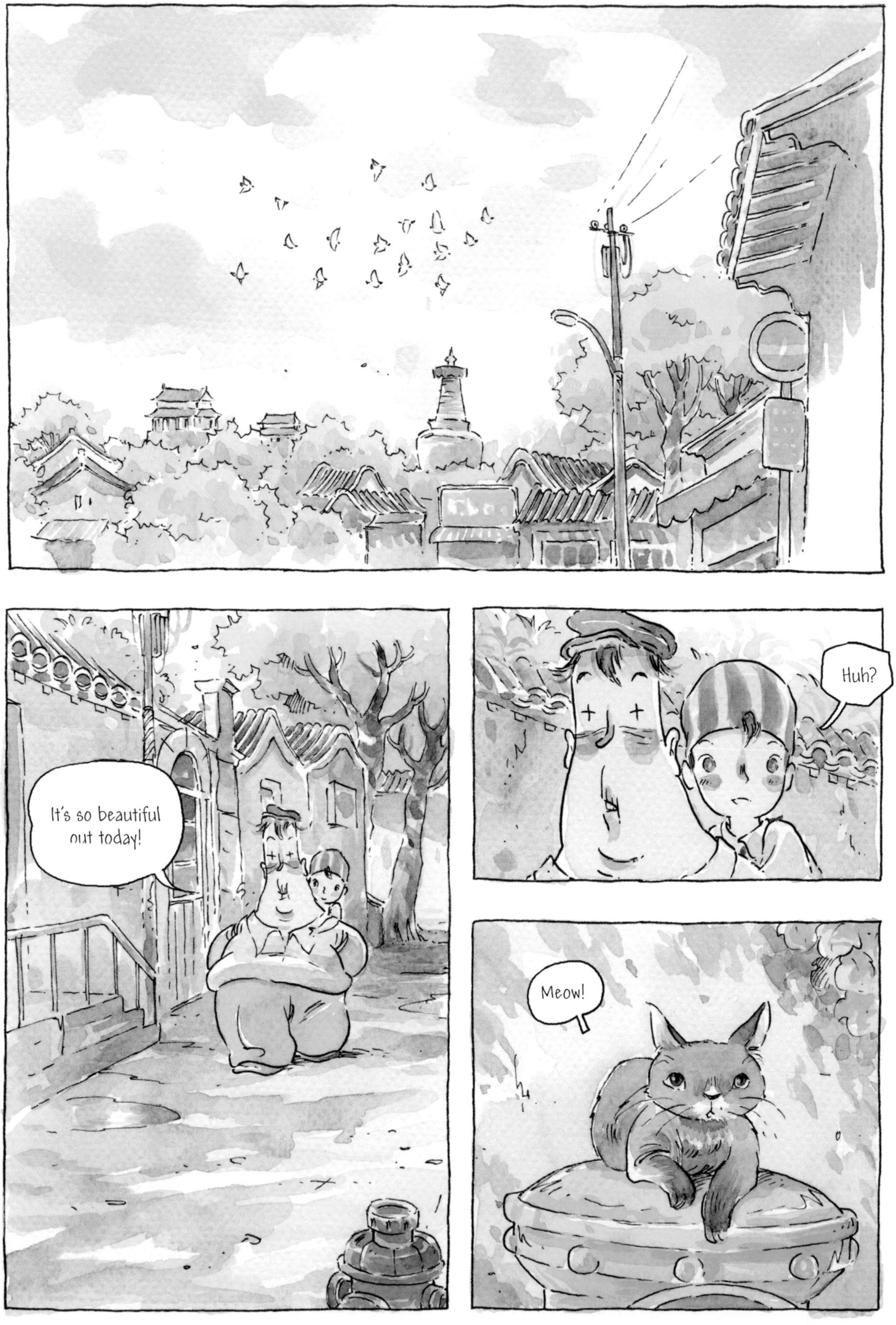
It's so beautiful out today!
Huh?
Meow!

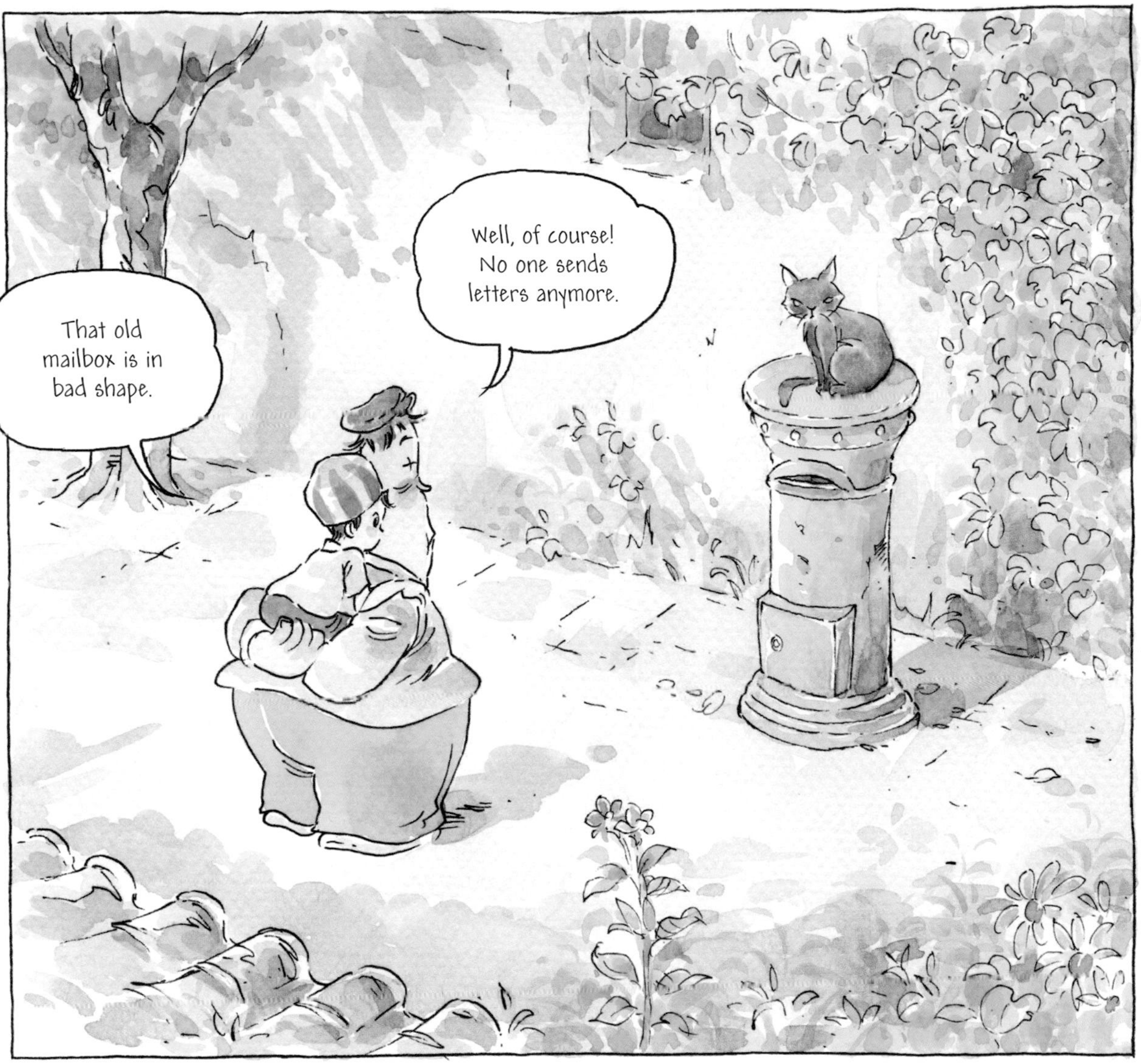
That old mailbox is in bad shape.
Well, of course! No one sends letters anymore.

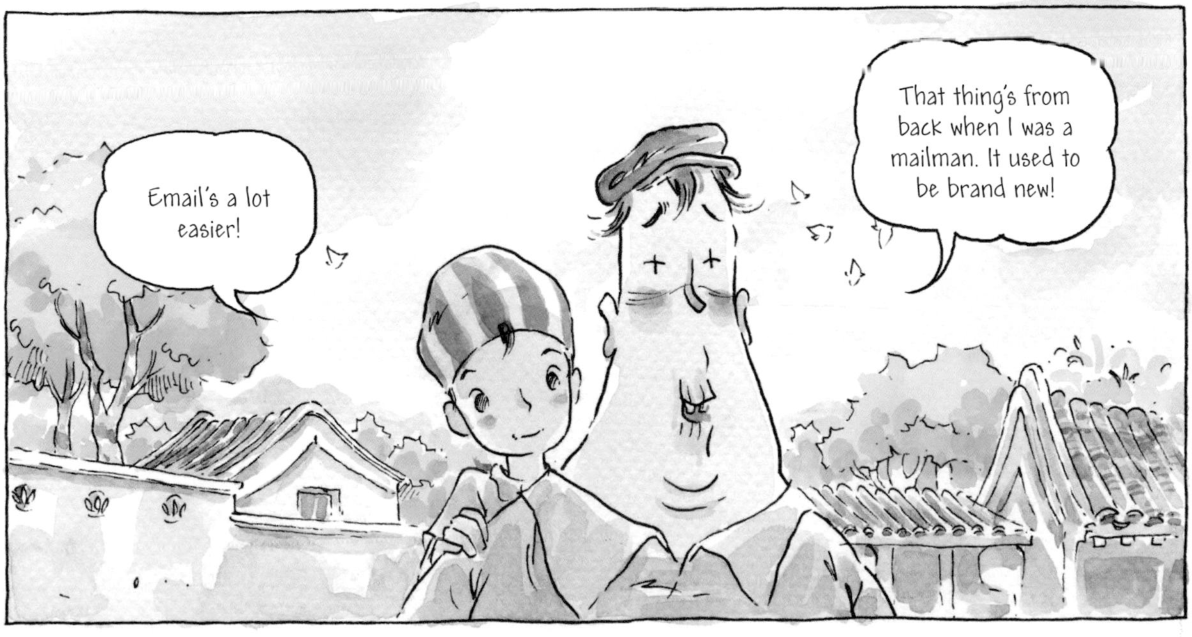
Email's a lot easier!
That thing's from back when I was a mailman. It used to be brand new!

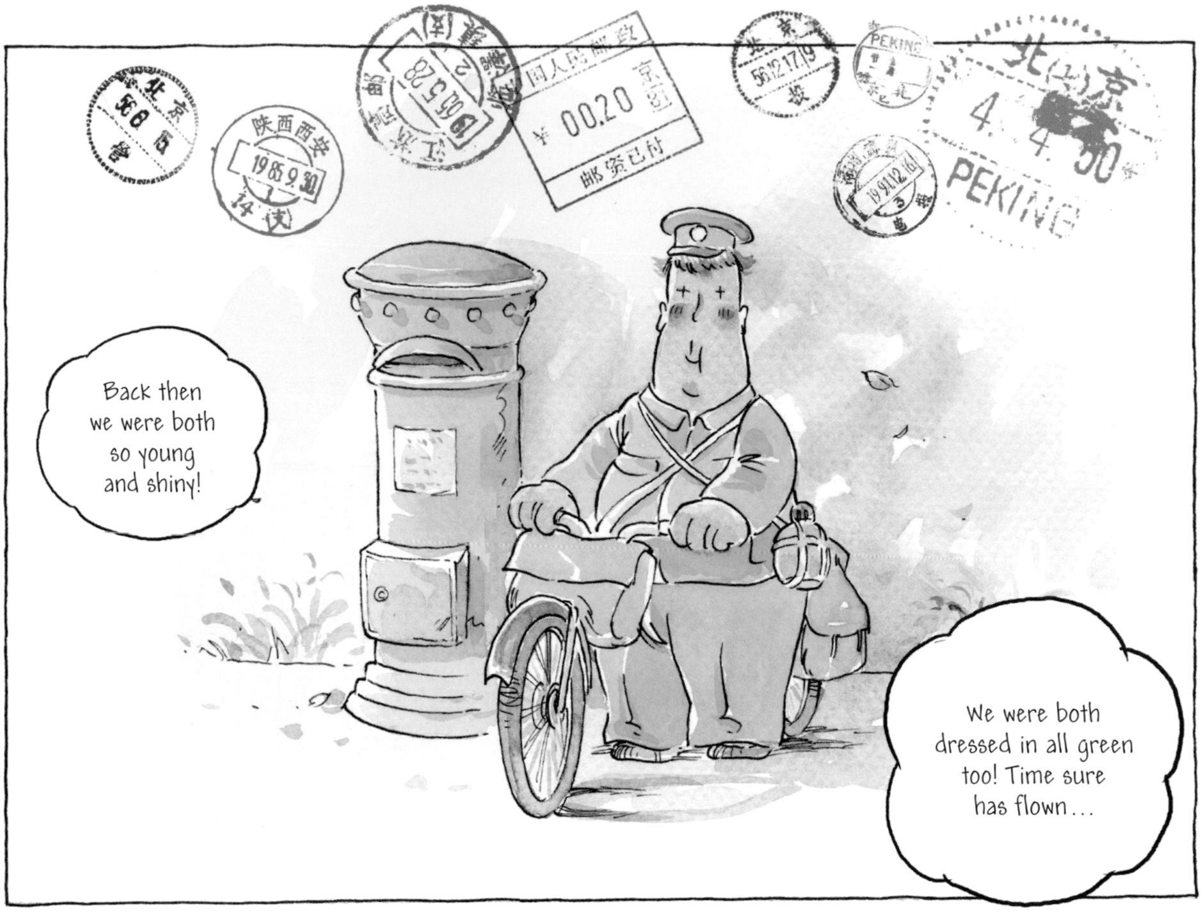
PEKING
Back then we were both so young and shiny!
We were both dressed in all green too! Time sure has flown...

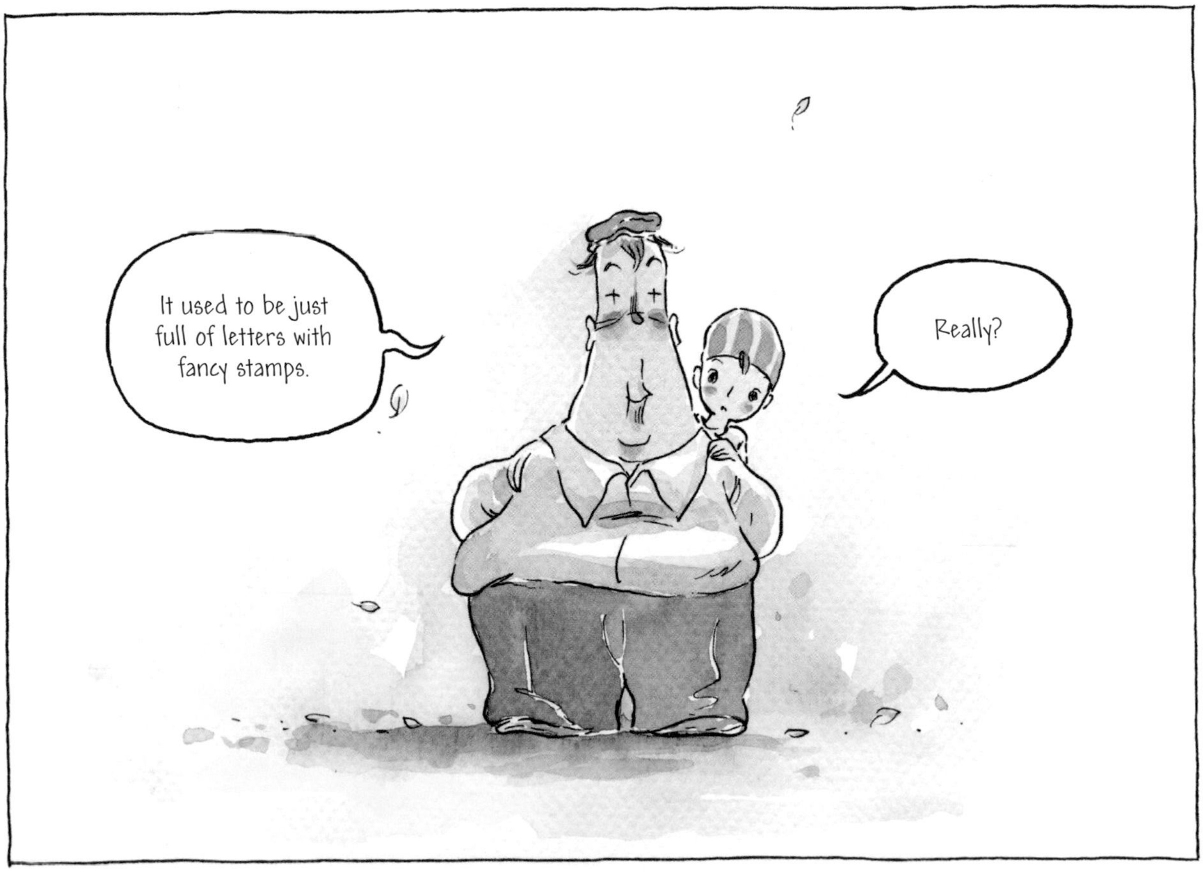
It used to be just full of letters with fancy stamps.
Really?

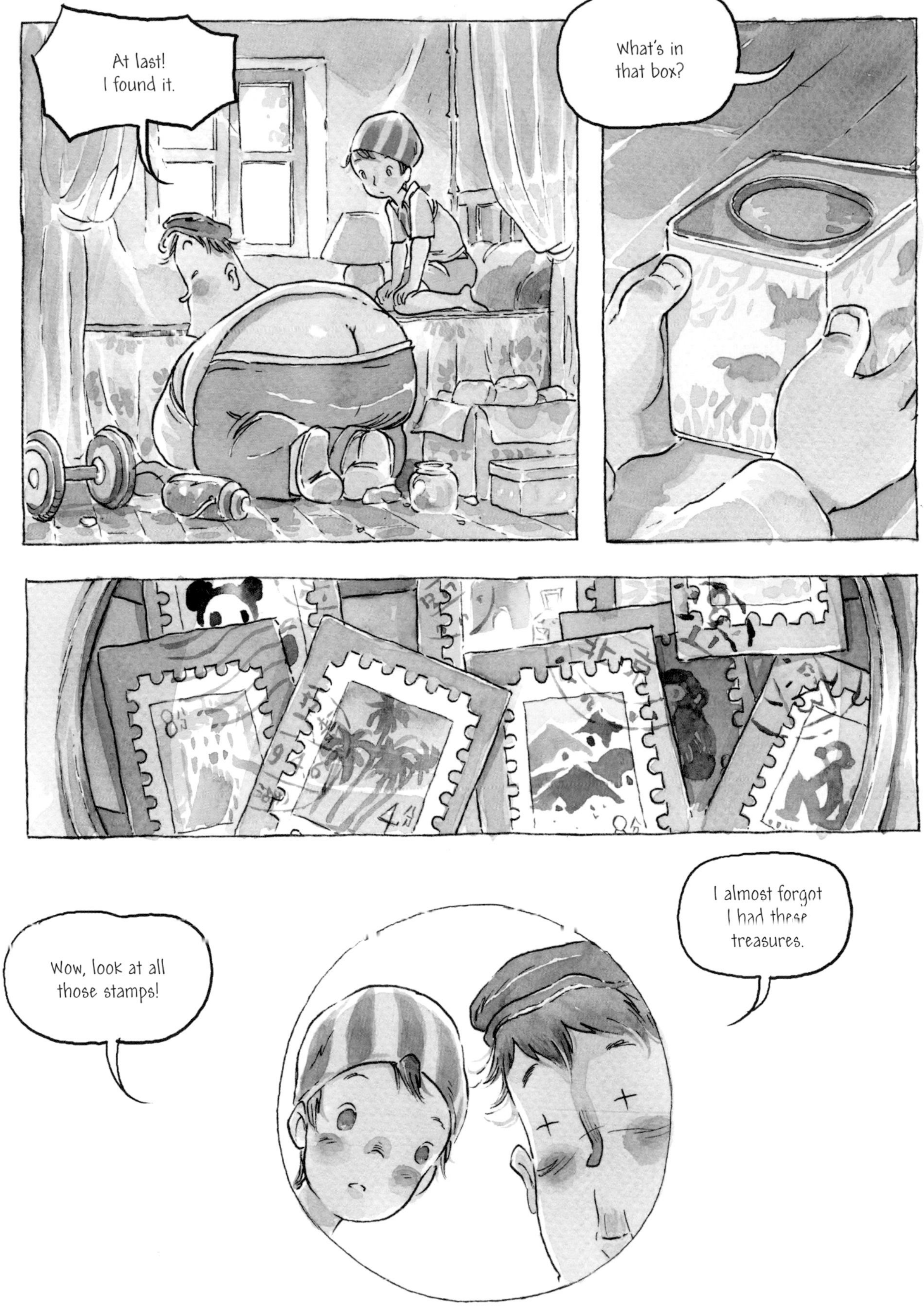
At last!
I found it.
What's in that box?
Wow, look at all those stamps!
I almost forgot I had these treasures.

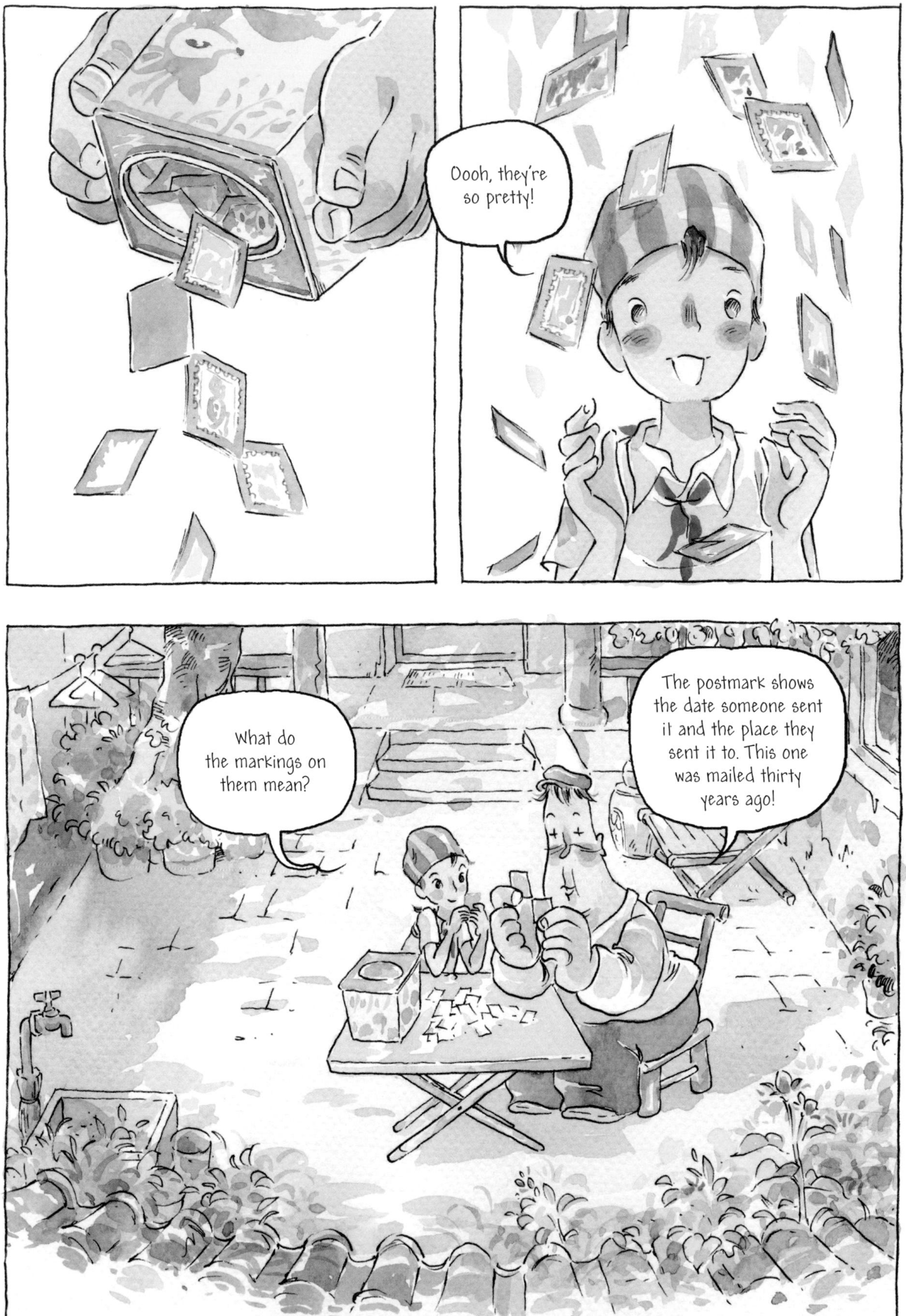
Oooh, they're so pretty!
What do the markings on them mean?
The postmark shows the date someone sent it and the place they sent it to. This one was mailed thirty years ago!

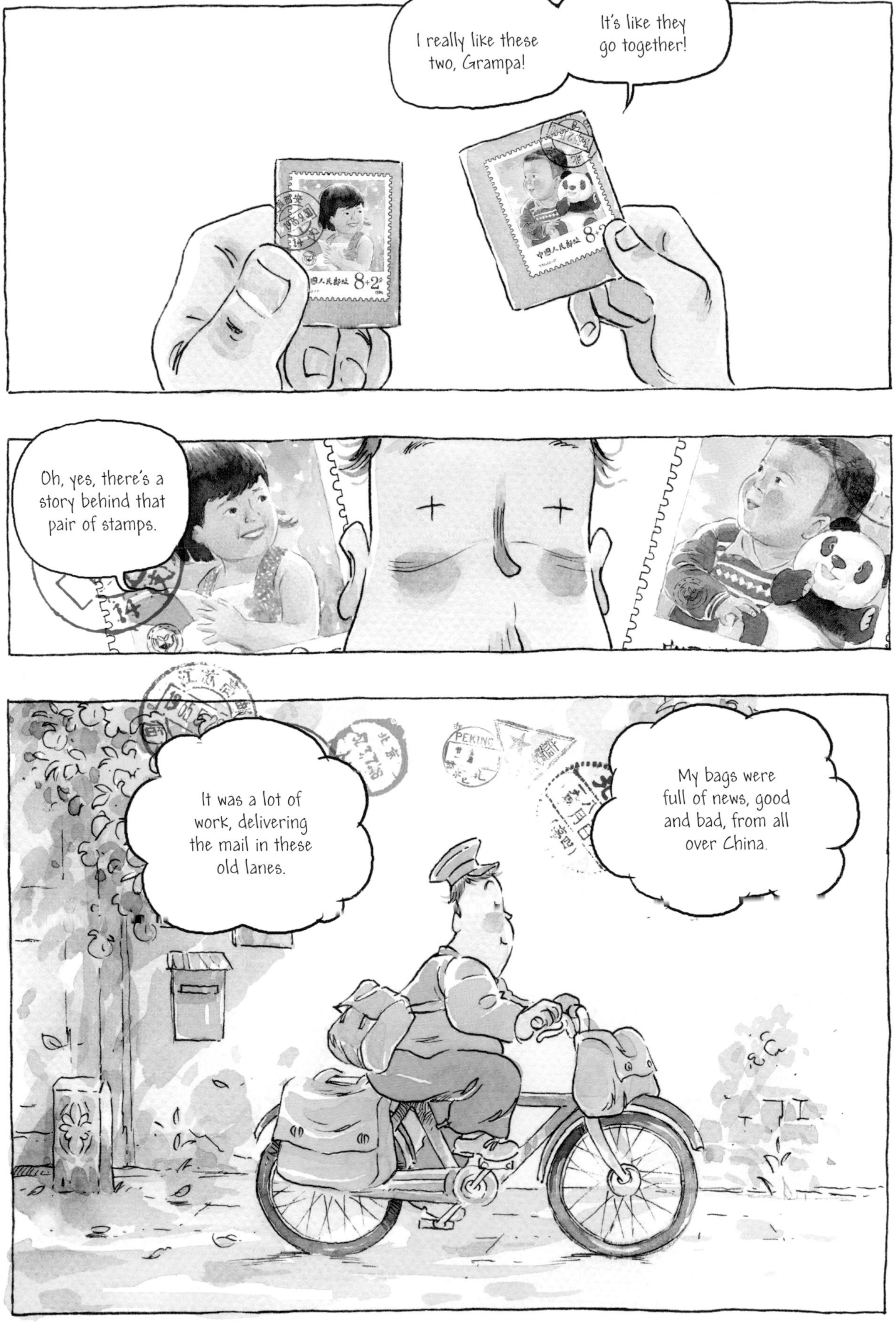
I really like these two, Grampa!
It's like they go together!
Oh, yes, there's a story behind that pair of stamps.
It was a lot of work, delivering the mail in these old lanes.
My bags were full of news, good and bad, from all over China.

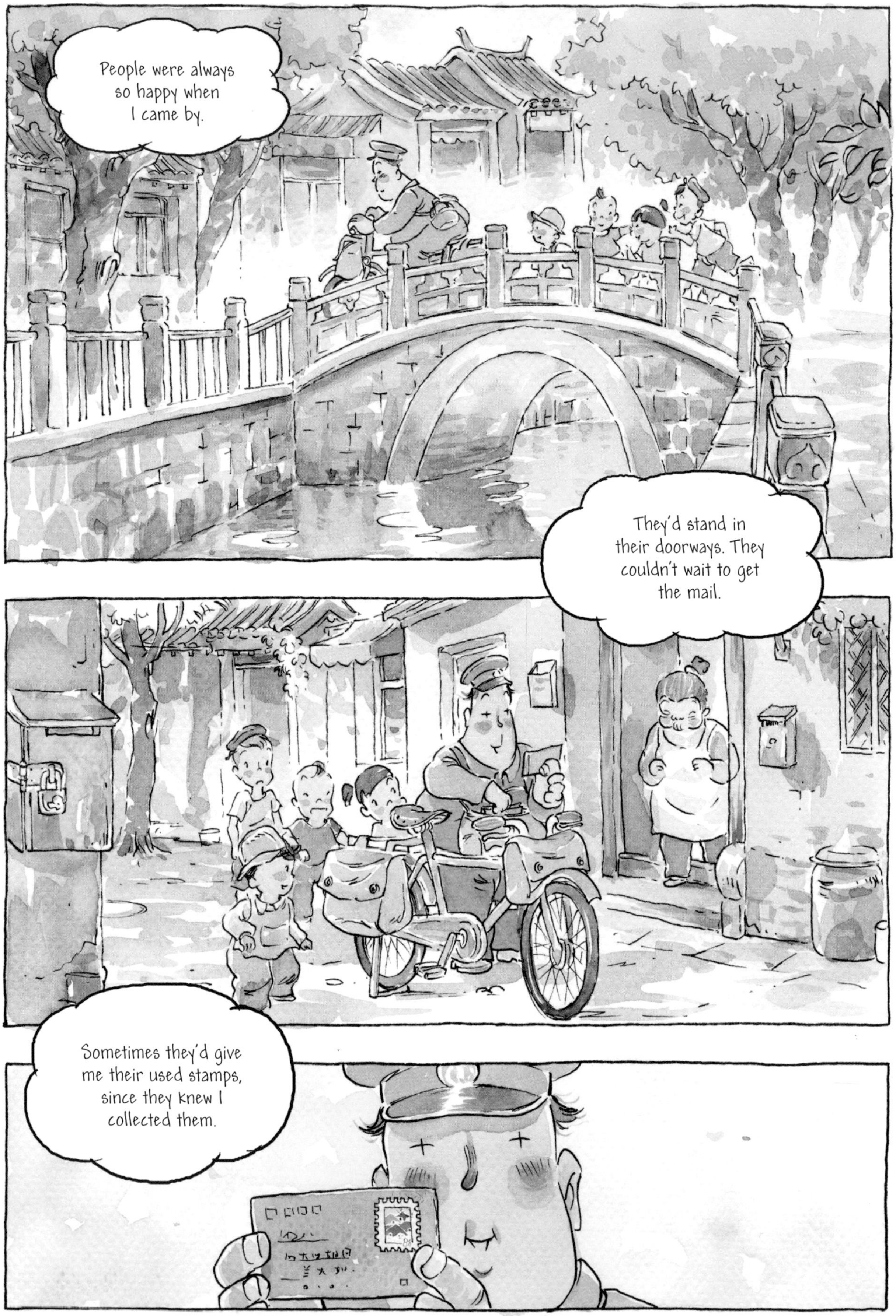
People were always so happy when I came by.
They'd stand in their doorways. They couldn't wait to get the mail.
Sometimes they'd give me their used stamps, since they knew I collected them.

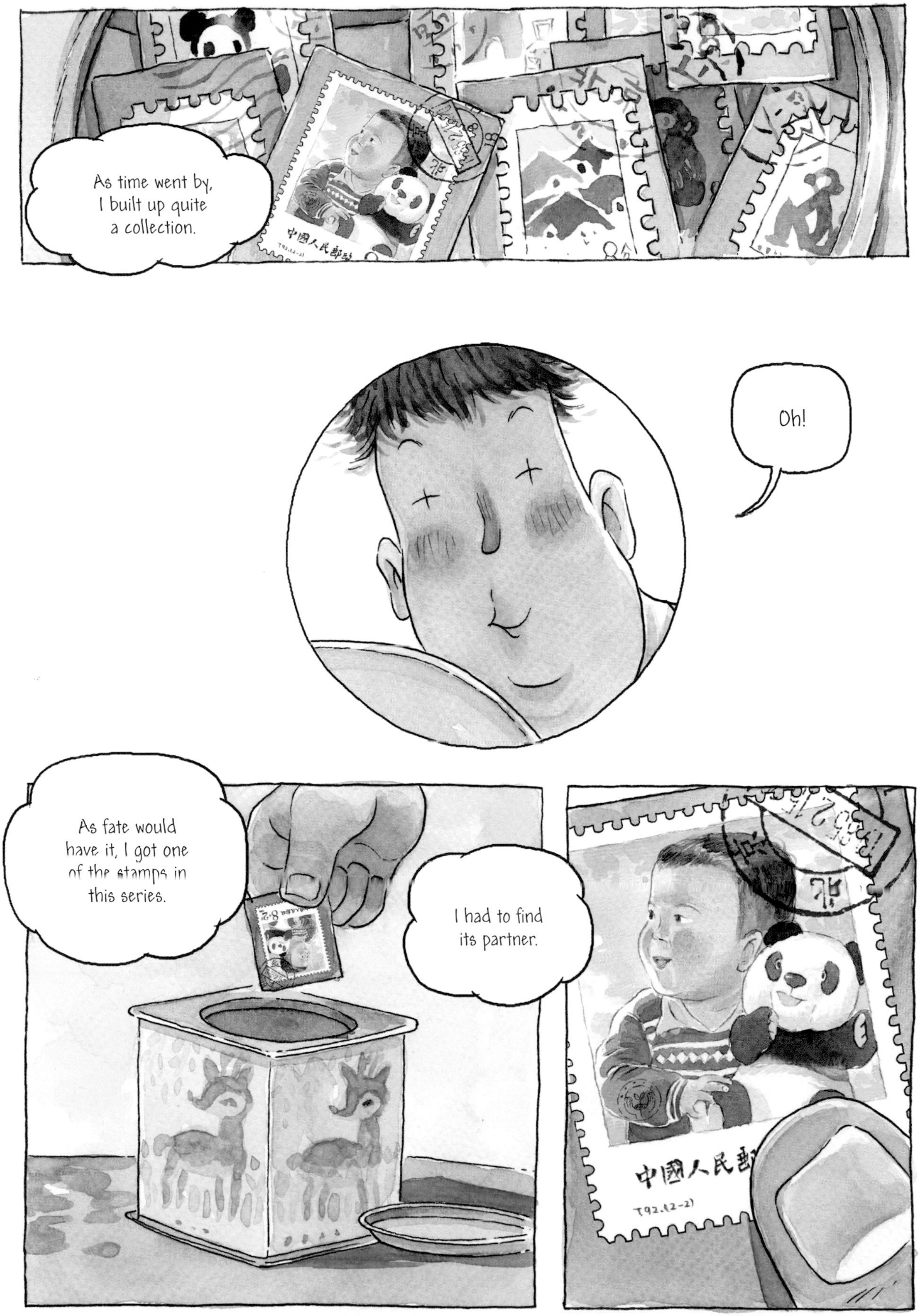
As time went by, I built up quite a collection.
Oh!
As fate would have it, I got one of the stamps in this series.
I had to find its partner.

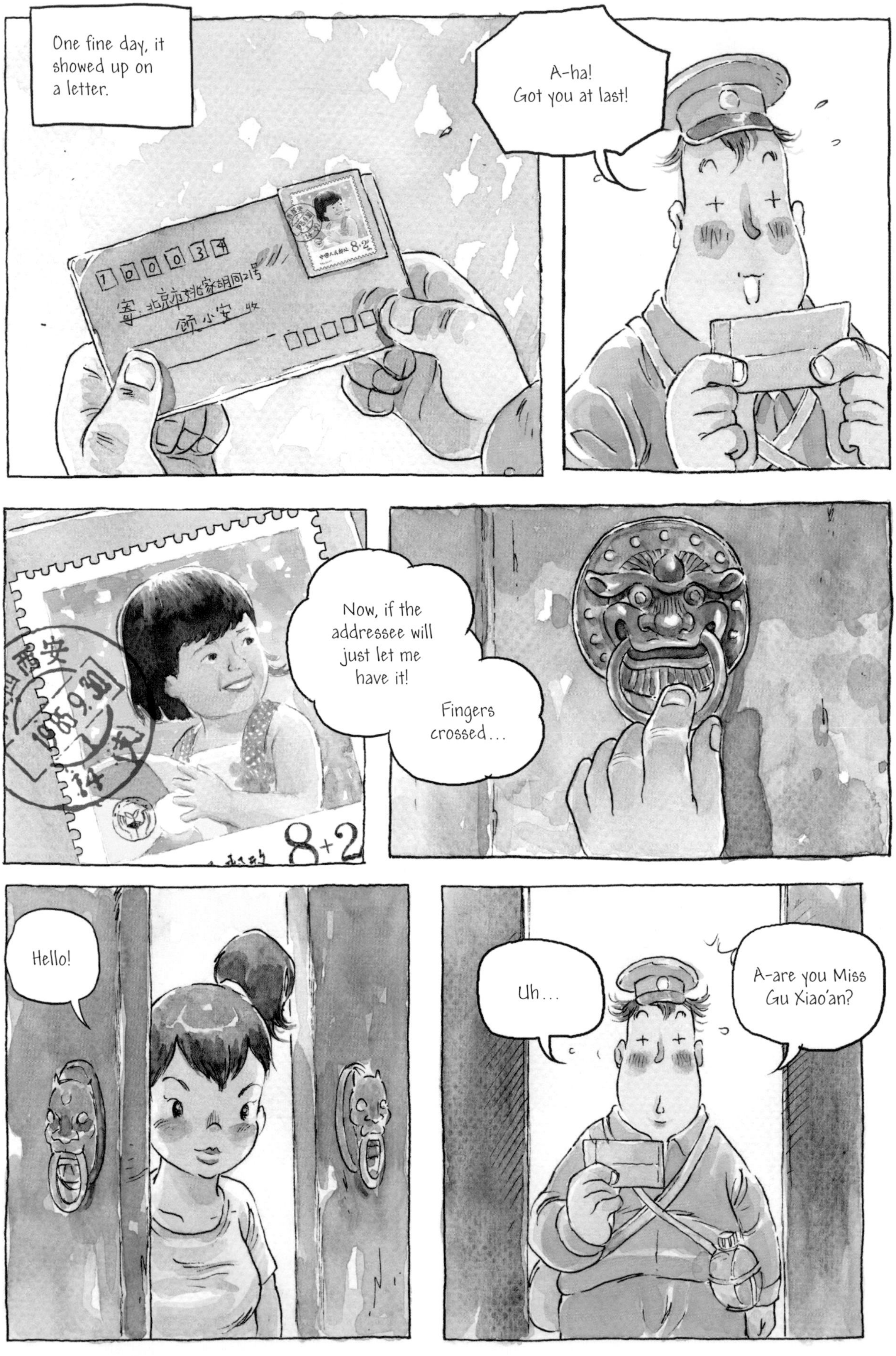

One fine day, it showed up on a letter.
A-ha! Got you at last!
Now, if the addressee will just let me have it!
Fingers crossed…
Hello!
Uh…
A-are you Miss Gu Xiao'an?

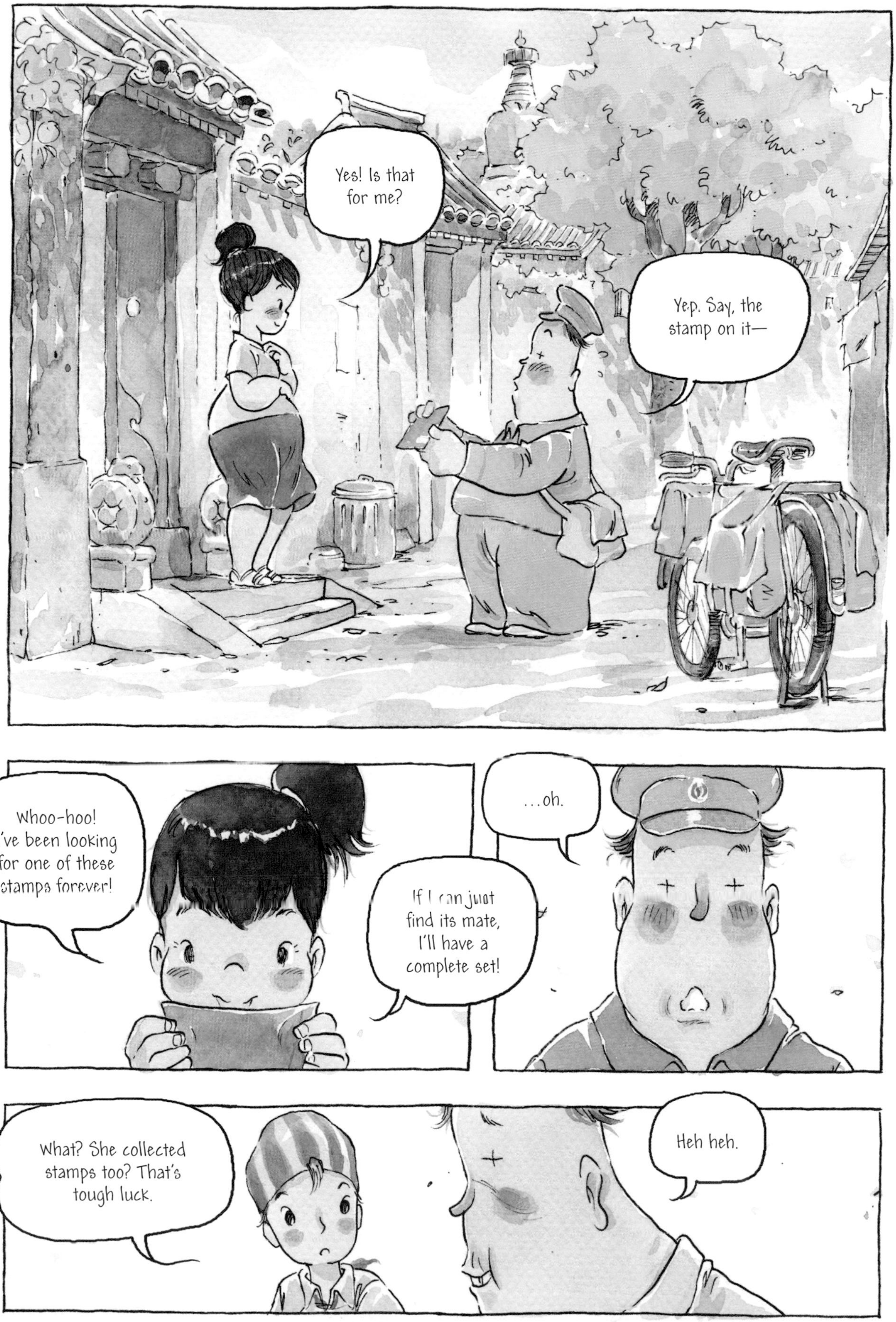
Yes! Is that for me?
Yep. Say, the stamp on it—
Whoo-hoo! I've been looking for one of these stamps forever!
If I can just find its mate, I'll have a complete set!
...oh.
What? She collected stamps too? That's tough luck.
Heh heh.

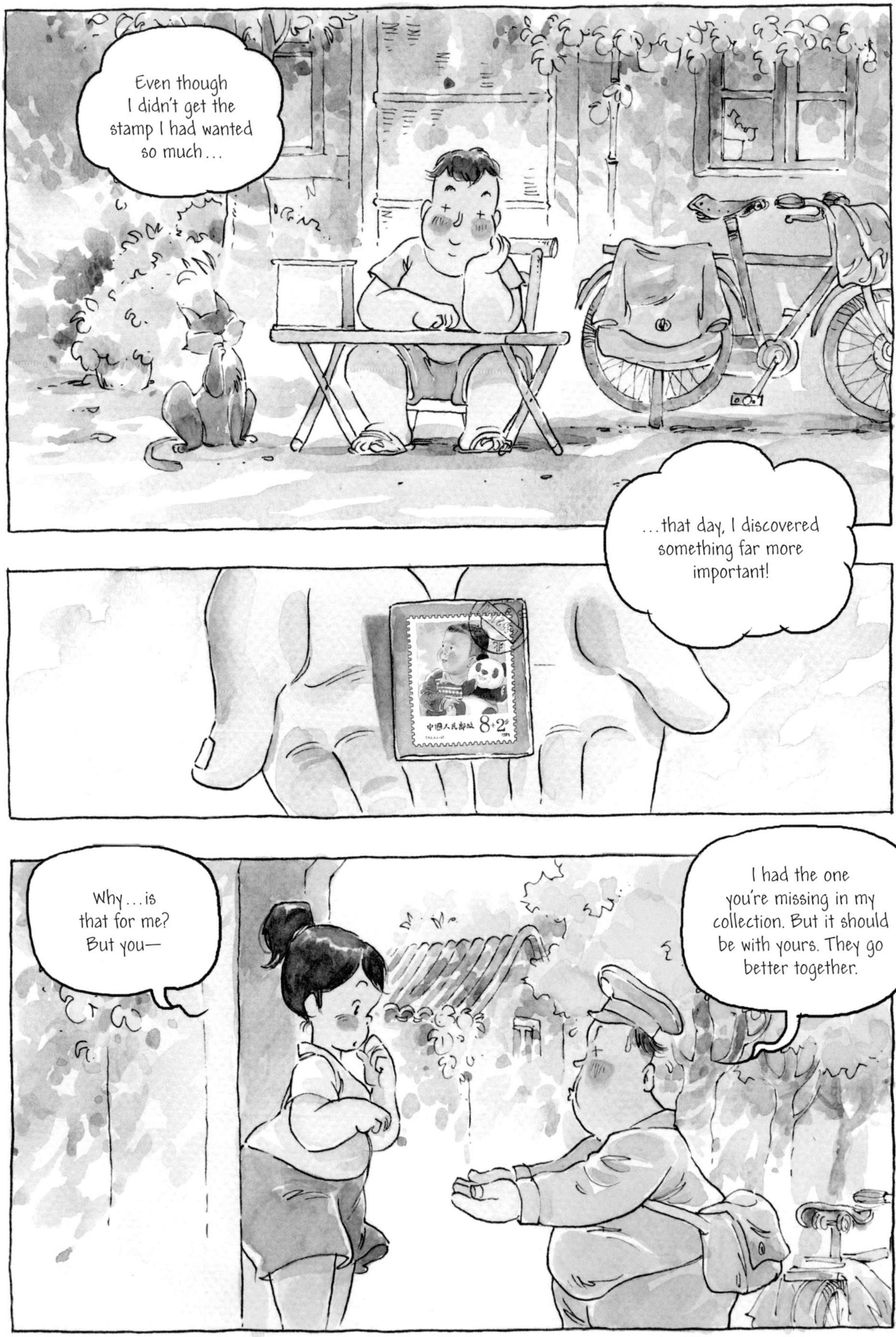
Even though I didn't get the stamp I had wanted so much…
…that day, I discovered something far more important!
Why…is that for me? But you—
I had the one you're missing in my collection. But it should be with yours. They go better together.

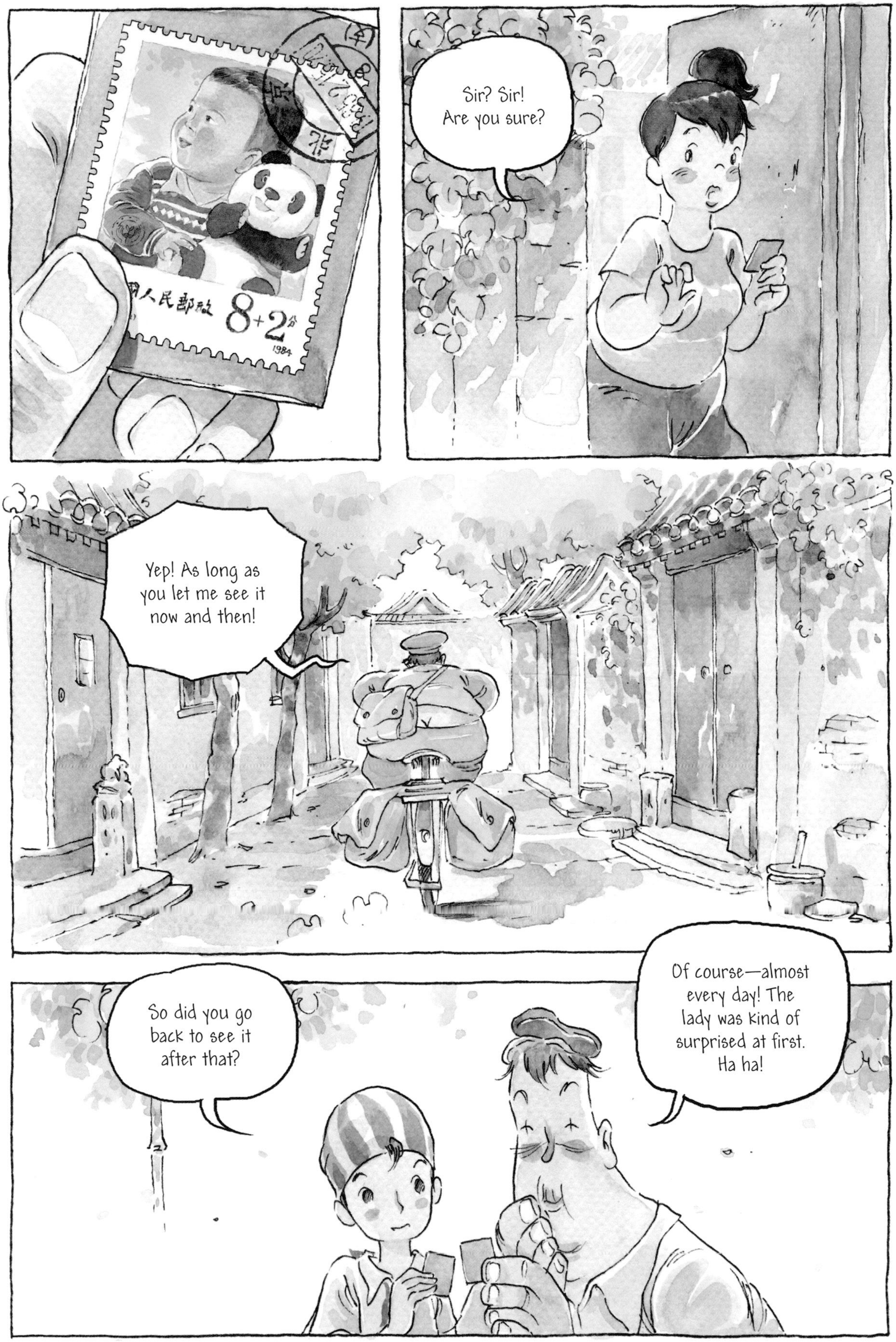

Sir? Sir! Are you sure?
Yep! As long as you let me see it now and then!
So did you go back to see it after that?
Of course—almost every day! The lady was kind of surprised at first. Ha ha!

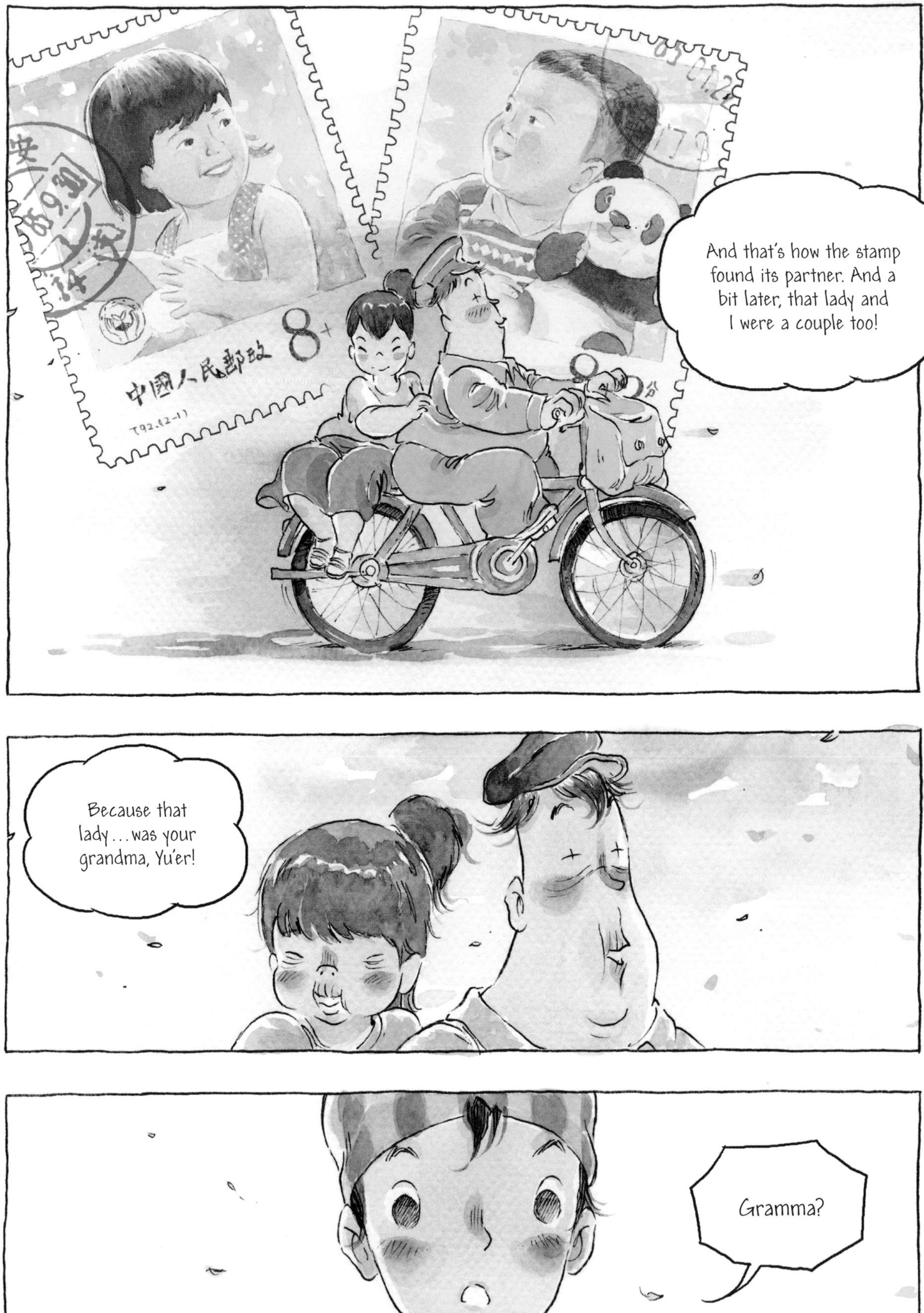
中國人民郵政
And that's how the stamp found its partner. And a bit later, that lady and I were a couple too!
Because that lady...was your grandma, Yu'er!
Gramma?

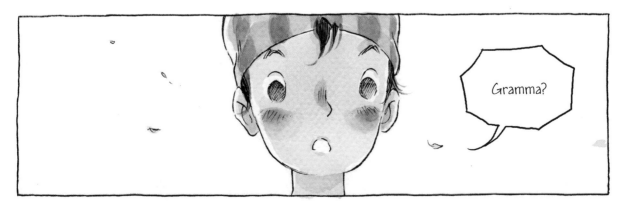

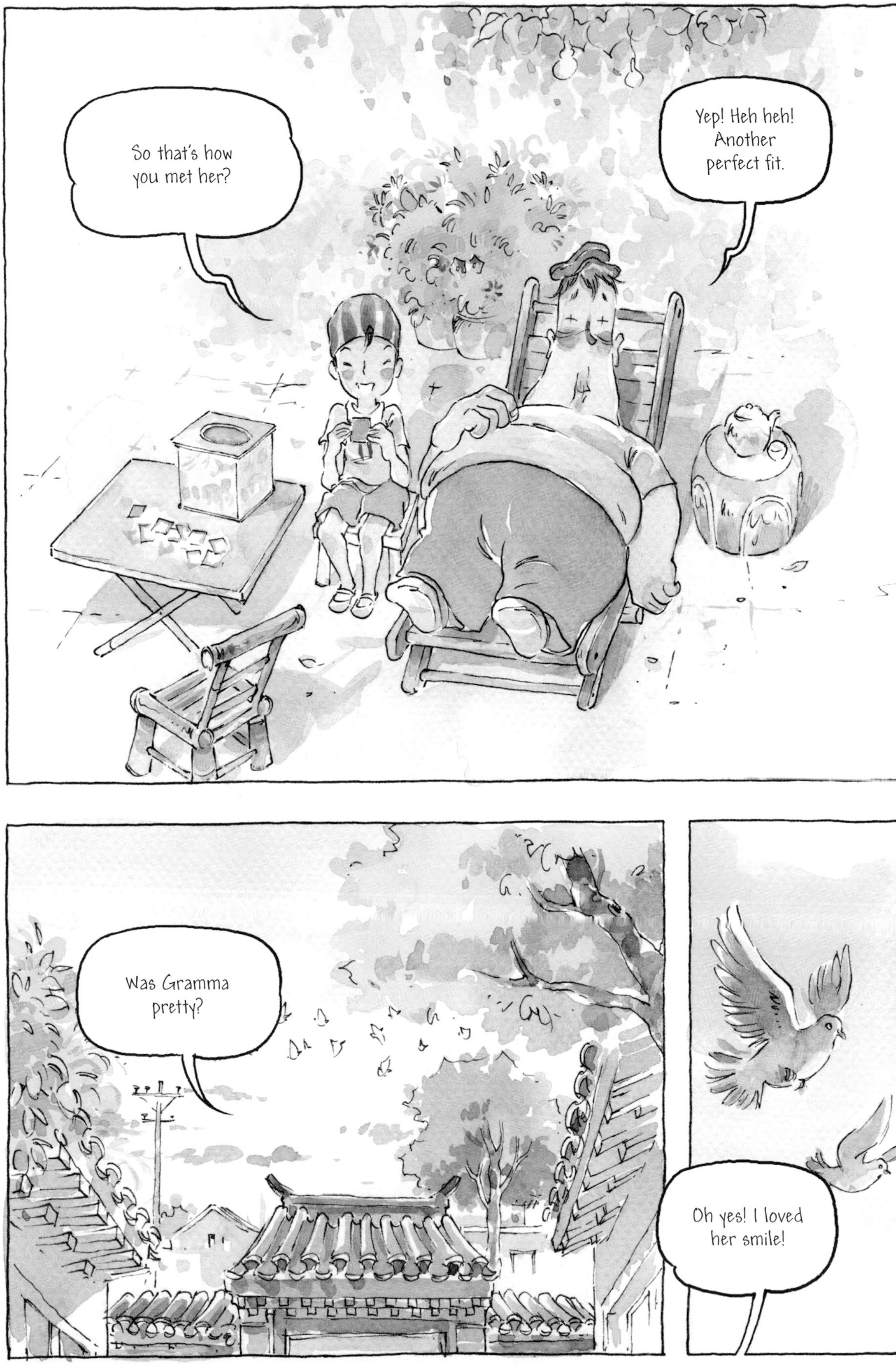
So that's how you met her?
Yep! Heh heh! Another perfect fit.
Was Gramma pretty?
Oh yes! I loved her smile!

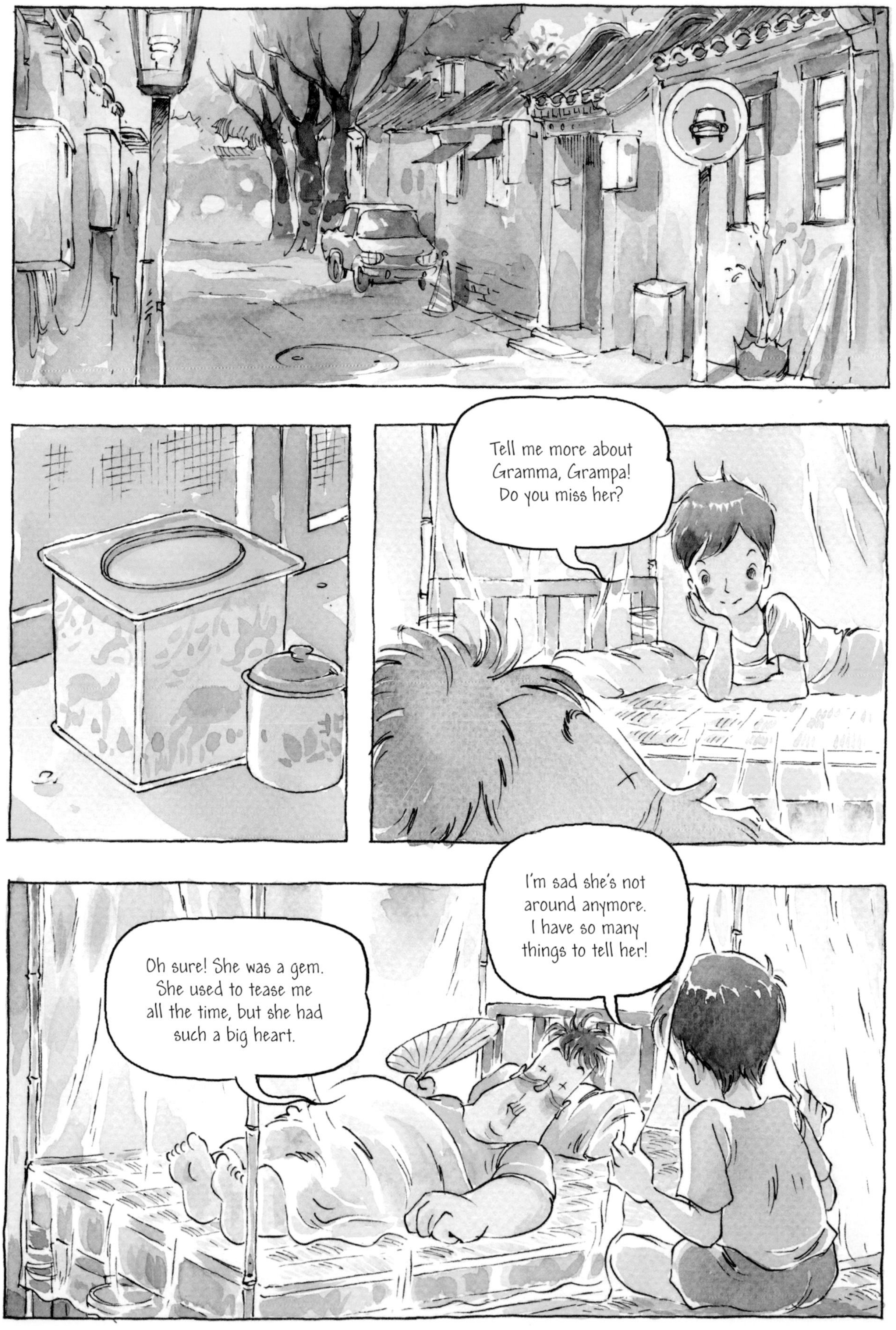
Tell me more about Gramma, Grampa! Do you miss her?
I'm sad she's not around anymore. I have so many things to tell her!
Oh sure! She was a gem. She used to tease me all the time, but she had such a big heart.

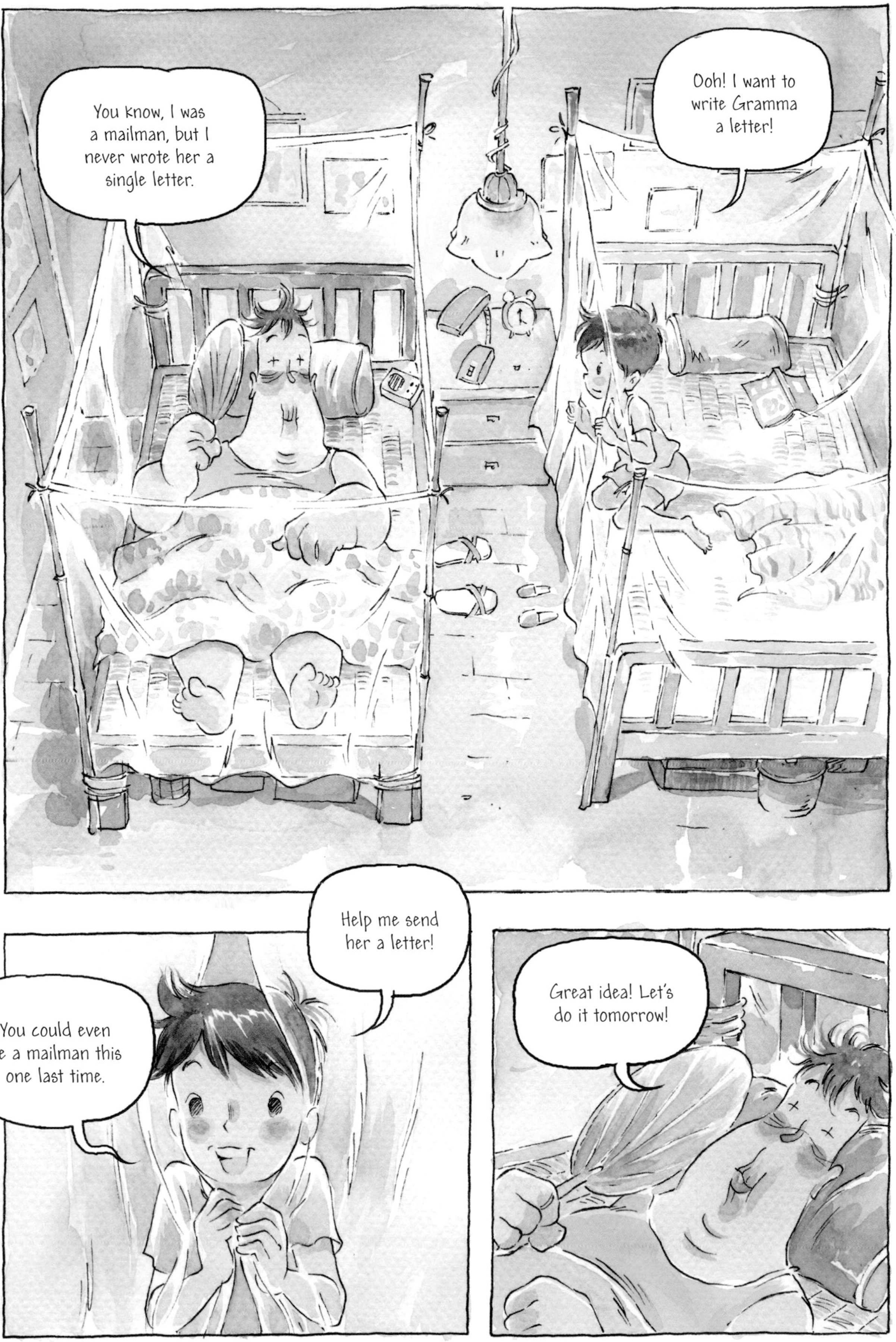
You know, I was a mailman, but I never wrote her a single letter.
Ooh! I want to write Gramma a letter!
Help me send her a letter!
You could even be a mailman this one last time.
Great idea! Let's do it tomorrow!

That night Yu'er's grandpa had an incredible dream. He was a mailman again, and the people who lived along the hutong were lining up to post their letters.

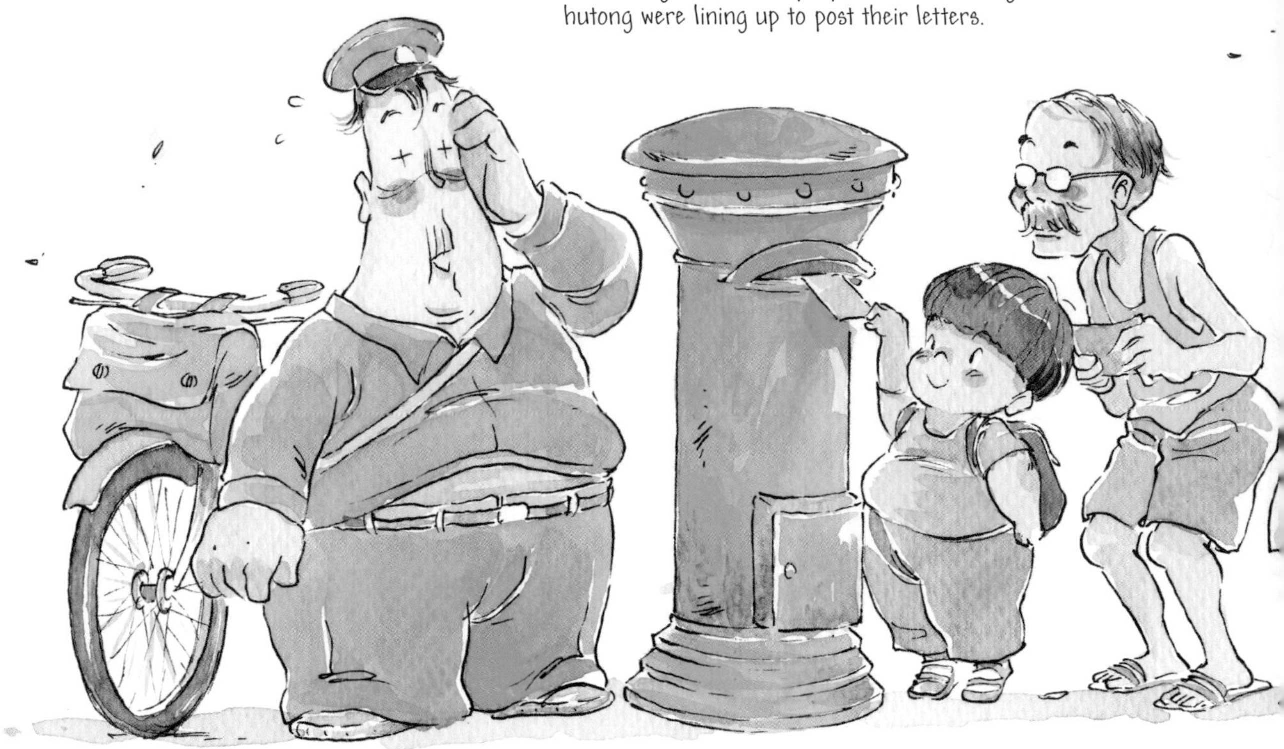

Yu'er dreamed about her grandma too.
It was something pretty special...

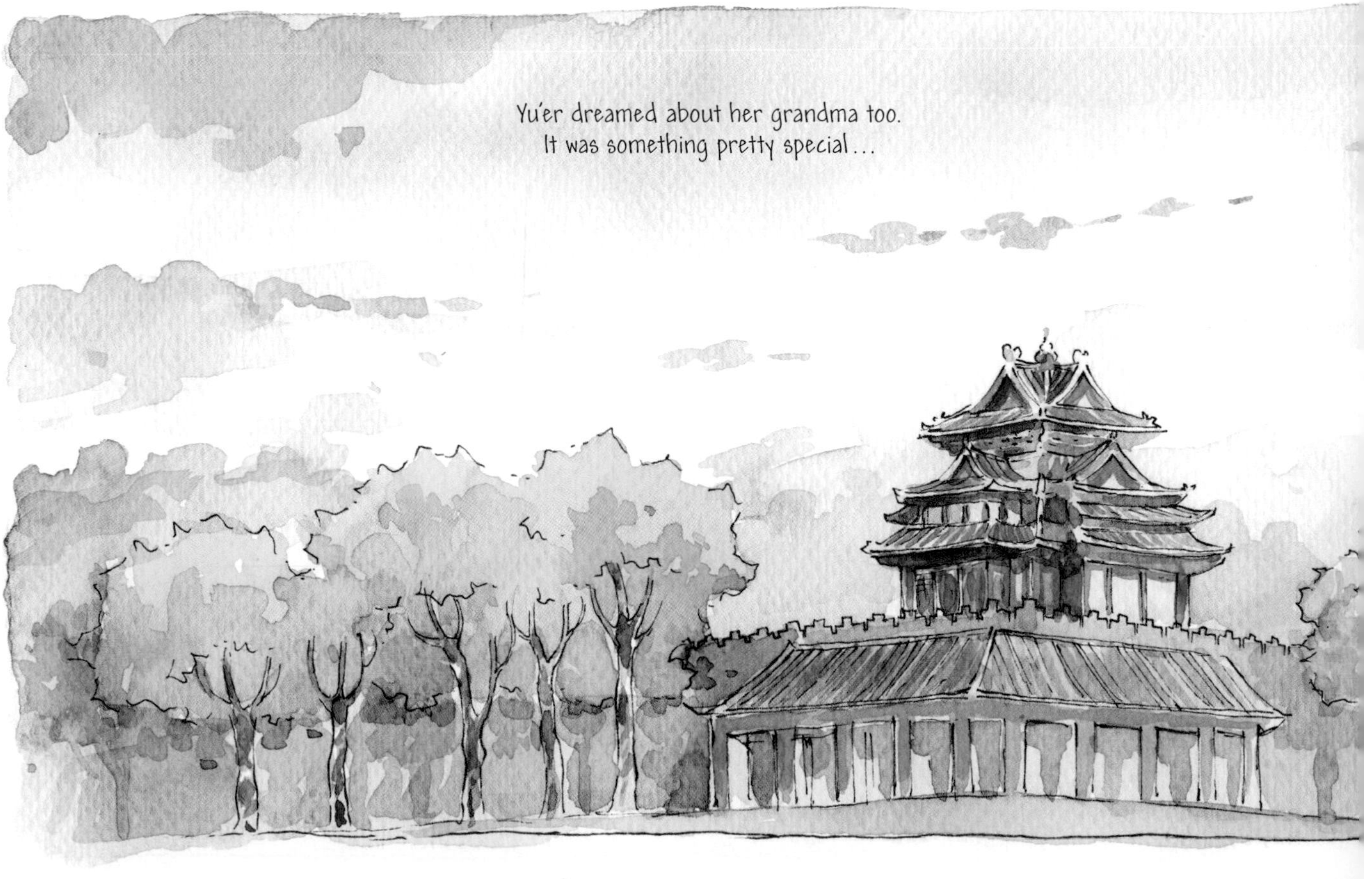

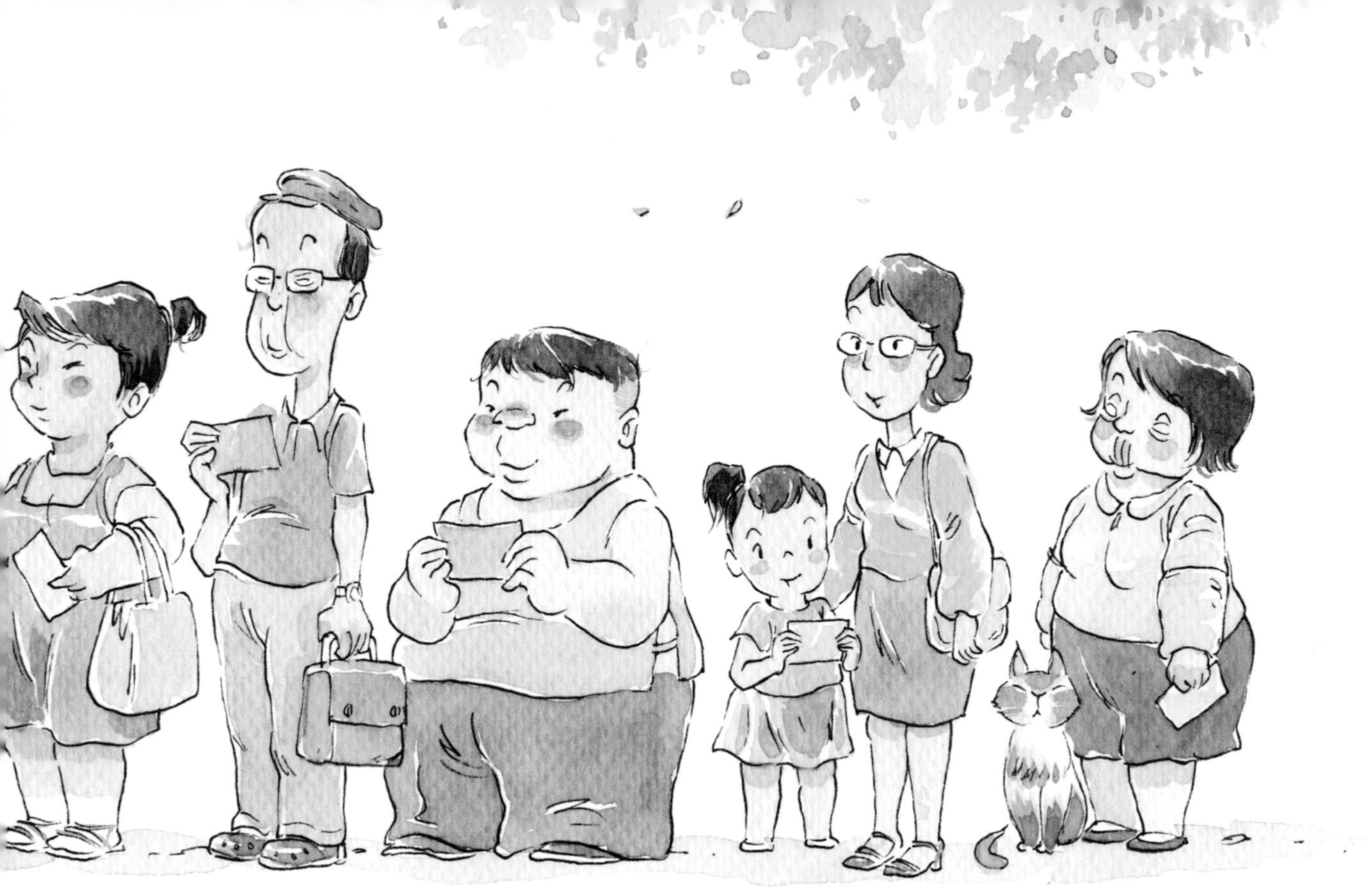

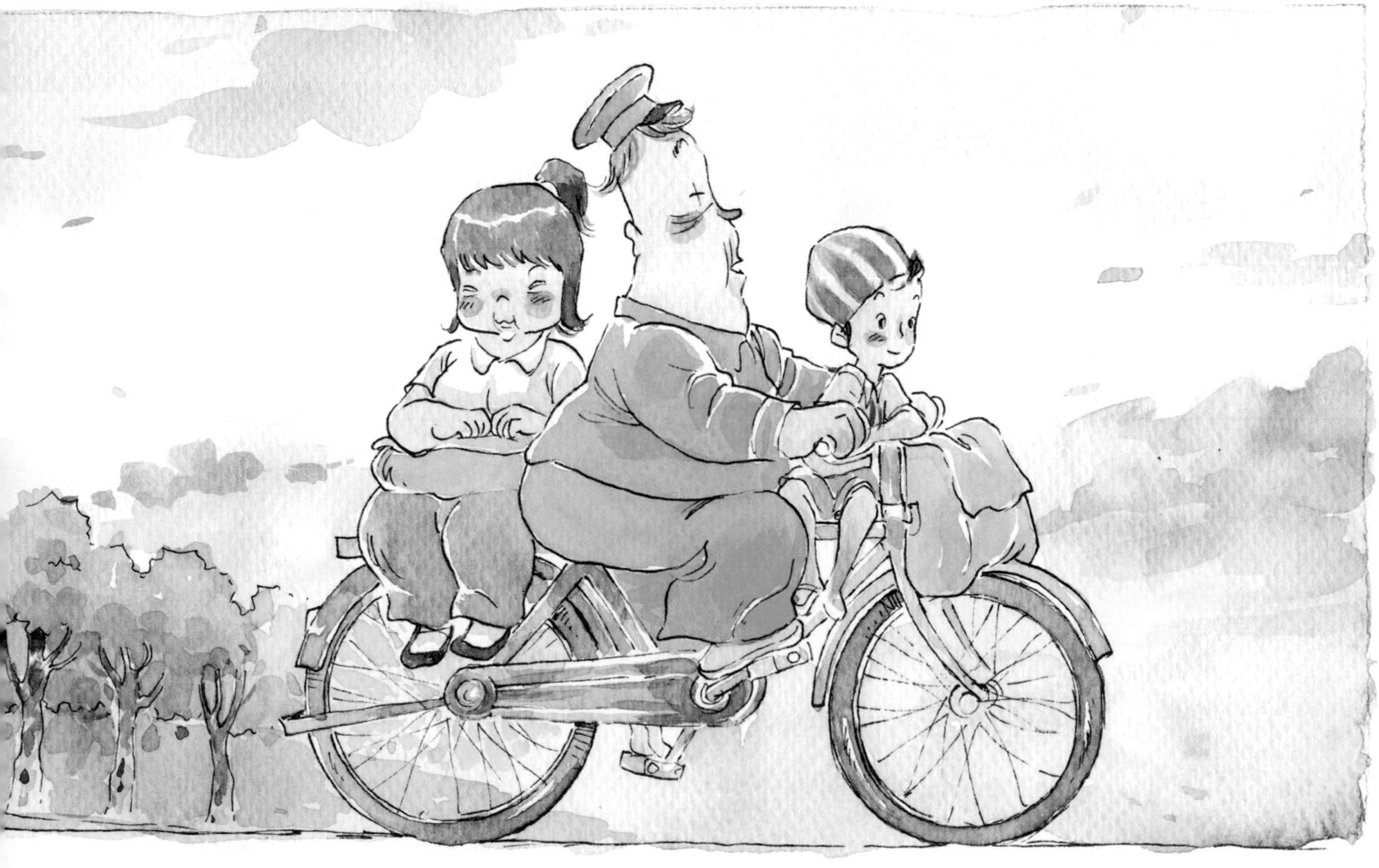

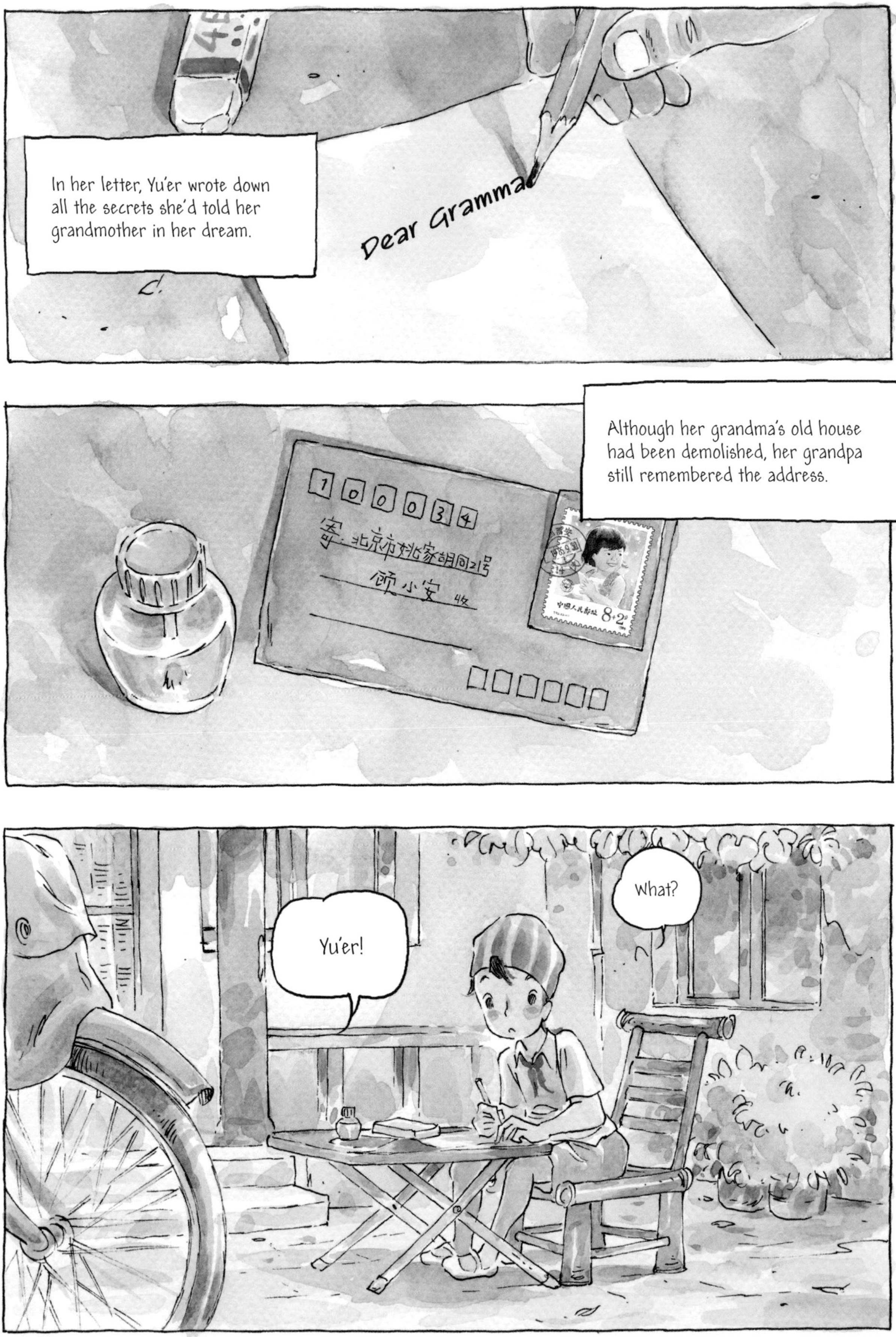
In her letter, Yu'er wrote down all the secrets she'd told her grandmother in her dream.
Dear Gramma
Although her grandma's old house had been demolished, her grandpa still remembered the address.
100034
寄: 北京市姚家胡同2号
颜小安 收
中国人民邮政 8+2分
Yu'er!
What?

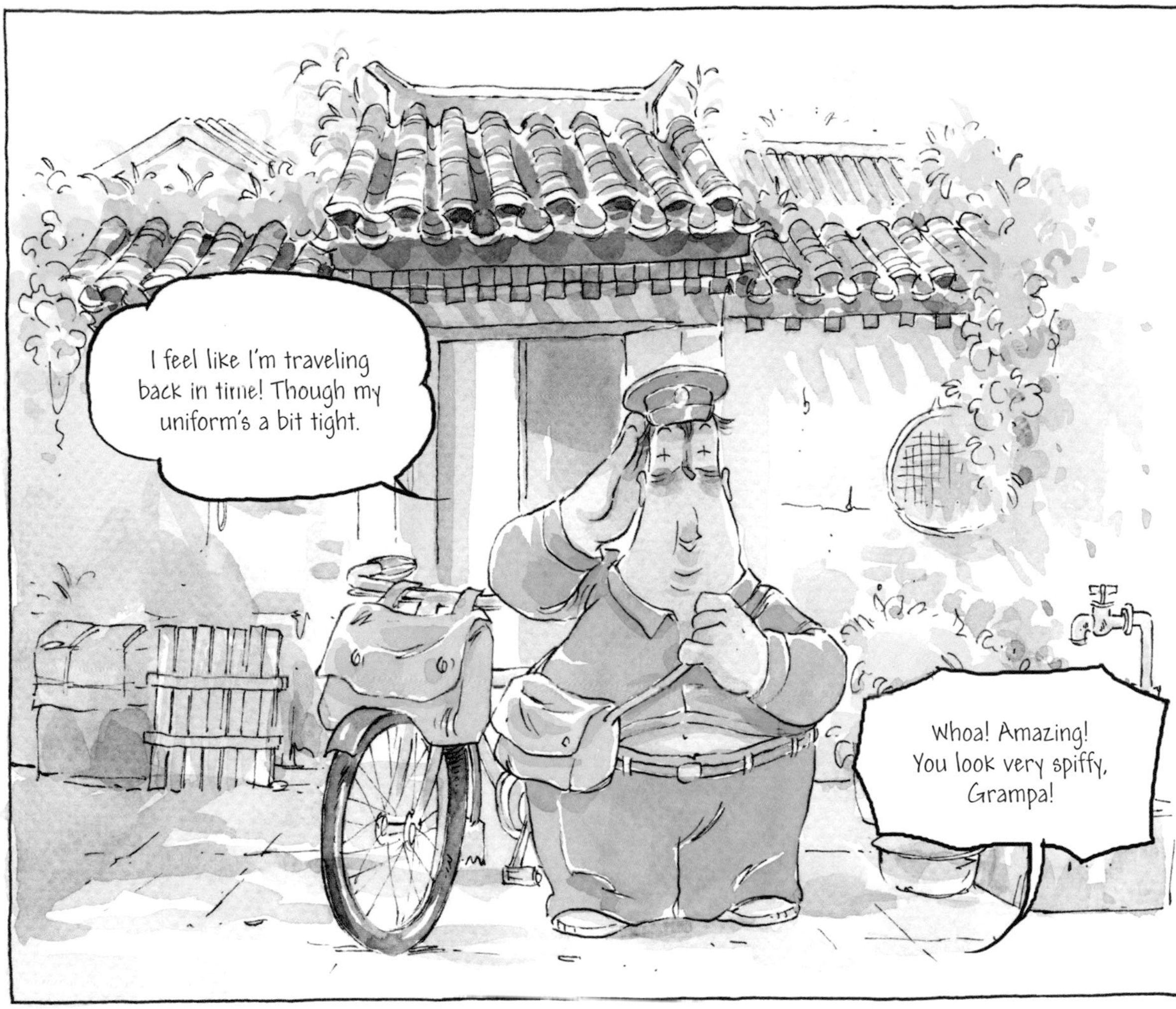
I feel like I'm traveling back in time! Though my uniform's a bit tight.
Whoa! Amazing! You look very spiffy, Grampa!
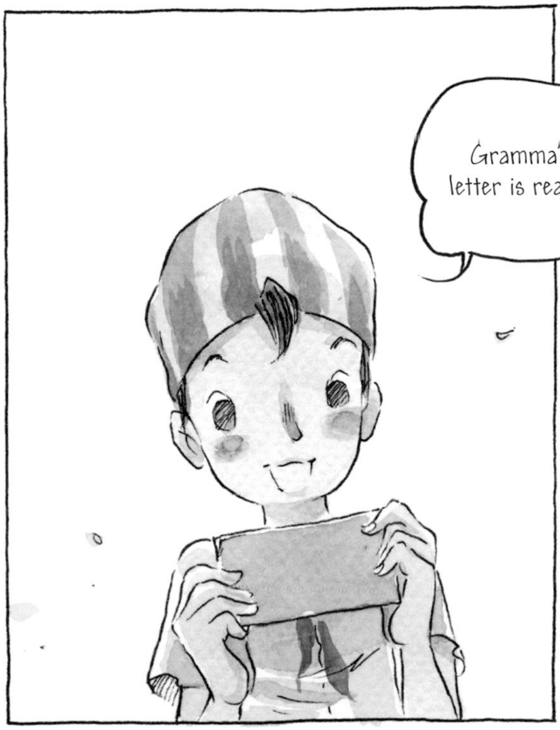
Gramma's letter is ready!
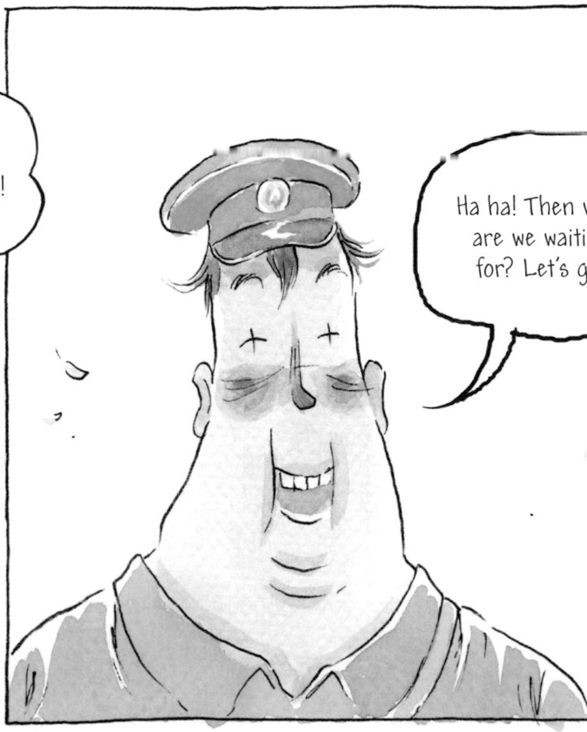
Ha ha! Then what are we waiting for? Let's go!

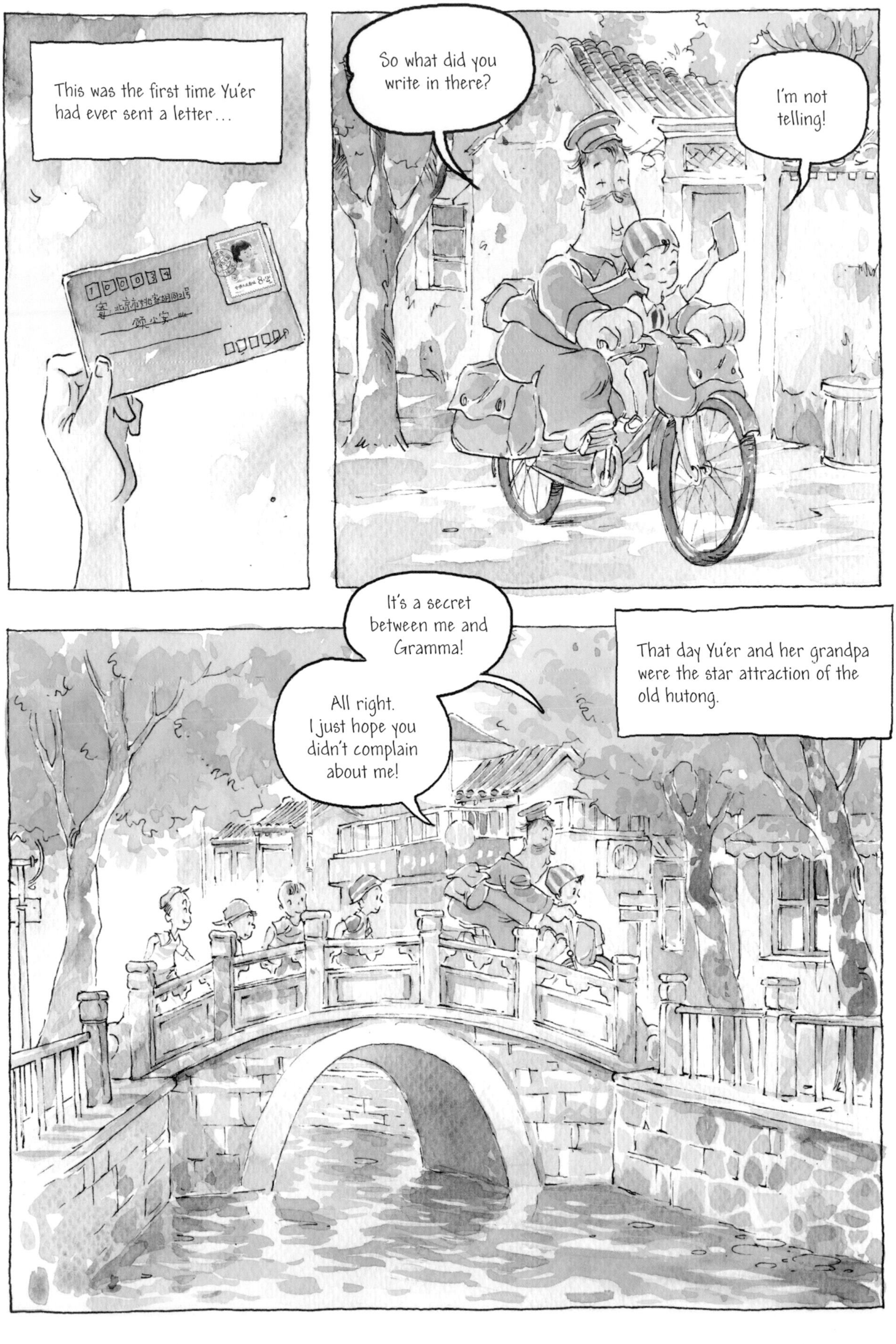
This was the first time Yu'er had ever sent a letter…
So what did you write in there?
I'm not telling!
It's a secret between me and Gramma!
All right. I just hope you didn't complain about me!
That day Yu'er and her grandpa were the star attraction of the old hutong.

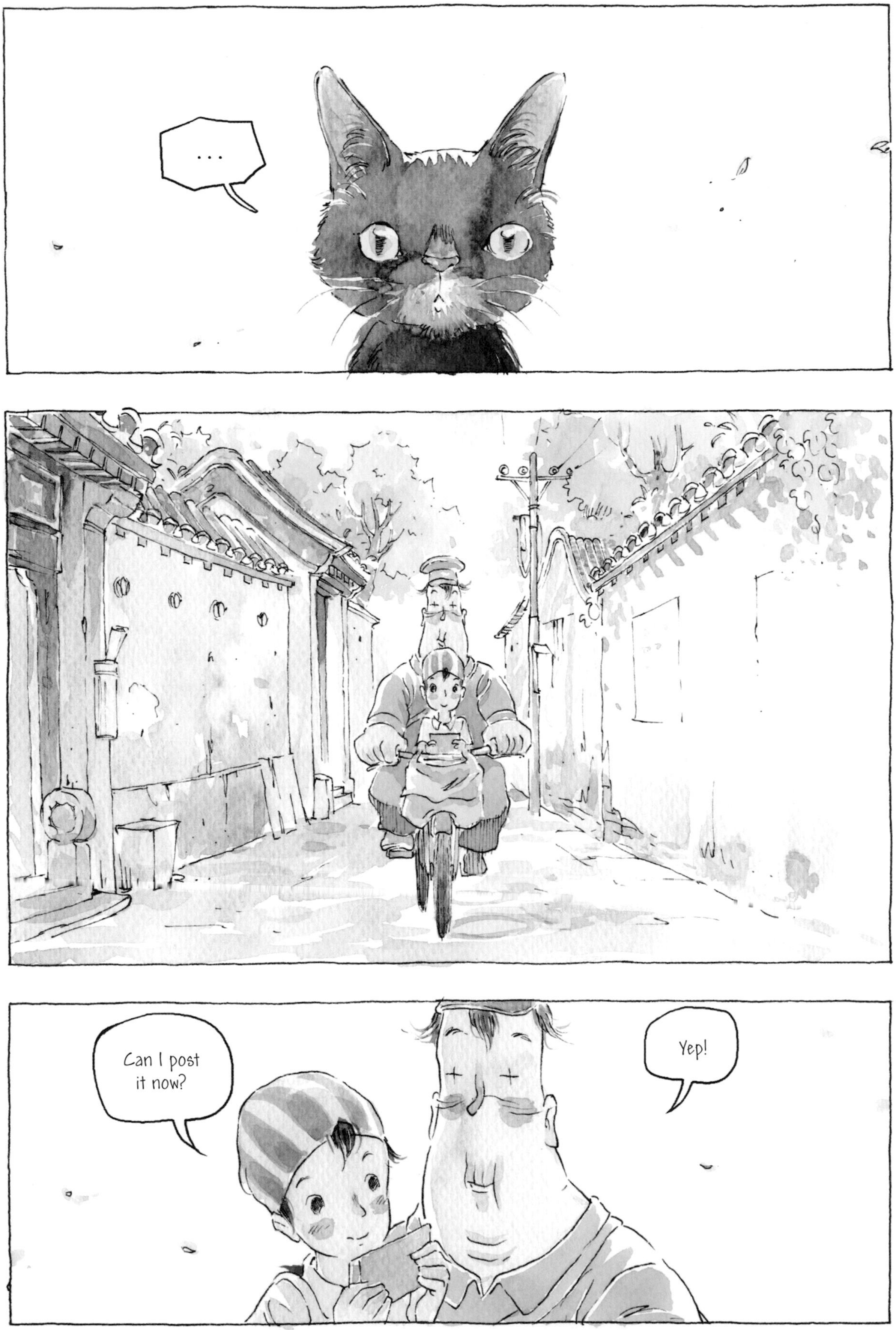
...
Can I post it now?
Yep!

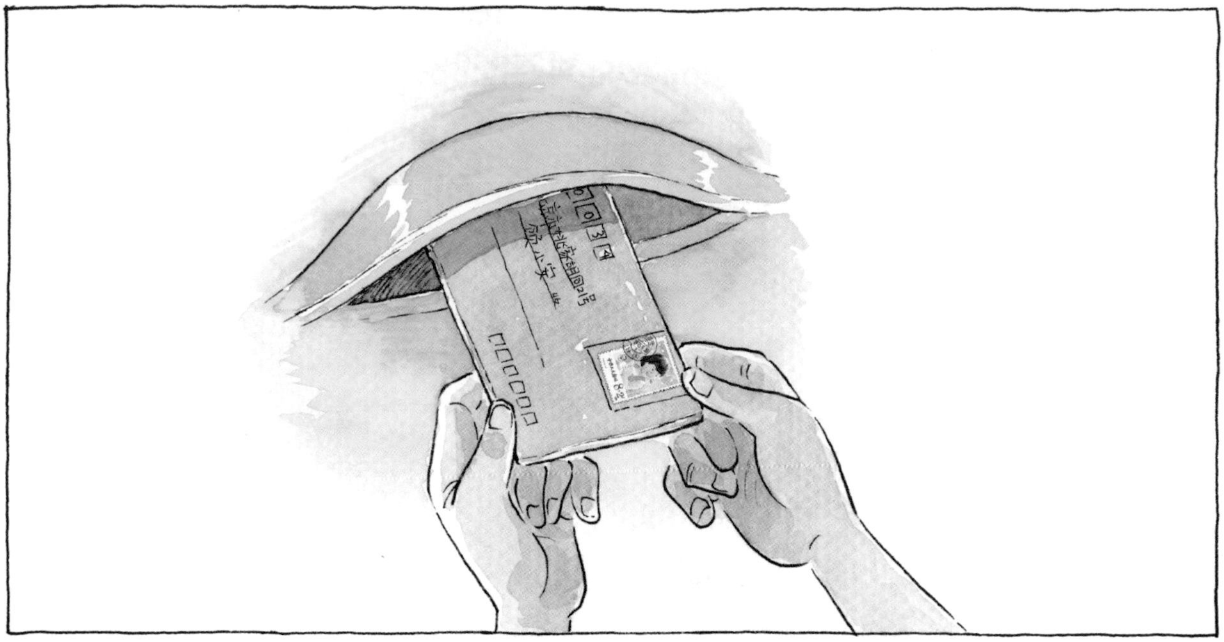

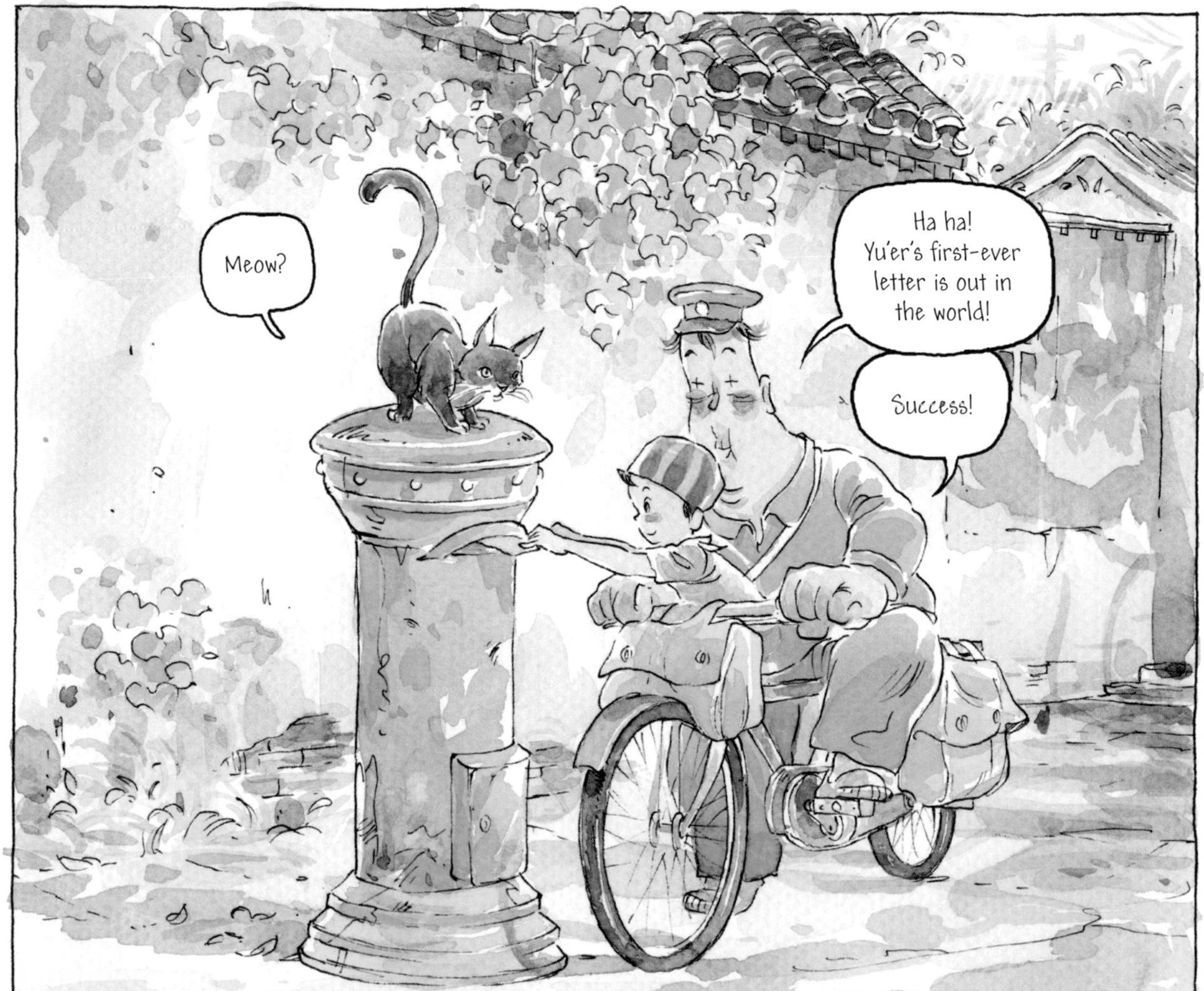
Meow?
Ha ha! Yu'er's first-ever letter is out in the world!
Success!

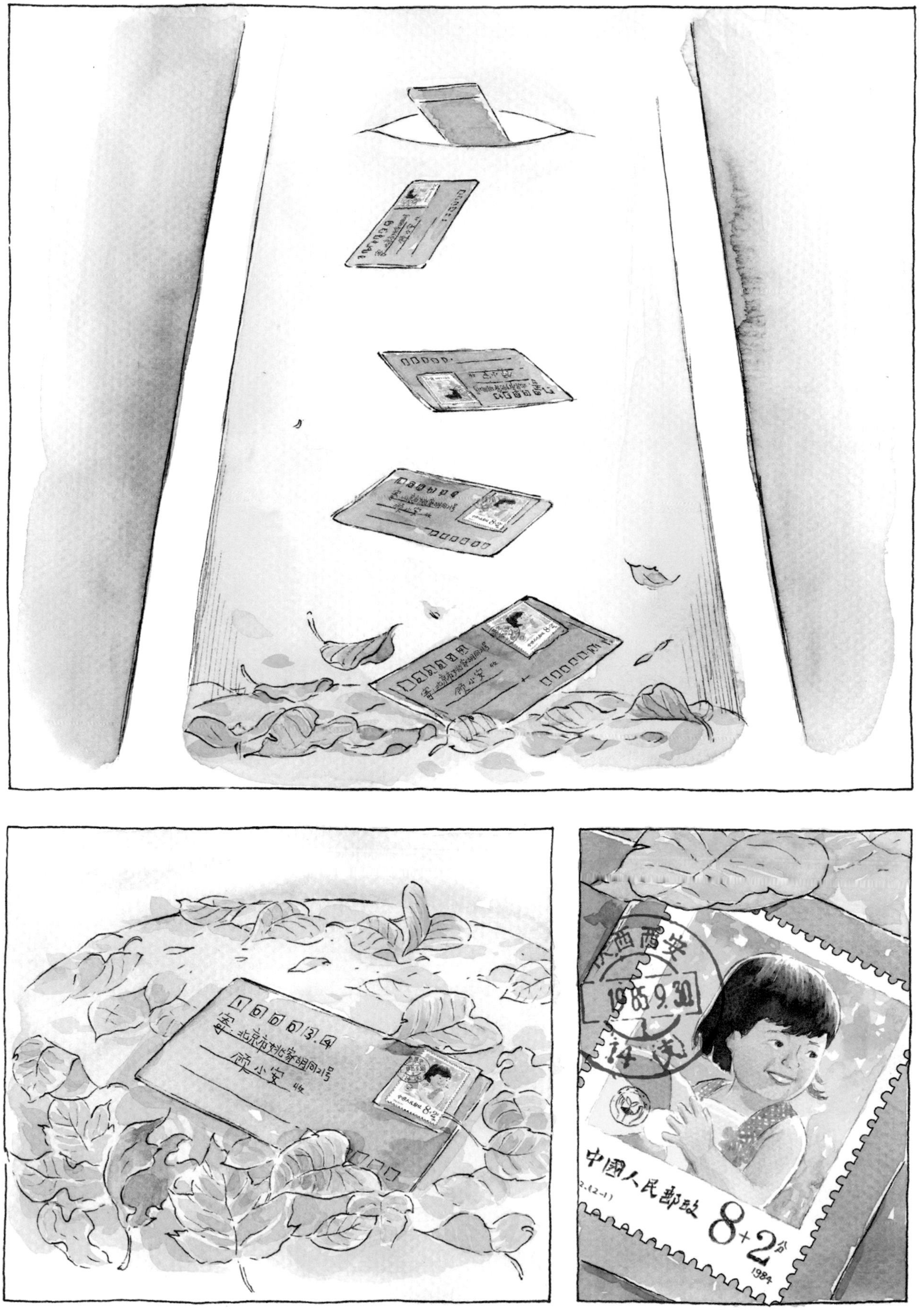
100034
寄: 北京市姚家胡同21号
顾小安 收
1985.9.30
14
中国人民邮政
8+2分
1984

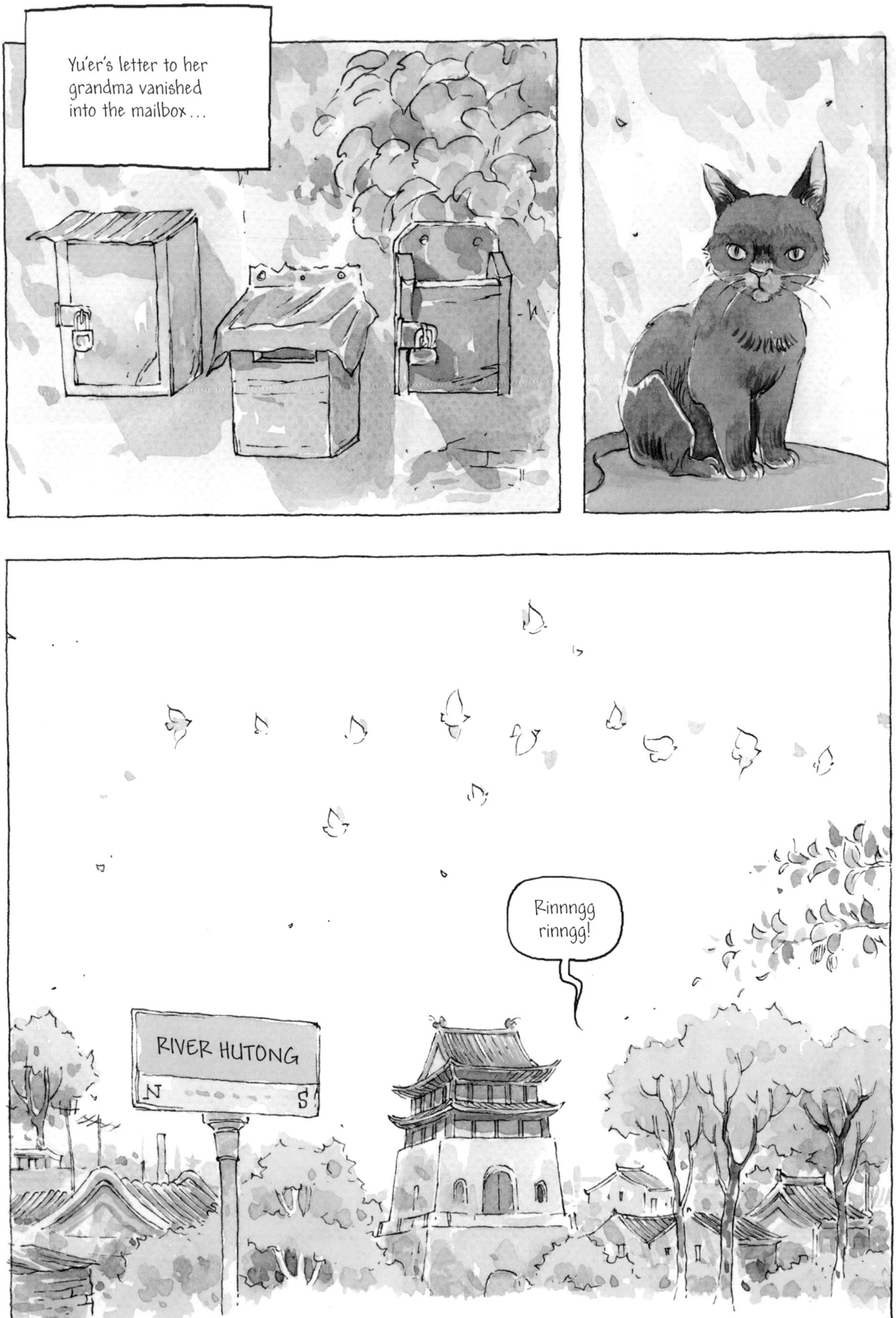
Yu'er's letter to her grandma vanished into the mailbox...
Rinnngg rinngg!
RIVER HUTONG
N
S

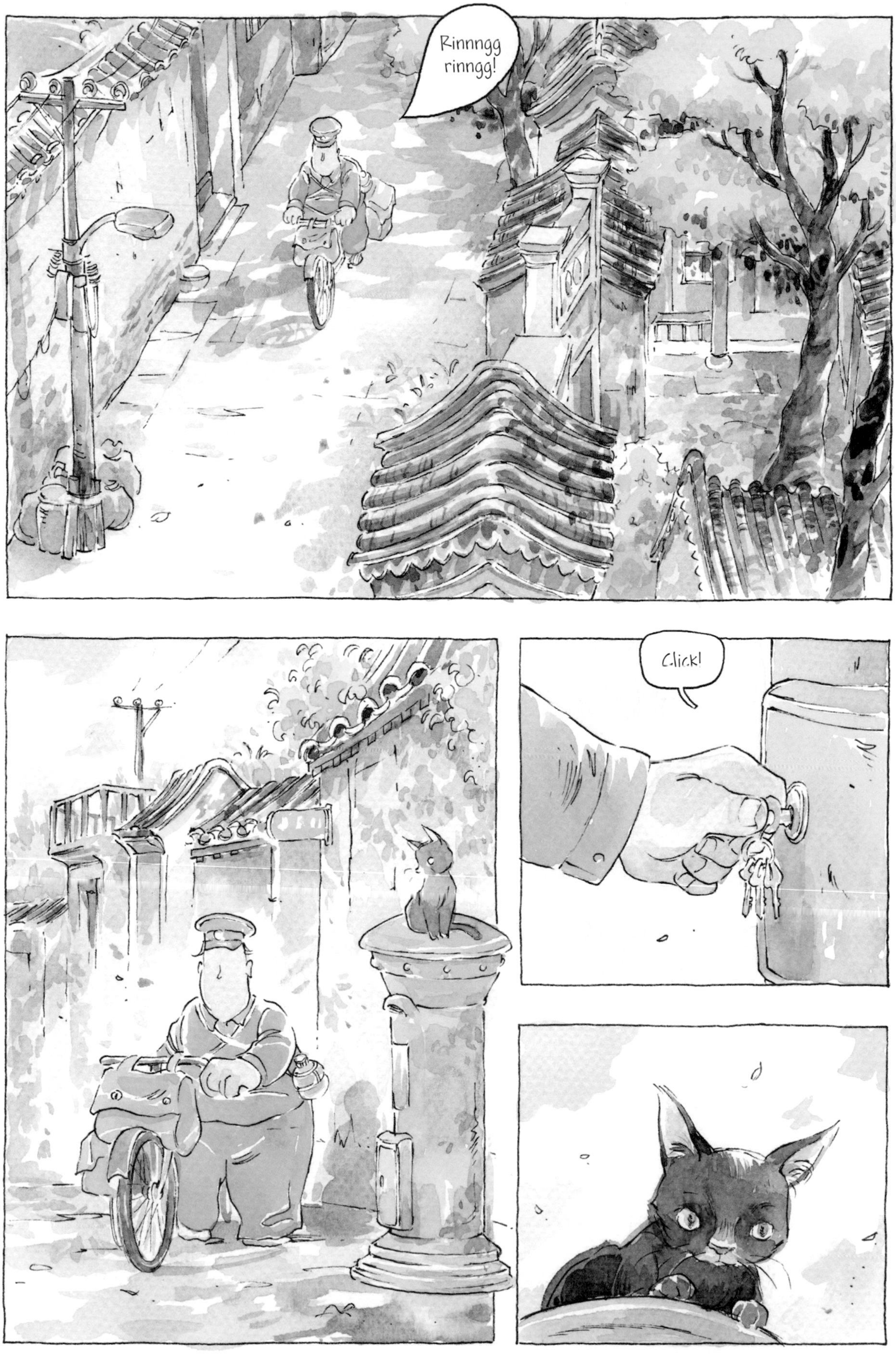
Rinnngg
rinngg!
Click!

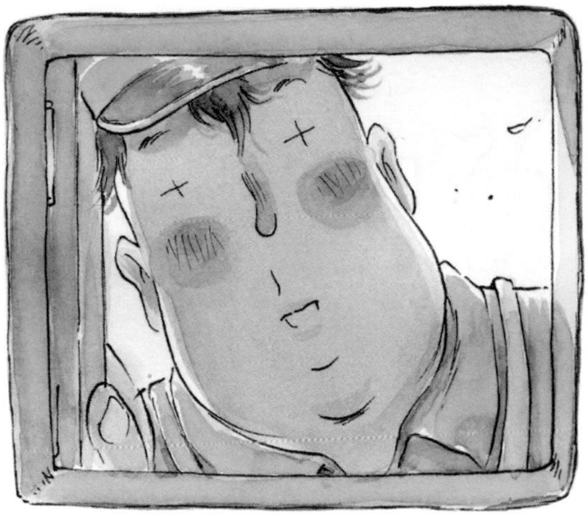

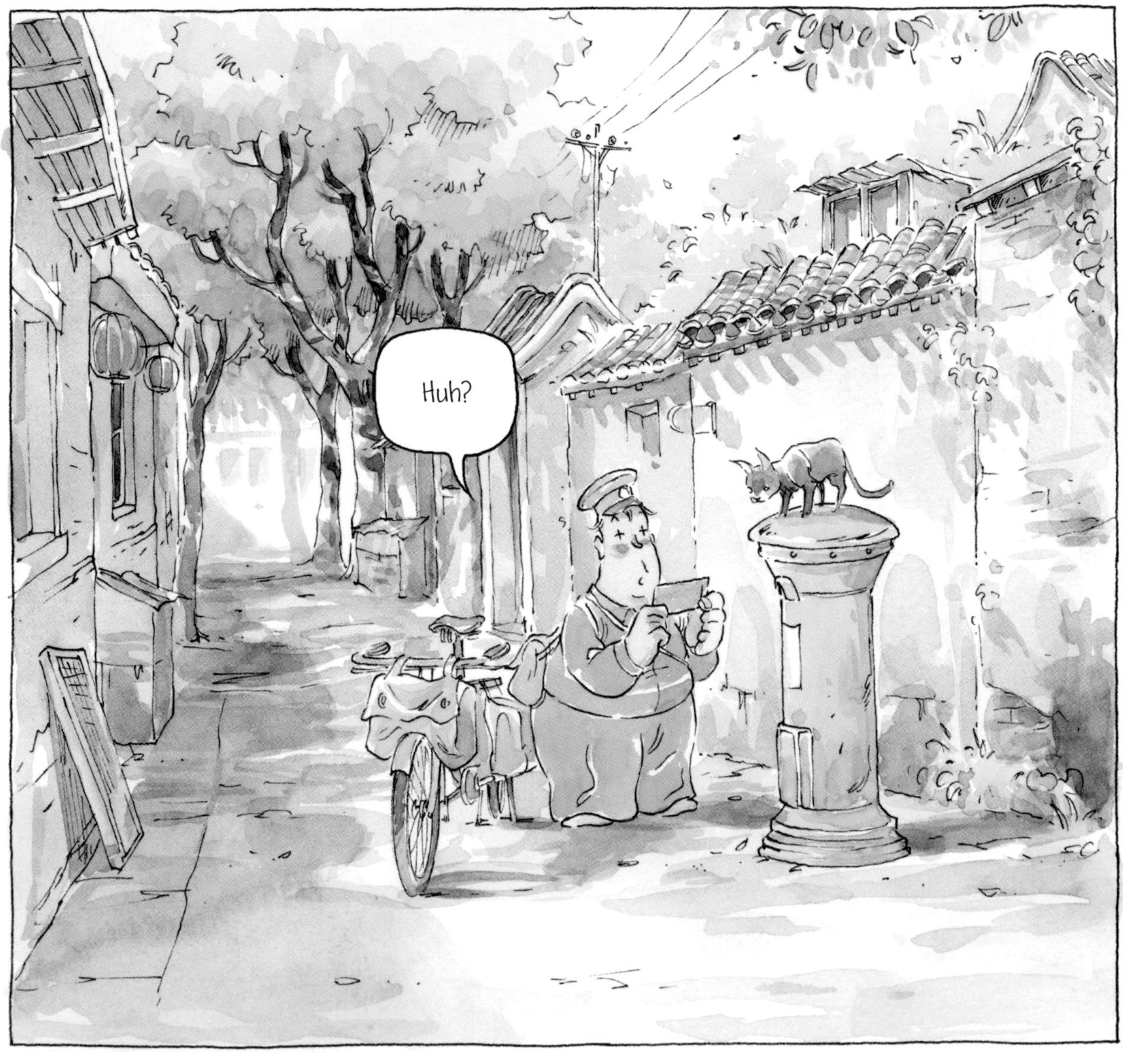
Huh?

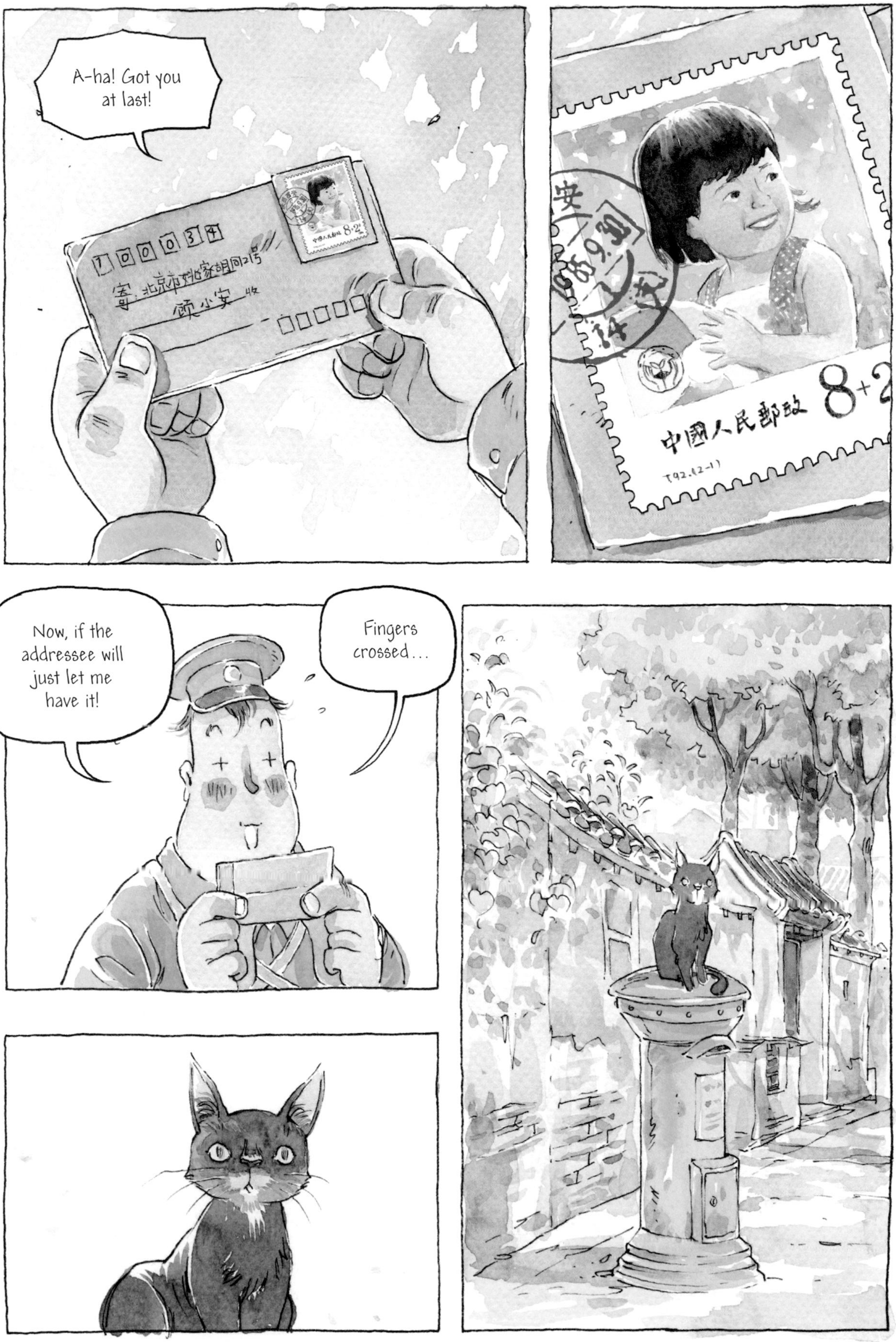
A-ha! Got you at last!
中國人民郵政
8+2
T92.(2-1)
Now, if the addressee will just let me have it!
Fingers crossed...

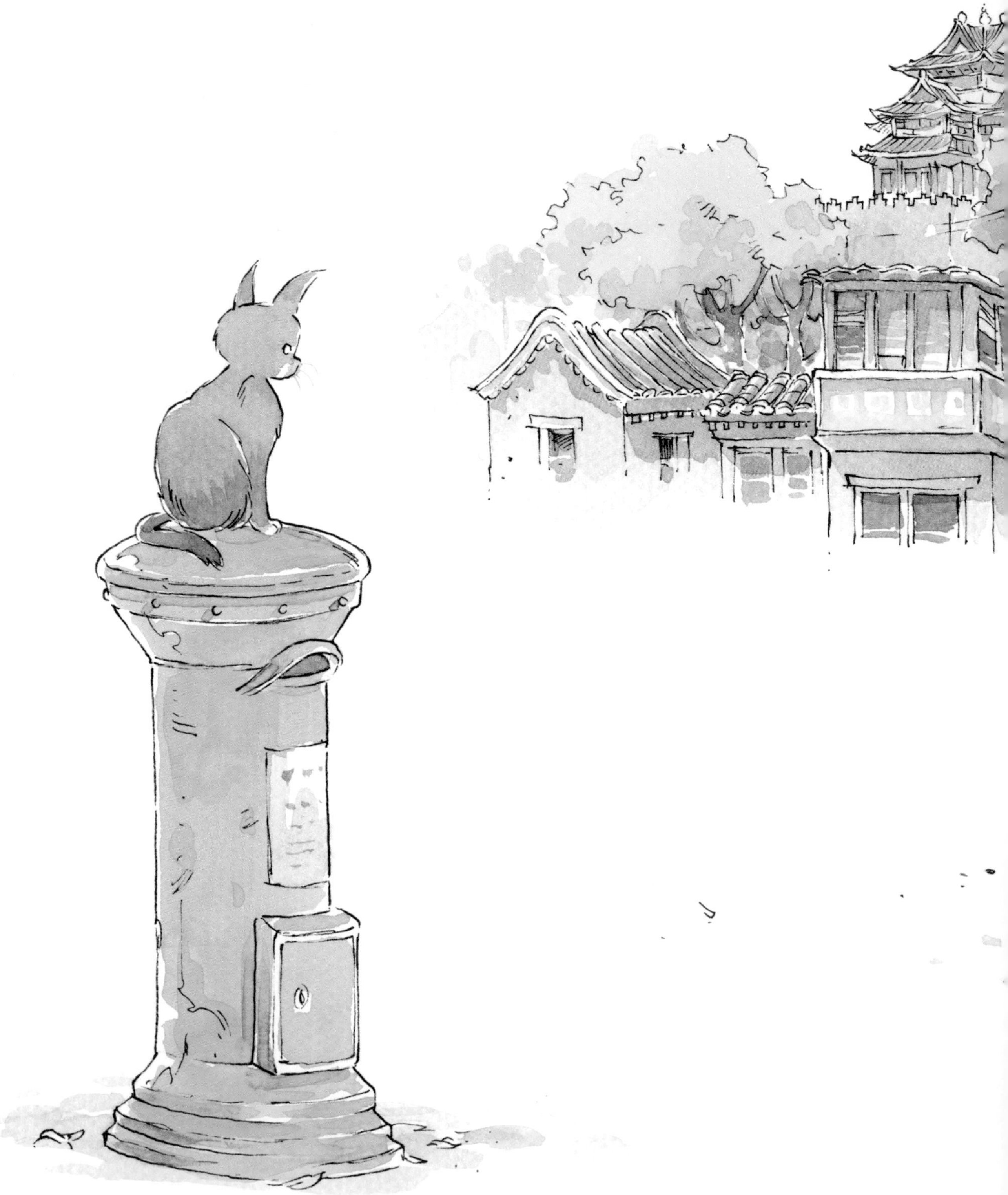

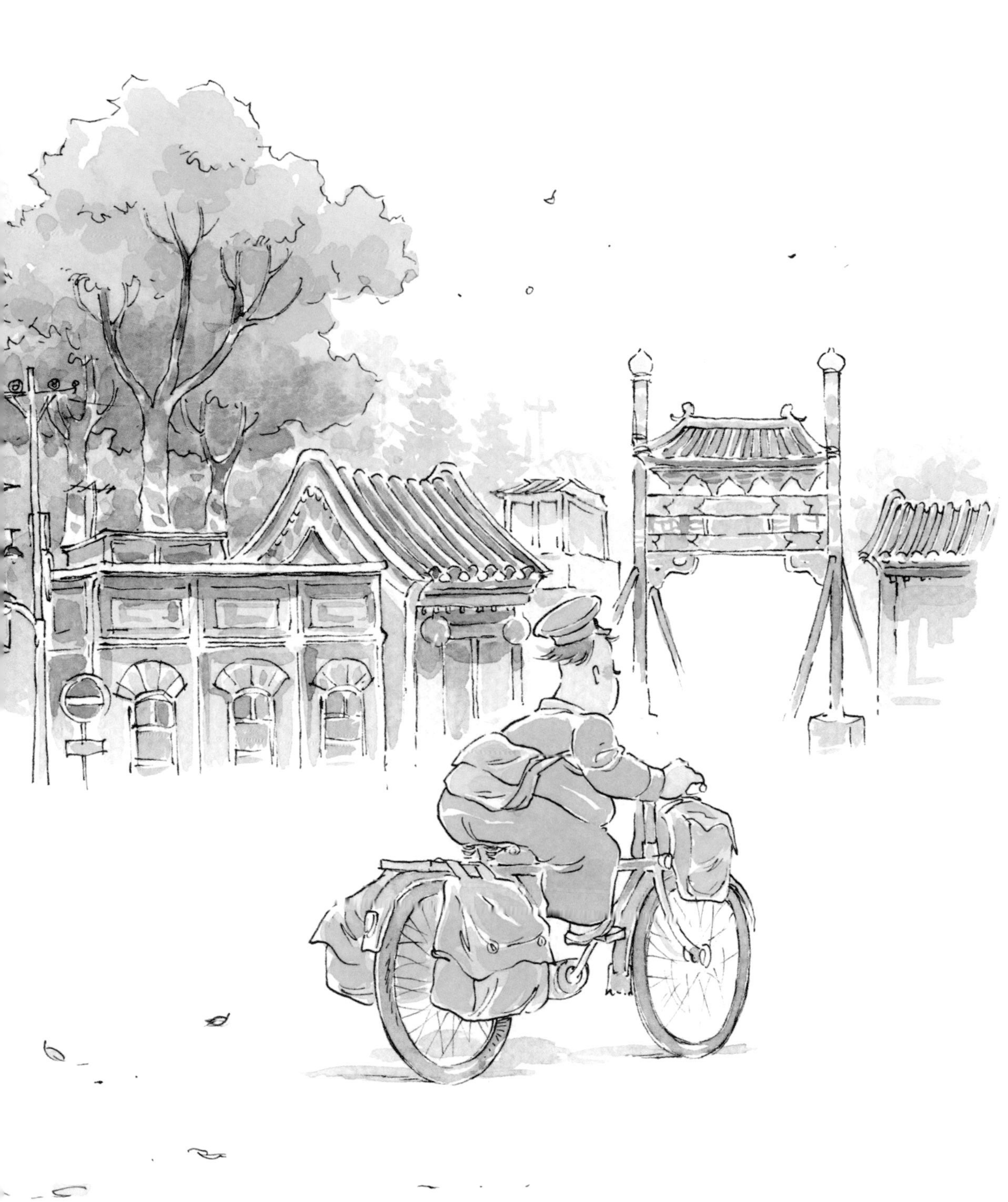

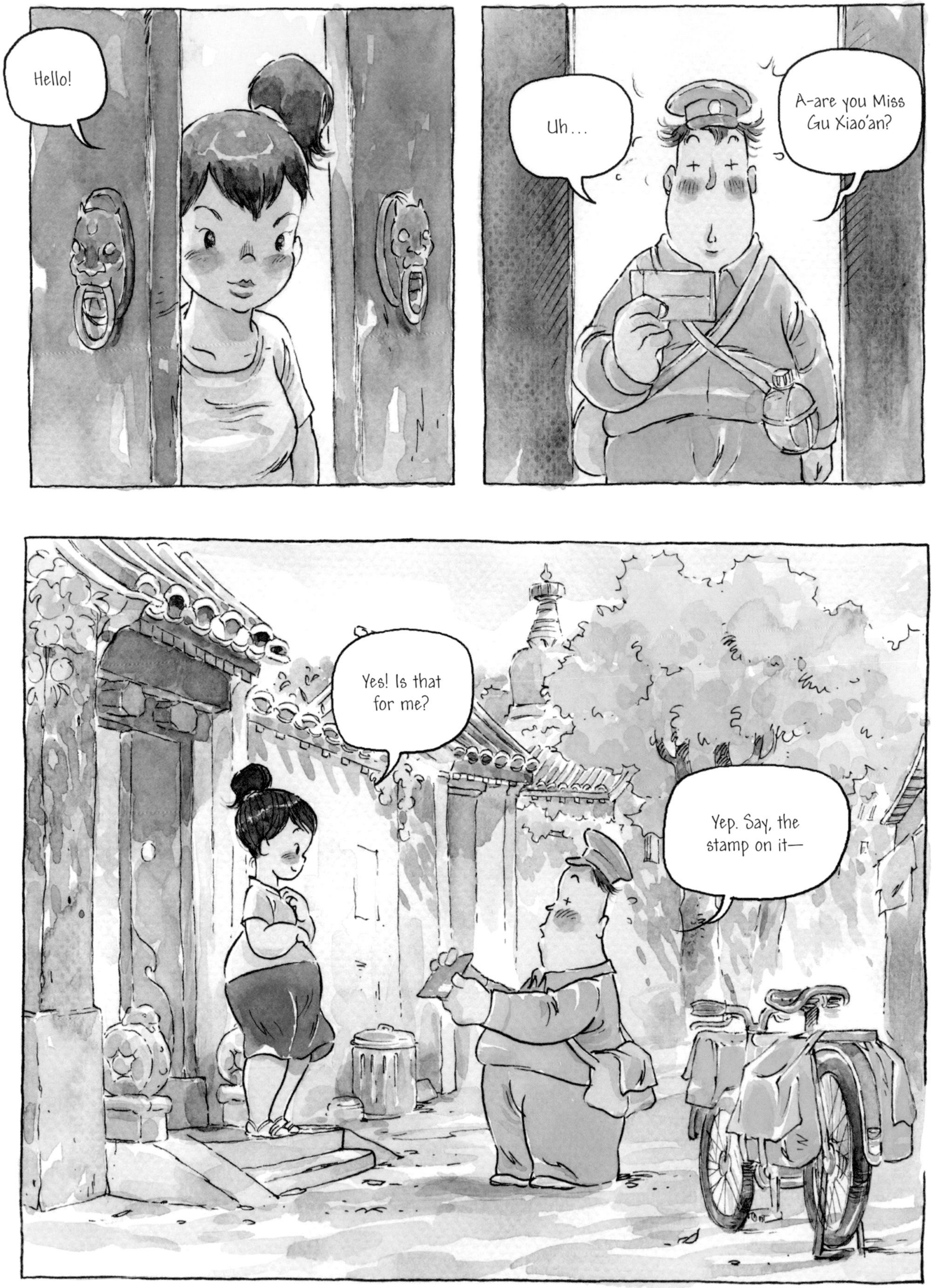
Hello!
Uh...
A-are you Miss Gu Xiao'an?
Yes! Is that for me?
Yep. Say, the stamp on it—

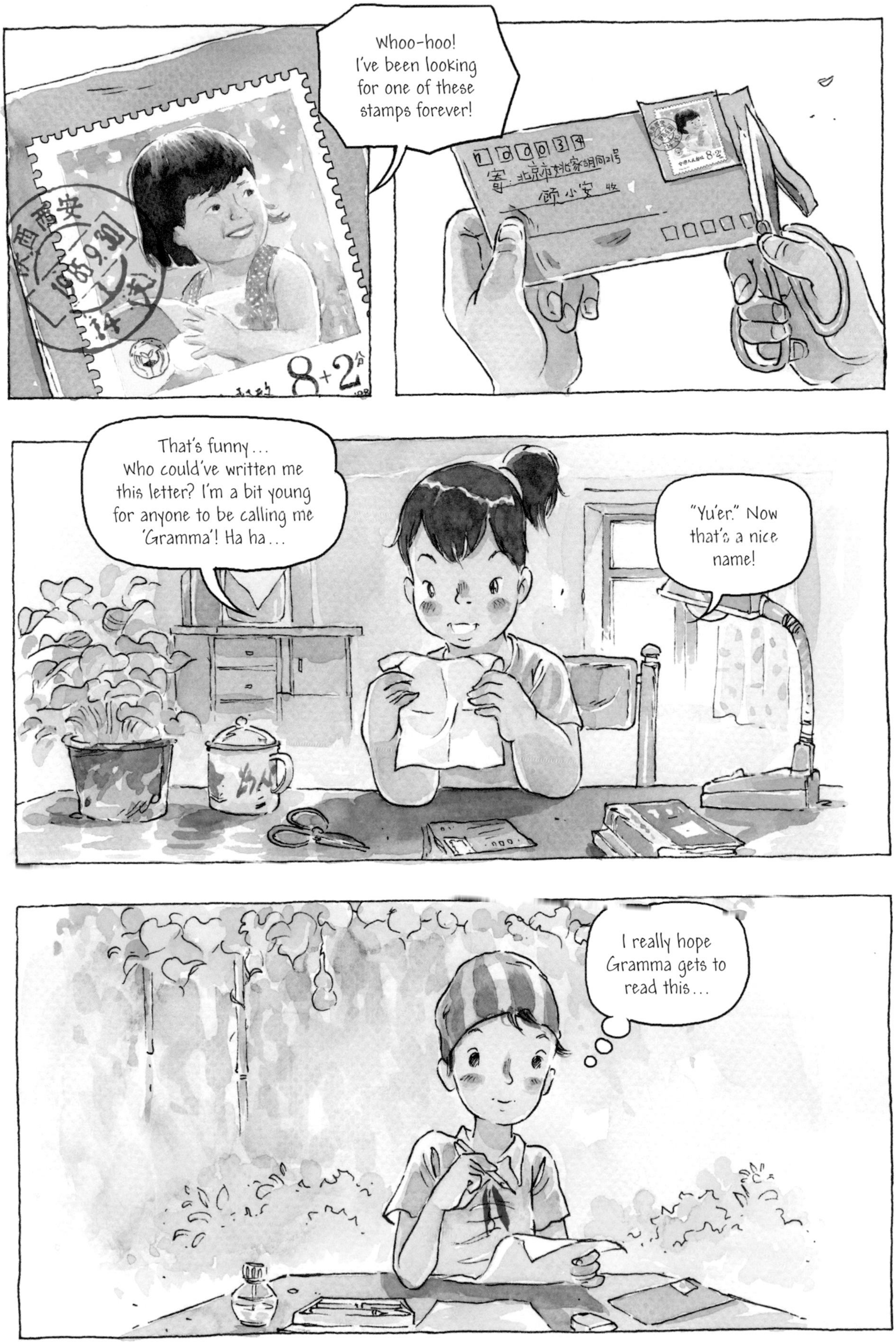
Whoo-hoo! I've been looking for one of these stamps forever!
That's funny... Who could've written me this letter? I'm a bit young for anyone to be calling me 'Gramma'! Ha ha...
"Yu'er." Now that's a nice name!
I really hope Gramma gets to read this...

Dear Gramma

My name is Yu'er. I'm your granddaughter! We sort of met already, in my dream. Grampa thinks about you all the time and misses you a lot. I hope you get this letter. We love you. oh, also—the mailman who comes by your house is really sweet! Be nice to him! Hee hee!

Yu'er

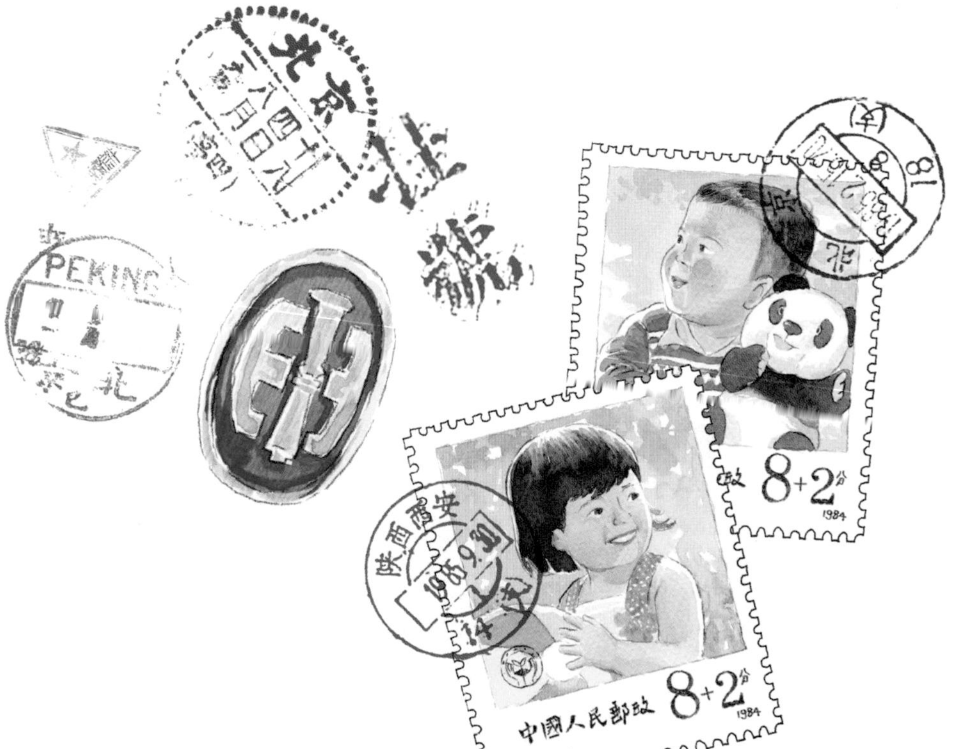
PEKING
8+2
1984

THE END

KIDS AT HEART

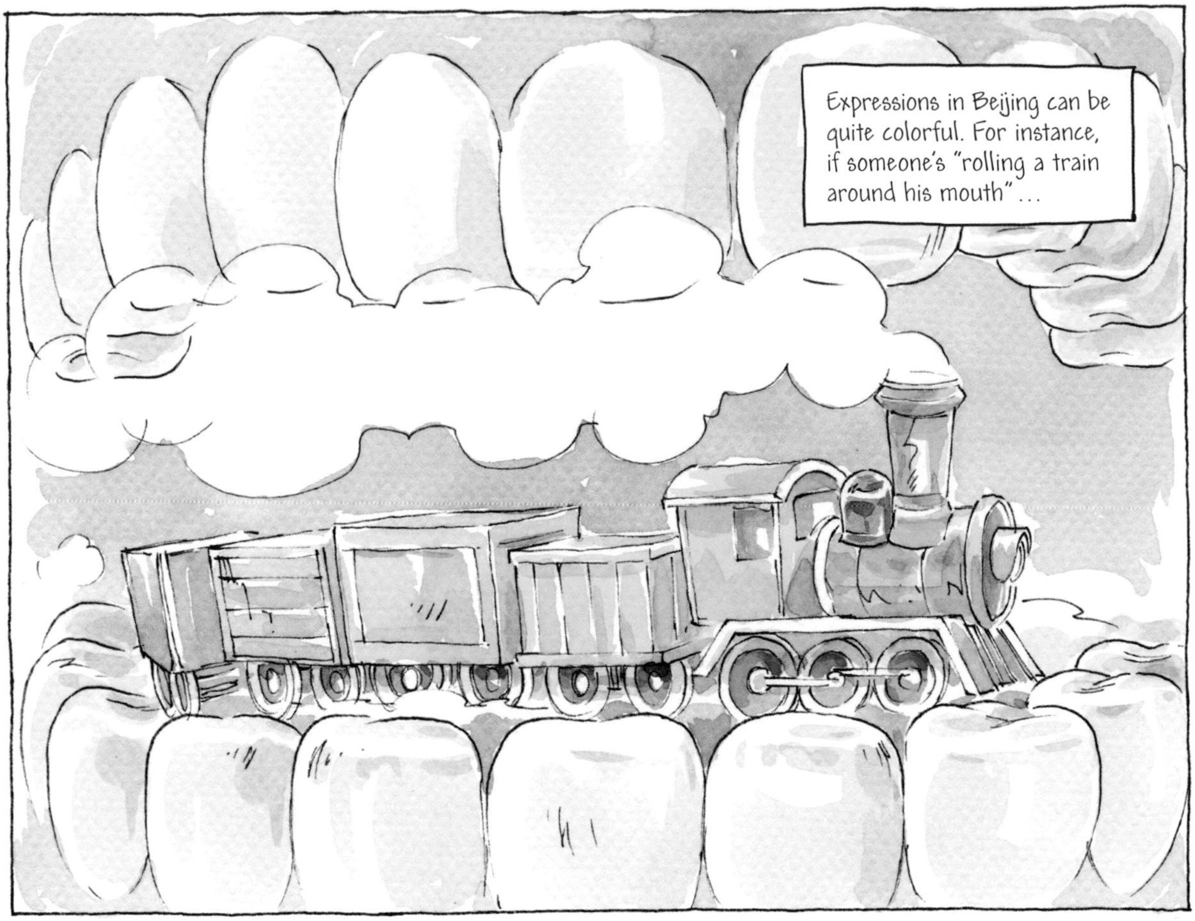
Expressions in Beijing can be quite colorful. For instance, if someone's "rolling a train around his mouth"...

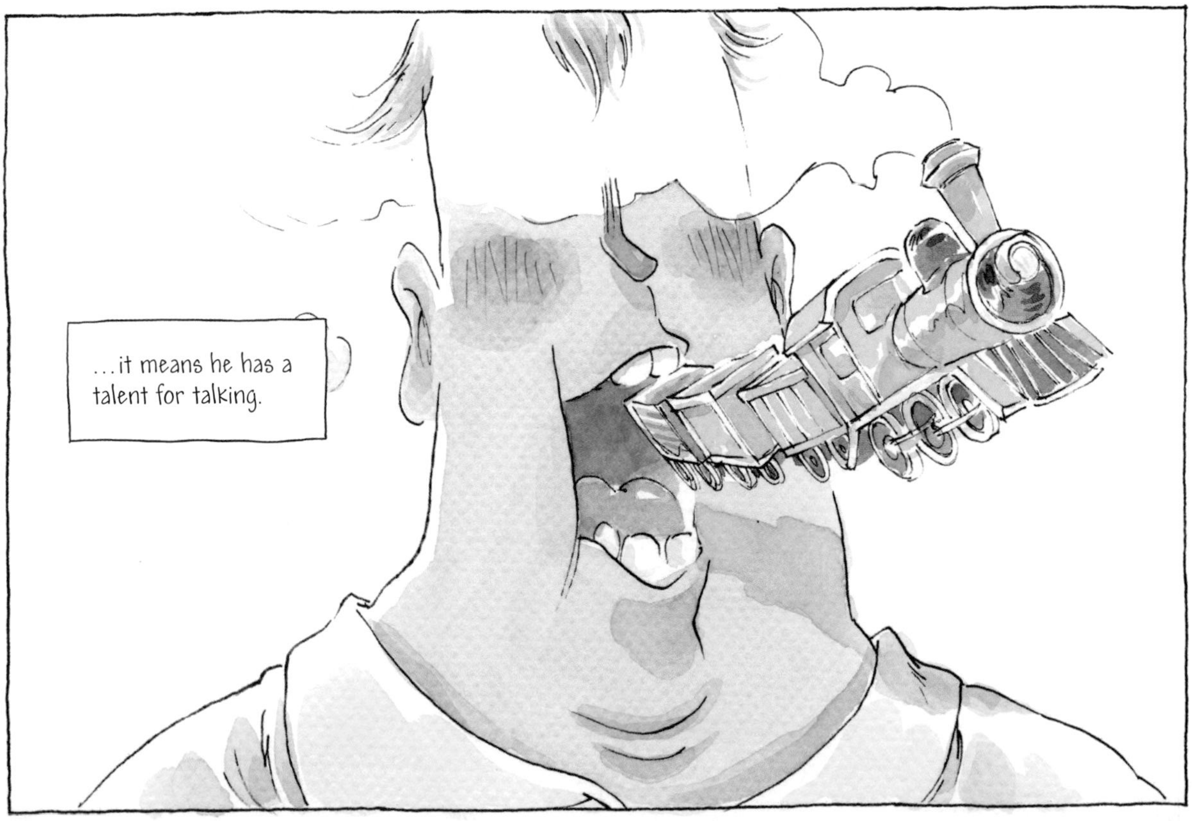
...it means he has a talent for talking.

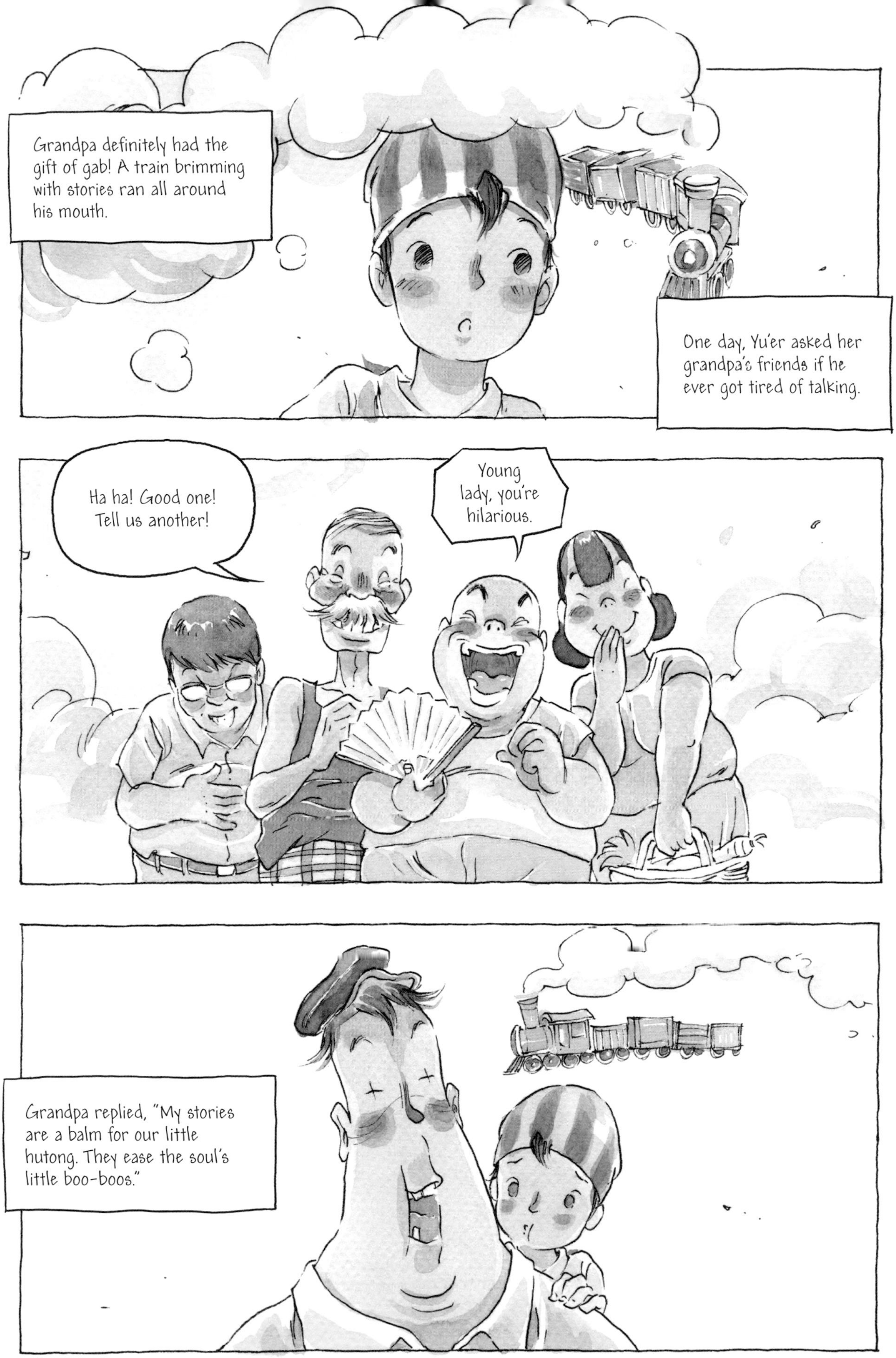
Grandpa definitely had the gift of gab! A train brimming with stories ran all around his mouth.
One day, Yu'er asked her grandpa's friends if he ever got tired of talking.
Ha ha! Good one! Tell us another!
Young lady, you're hilarious.
Grandpa replied, "My stories are a balm for our little hutong. They ease the soul's little boo-boos."

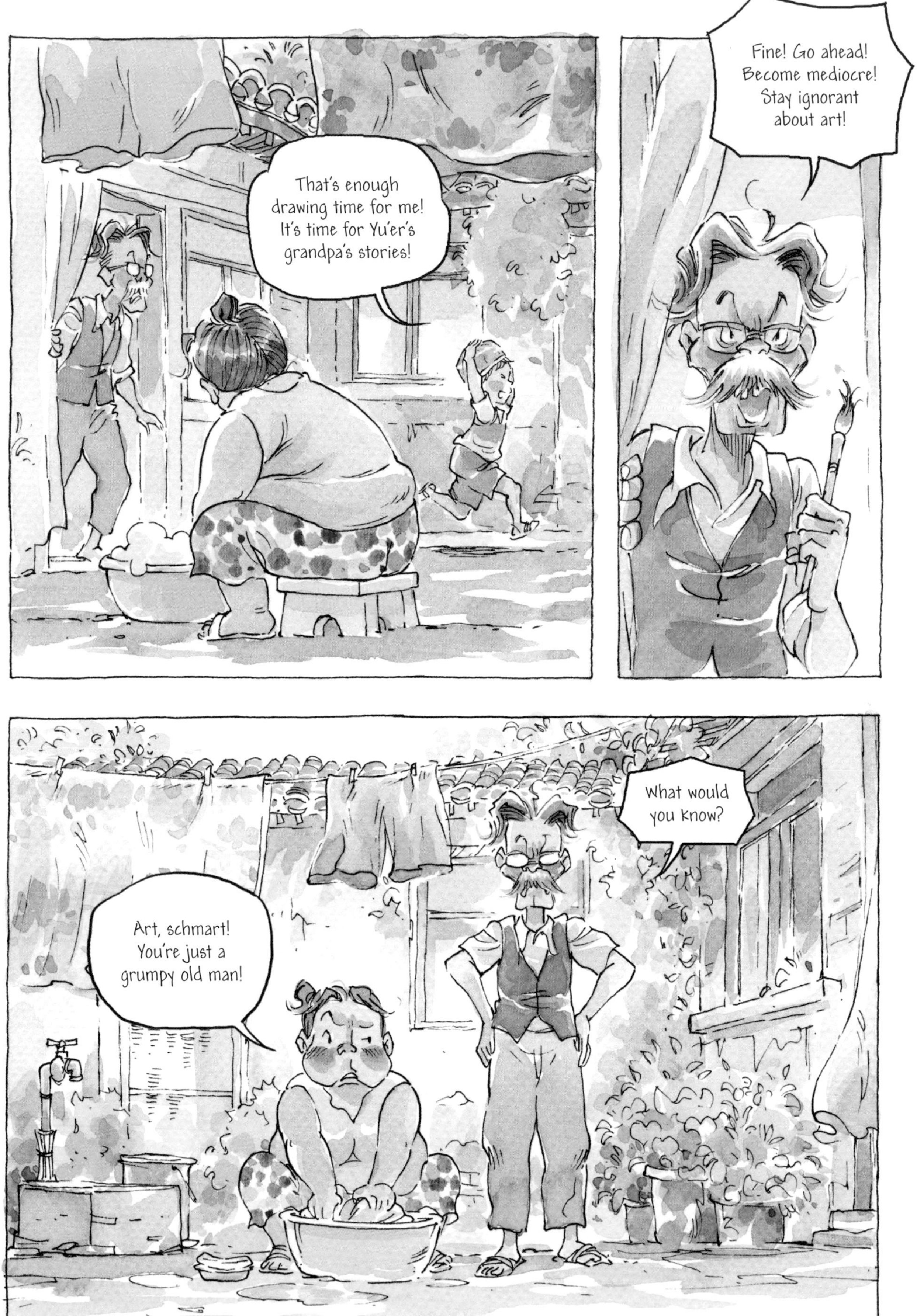
That's enough drawing time for me! It's time for Yu'er's grandpa's stories!
Fine! Go ahead! Become mediocre! Stay ignorant about art!
What would you know?
Art, schmart! You're just a grumpy old man!

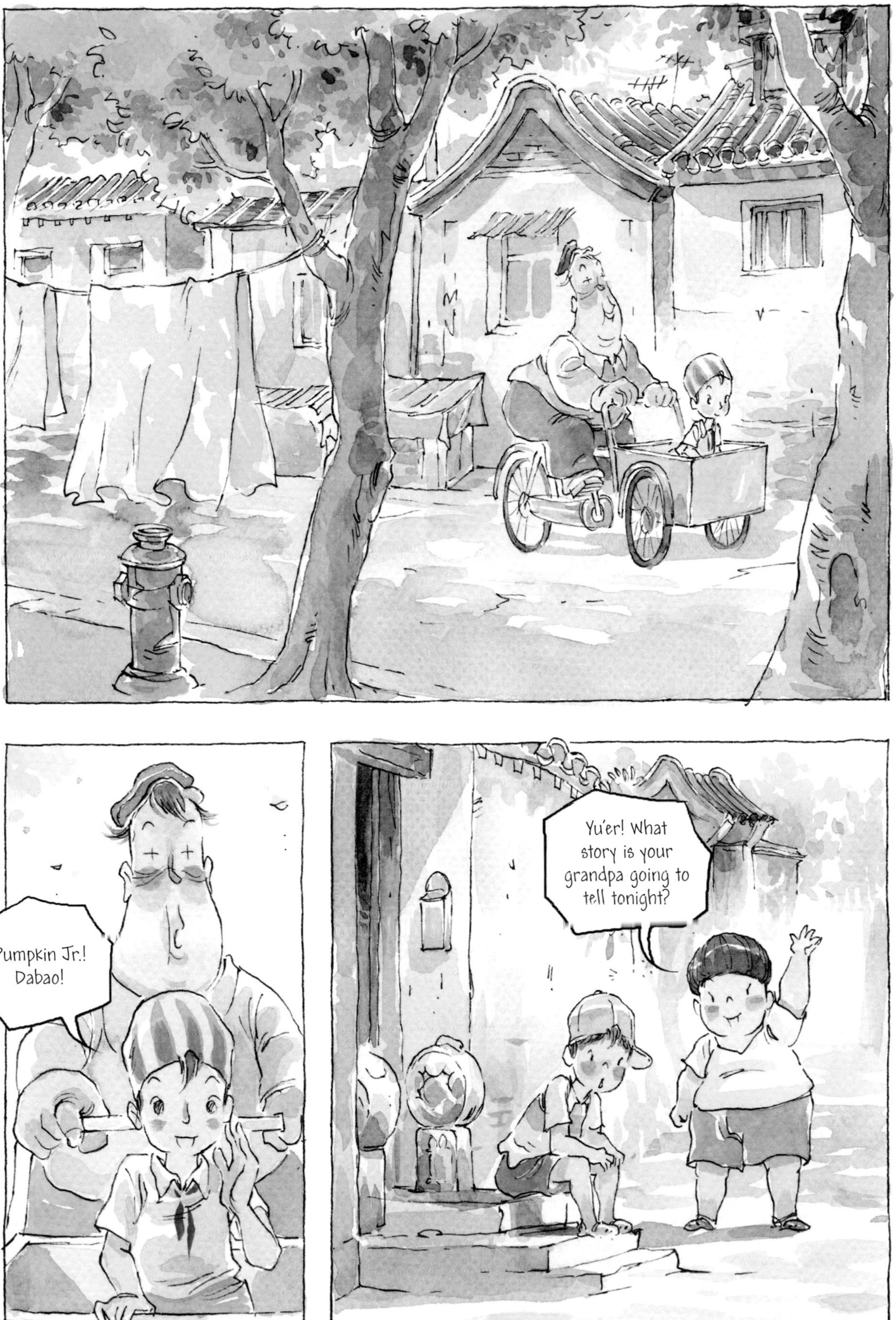
Pumpkin Jr.! Dabao!
Yu'er! What story is your grandpa going to tell tonight?

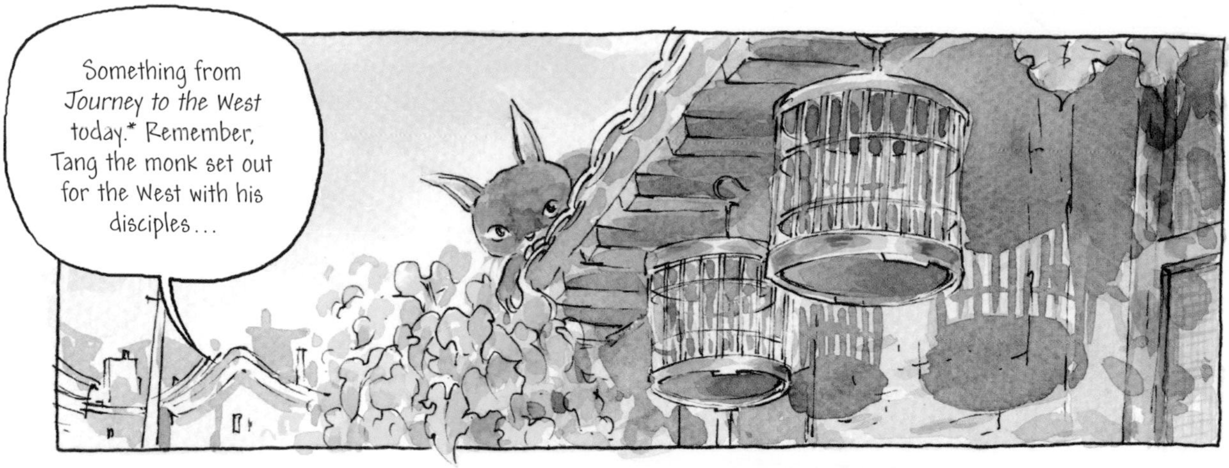
Something from *Journey to the West* today.* Remember, Tang the monk set out for the West with his disciples…

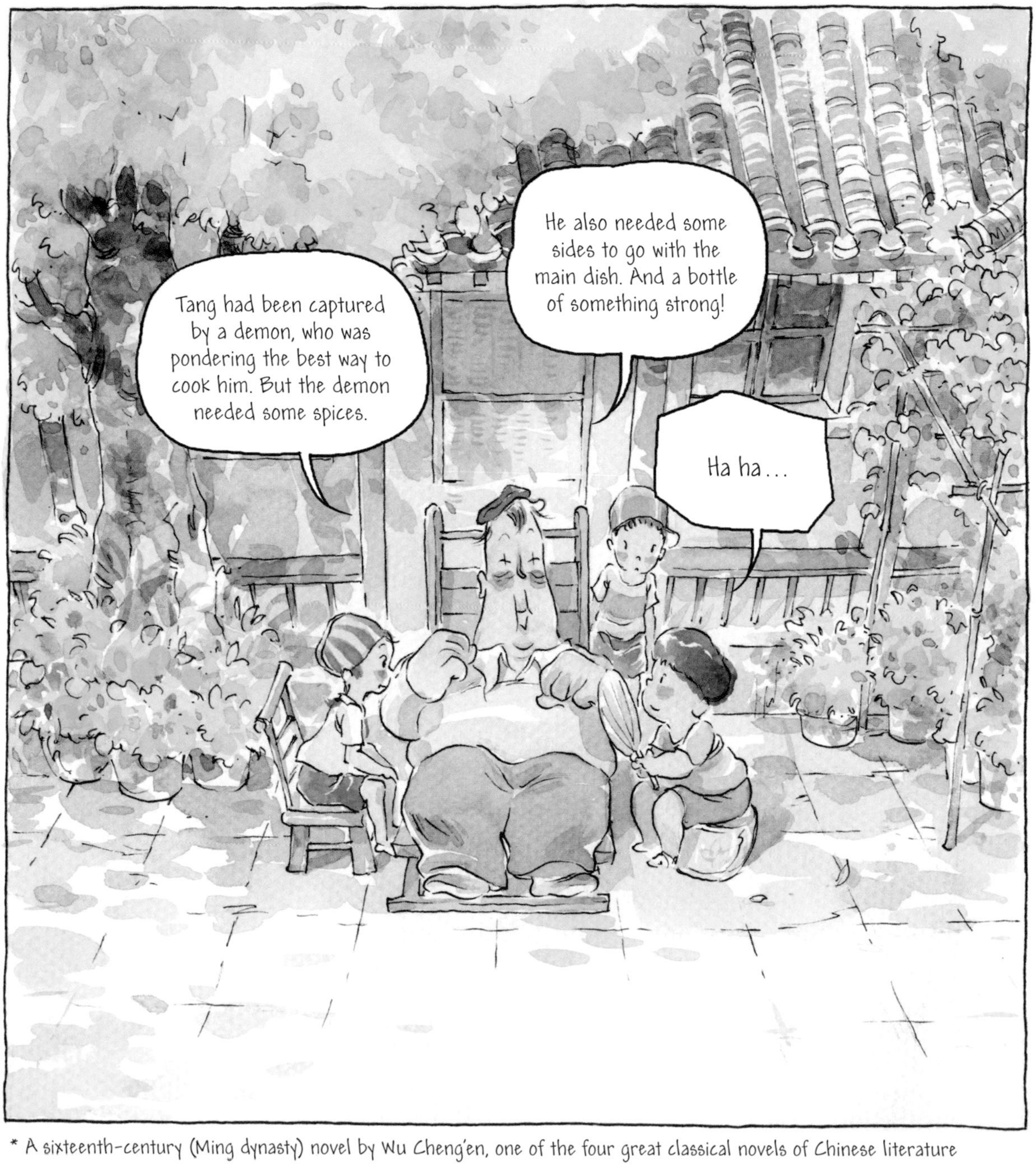
Tang had been captured by a demon, who was pondering the best way to cook him. But the demon needed some spices.
He also needed some sides to go with the main dish. And a bottle of something strong!
Ha ha…

* A sixteenth-century (Ming dynasty) novel by Wu Cheng'en, one of the four great classical novels of Chinese literature

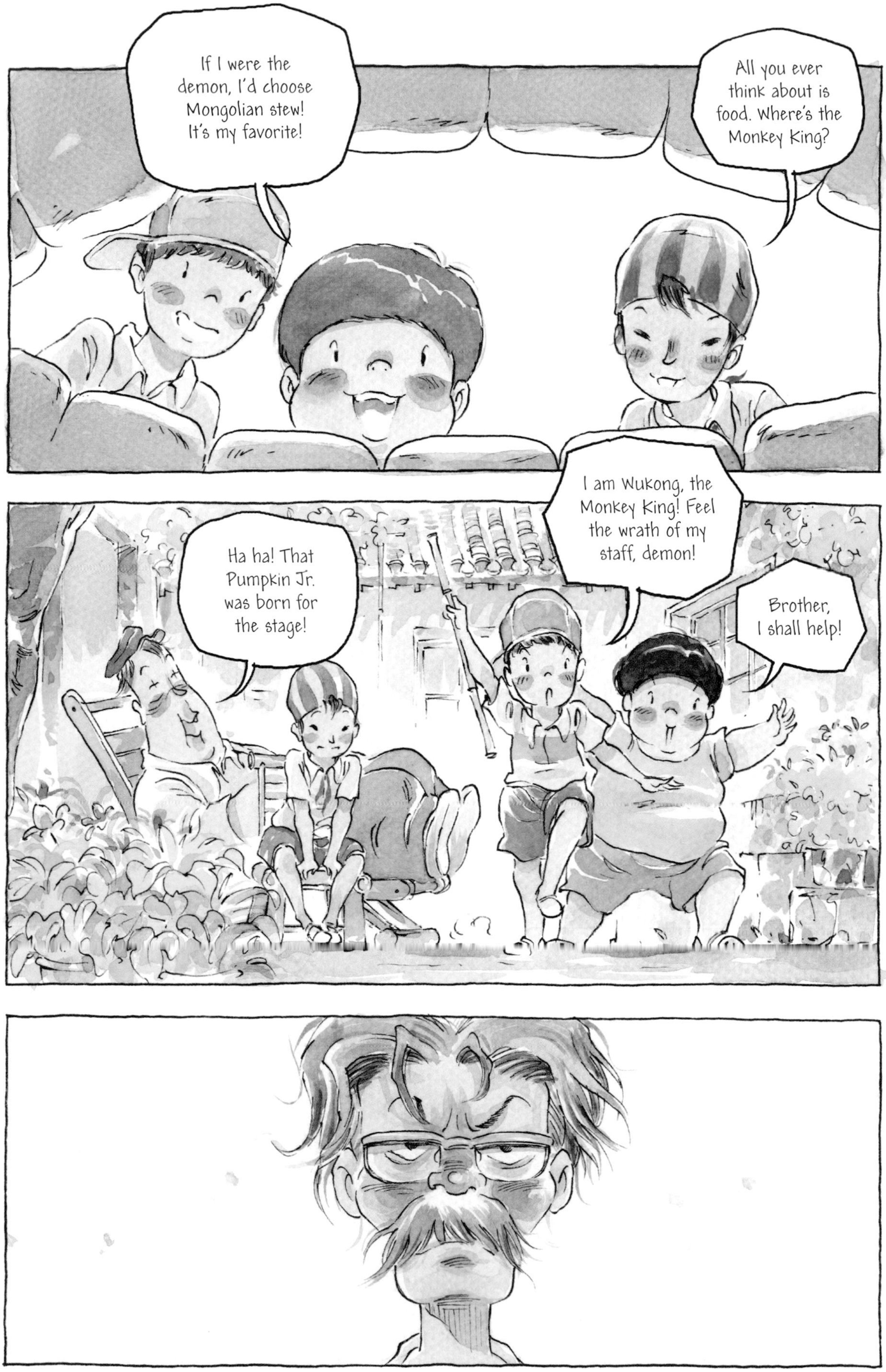
If I were the demon, I'd choose Mongolian stew! It's my favorite!
All you ever think about is food. Where's the Monkey King?
Ha ha! That Pumpkin Jr. was born for the stage!
I am Wukong, the Monkey King! Feel the wrath of my staff, demon!
Brother, I shall help!

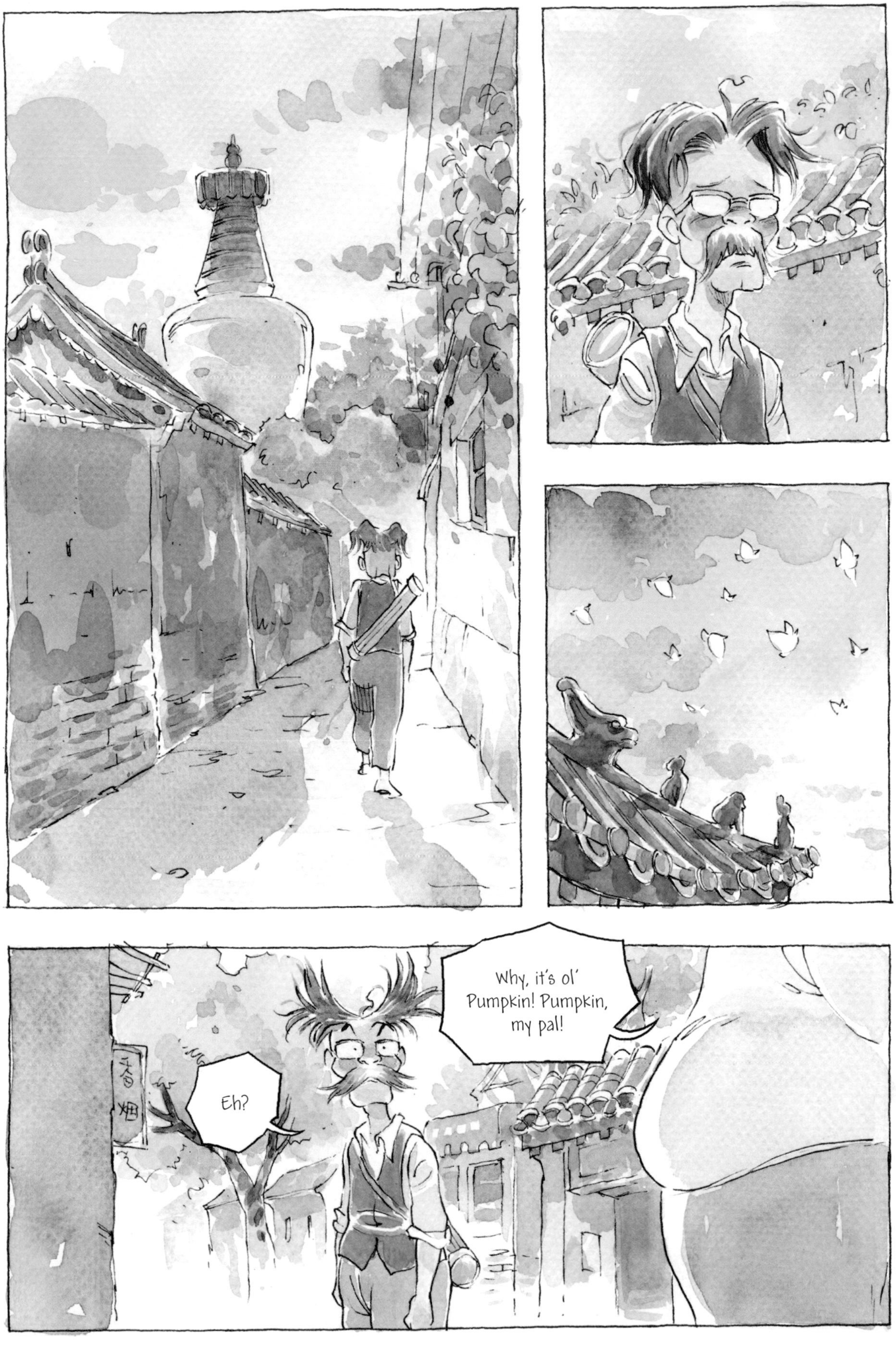
Why, it's ol' Pumpkin! Pumpkin, my pal!
Eh?
香烟

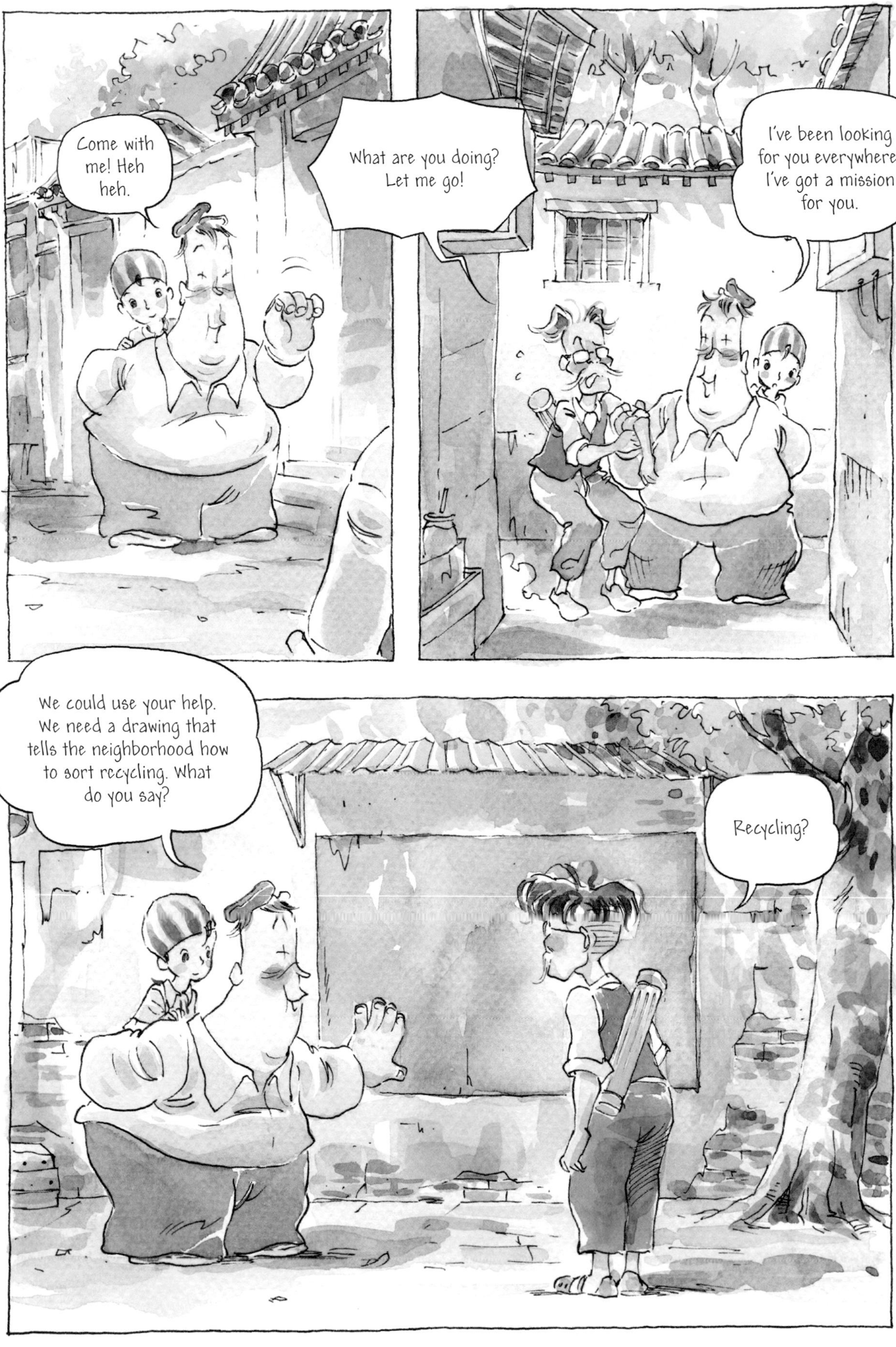
Come with me! Heh heh.
What are you doing? Let me go!
I've been looking for you everywhere! I've got a mission for you.
We could use your help. We need a drawing that tells the neighborhood how to sort recycling. What do you say?
Recycling?

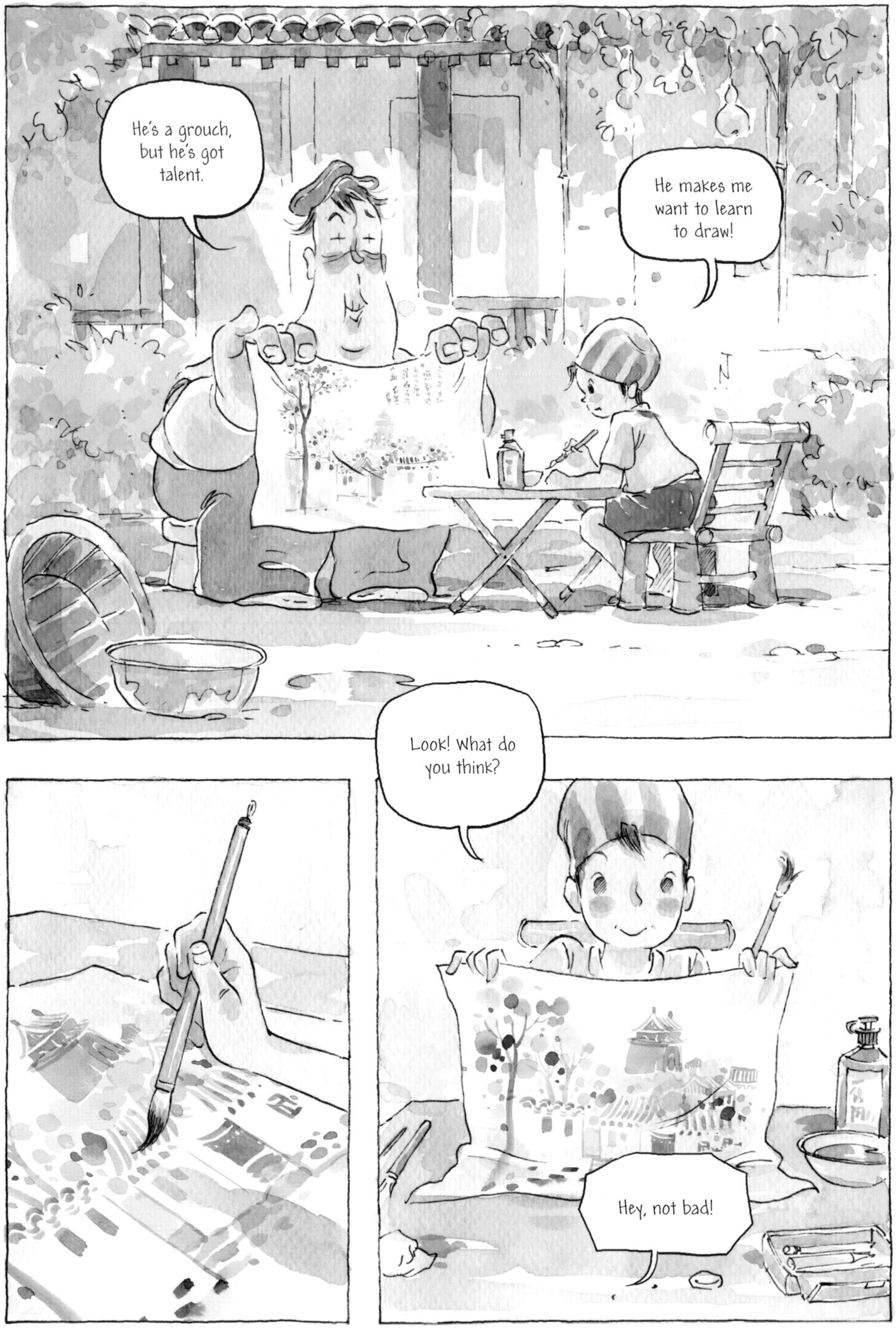
He's a grouch, but he's got talent.
He makes me want to learn to draw!
Look! What do you think?
Hey, not bad!

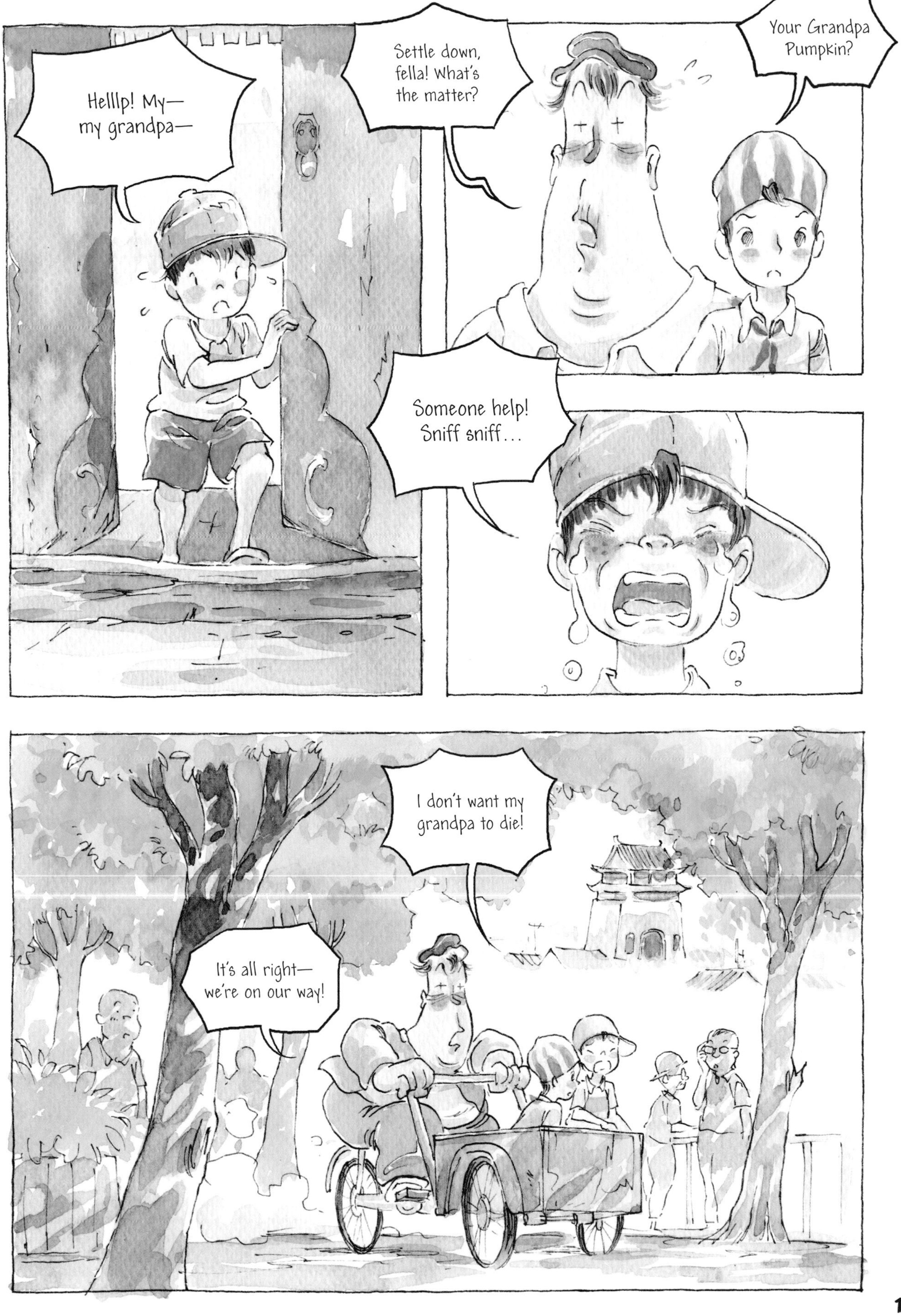
Helllp! My—
my grandpa—
Settle down,
fella! What's
the matter?
Your Grandpa
Pumpkin?
Someone help!
Sniff sniff...
I don't want my
grandpa to die!
It's all right—
we're on our way!

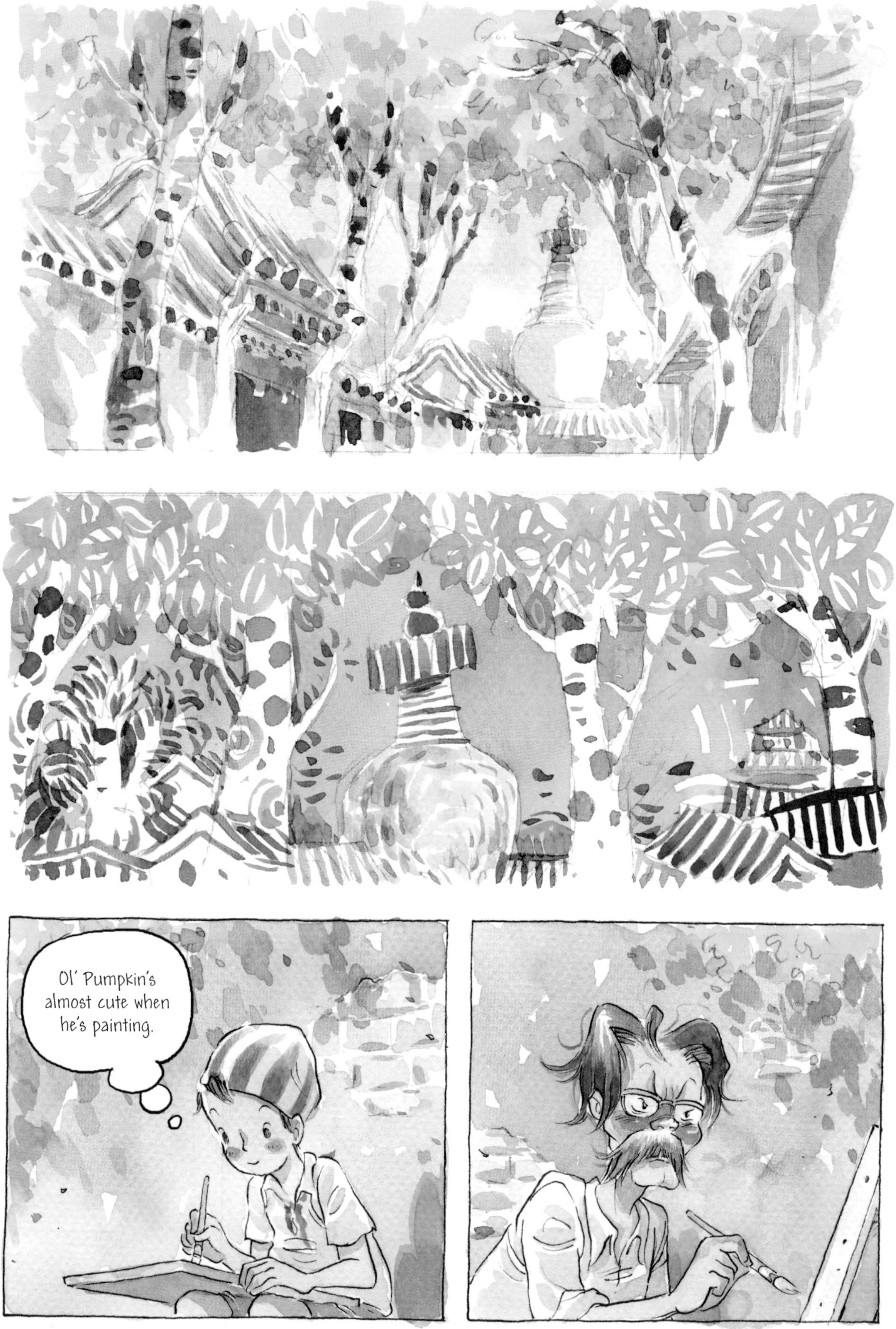
Ol' Pumpkin's almost cute when he's painting.

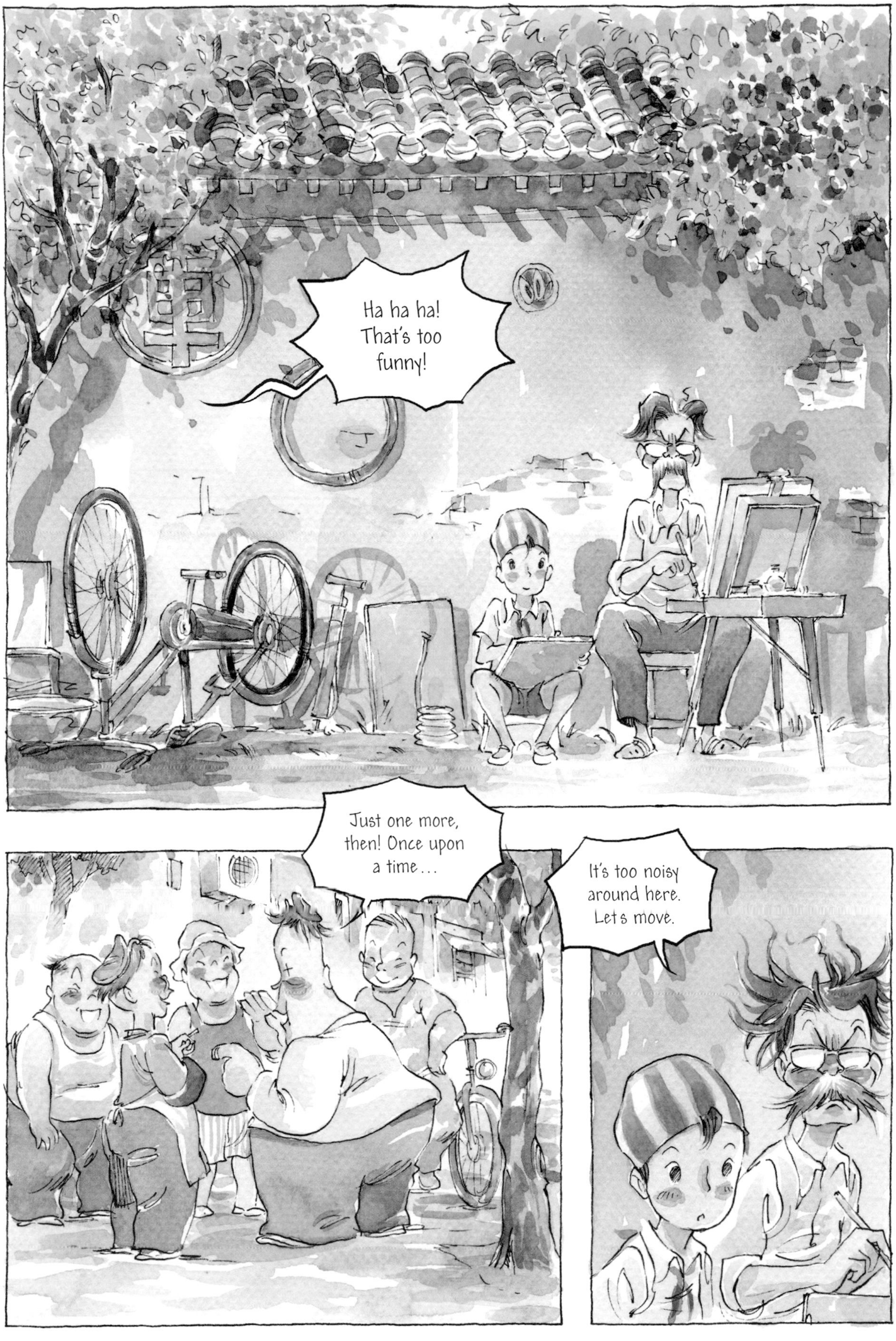
Ha ha ha! That's too funny!
Just one more, then! Once upon a time…
It's too noisy around here. Lets move.

THE END

A HUTONG SKETCHBOOK

Beijing is a city in the northern area of the People's Republic of China. It also serves as the country's capital. Beijing has one of the largest populations of any city across the world. It is home to more than 21,500,000 people. It has been China's capital during most points in Chinese history from 1297 onward. (The capital was elsewhere from 1368 to 1420 and from 1928 to 1949.) Both new buildings and older, more traditional spaces make up modern Beijing.

In *My Beijing*, Yu'er, her grandfather, and their neighbors live in an area known as a hutong. In a hutong, courtyard houses form a narrow lane or alleyway. The grounds of these houses have yards on the inside, beyond the houses' living spaces. Side by side, the homes' outer walls create the space of the hutong. Hutongs often join together to make larger neighborhoods.

Hutongs have been a part of Beijing's culture for hundreds of years. People began to create these spaces during China's Yuan dynasty (ca. 1271–1368). More hutongs appeared during the Ming (ca. 1368–1644) and Qing (ca. 1644–1912) dynasties. These neighborhoods capture both a traditional way of building homes and a traditional type of community. In more recent decades, many of Beijing's hutongs and surrounding homes were destroyed to create room for new buildings. However, other hutongs are treated as protected areas. They are also popular travel stops for visitors to Beijing.

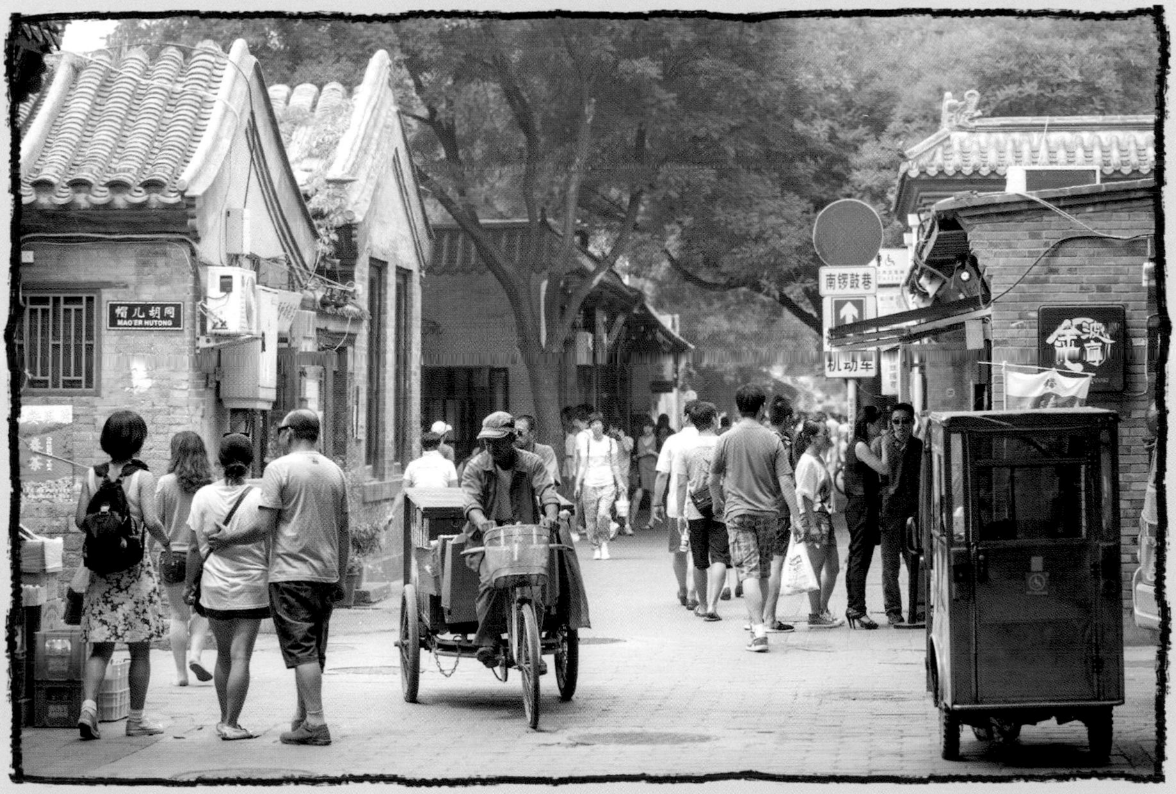
帽儿胡同
MAO'ER HUTONG
南锣鼓巷
机动车

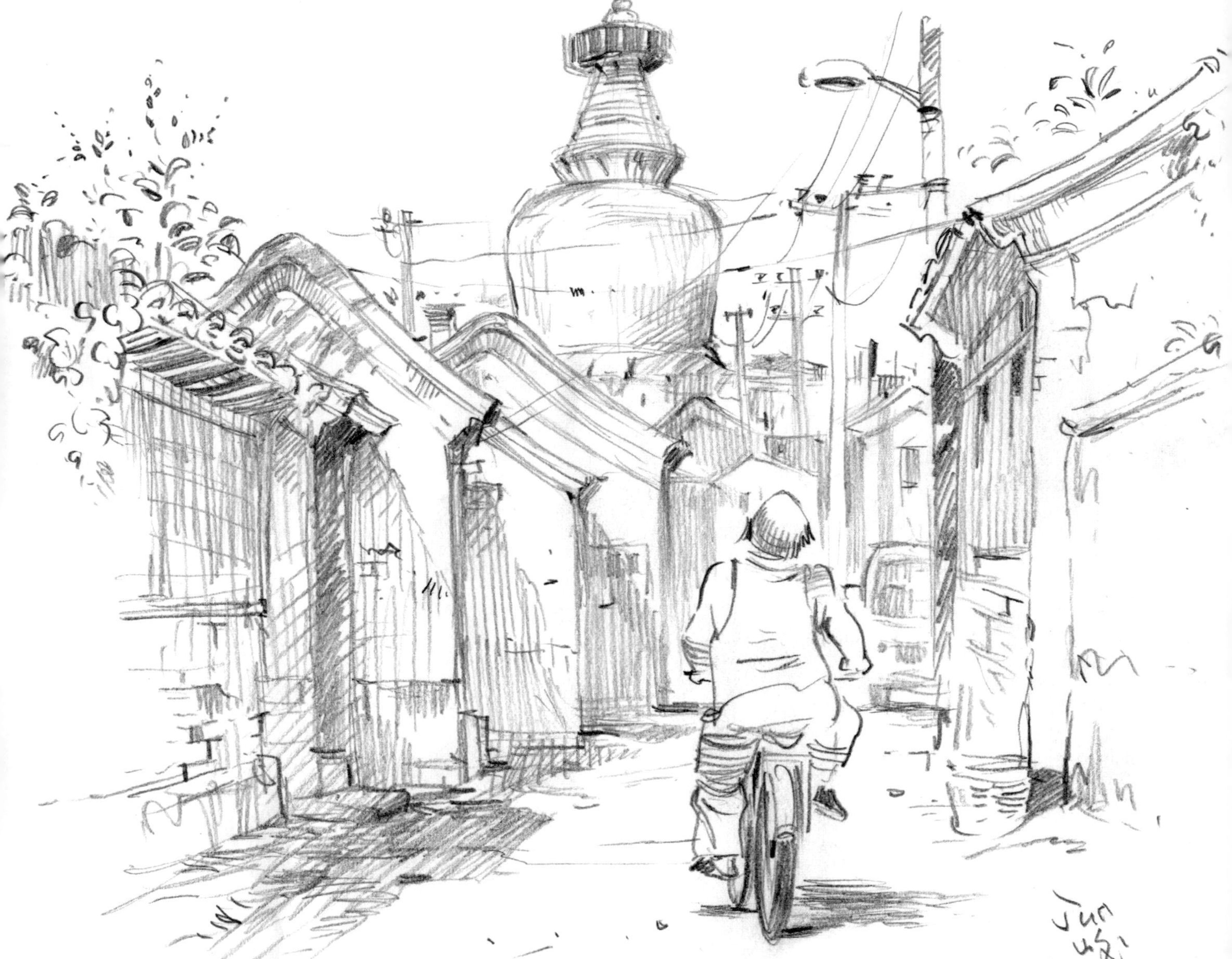

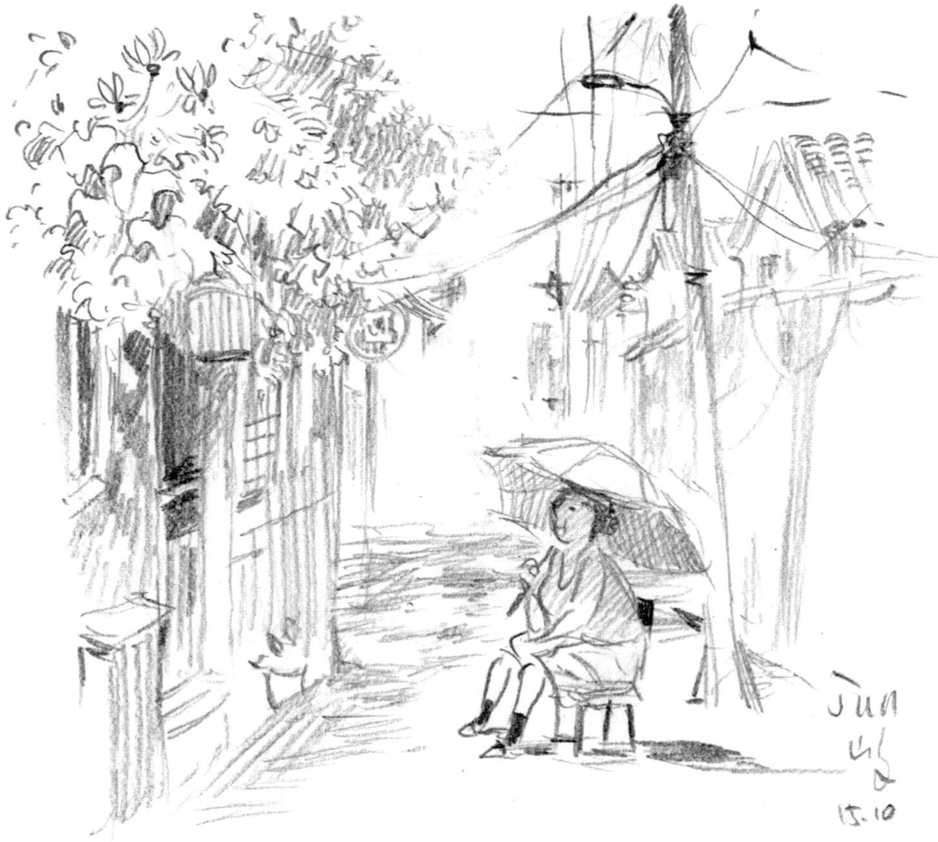
Jun
15.10

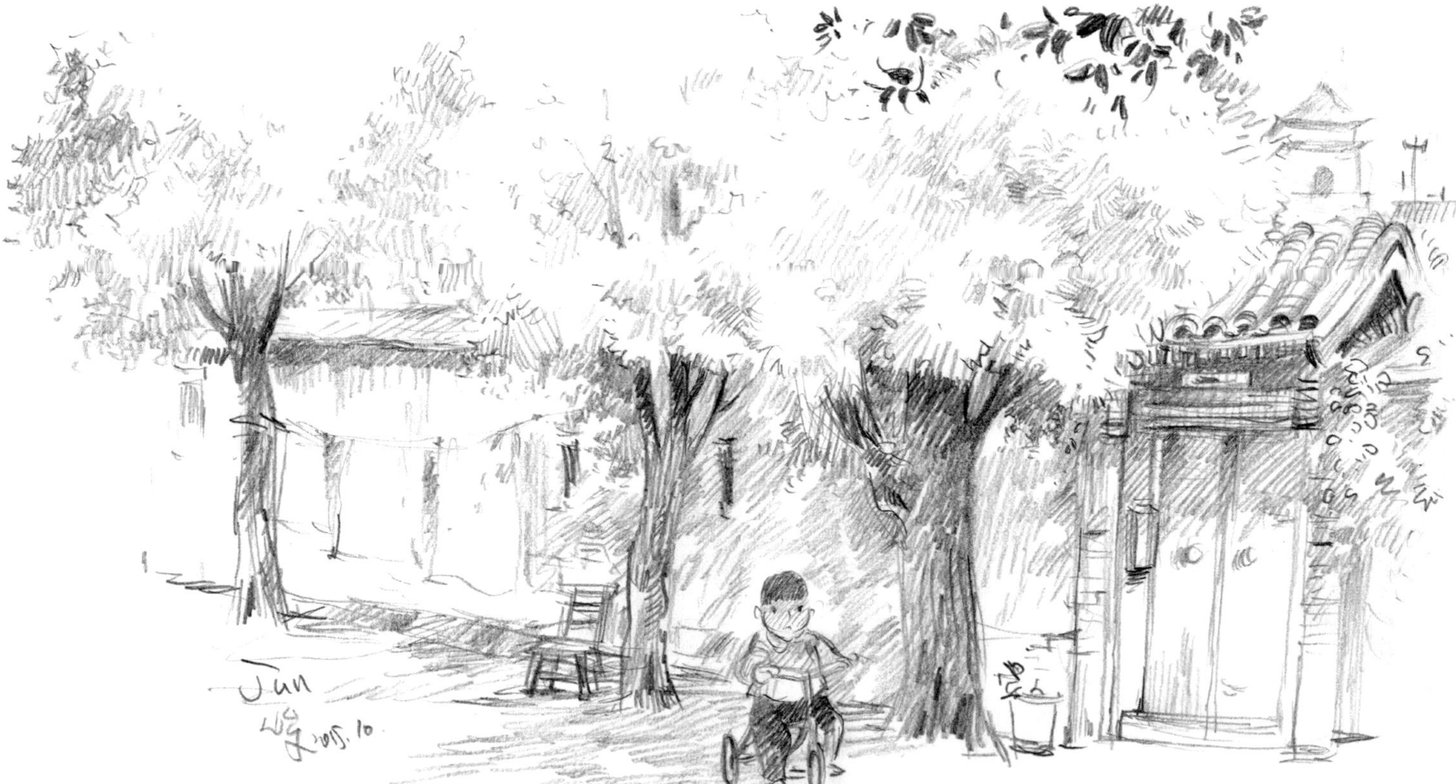
Jun
2015.10

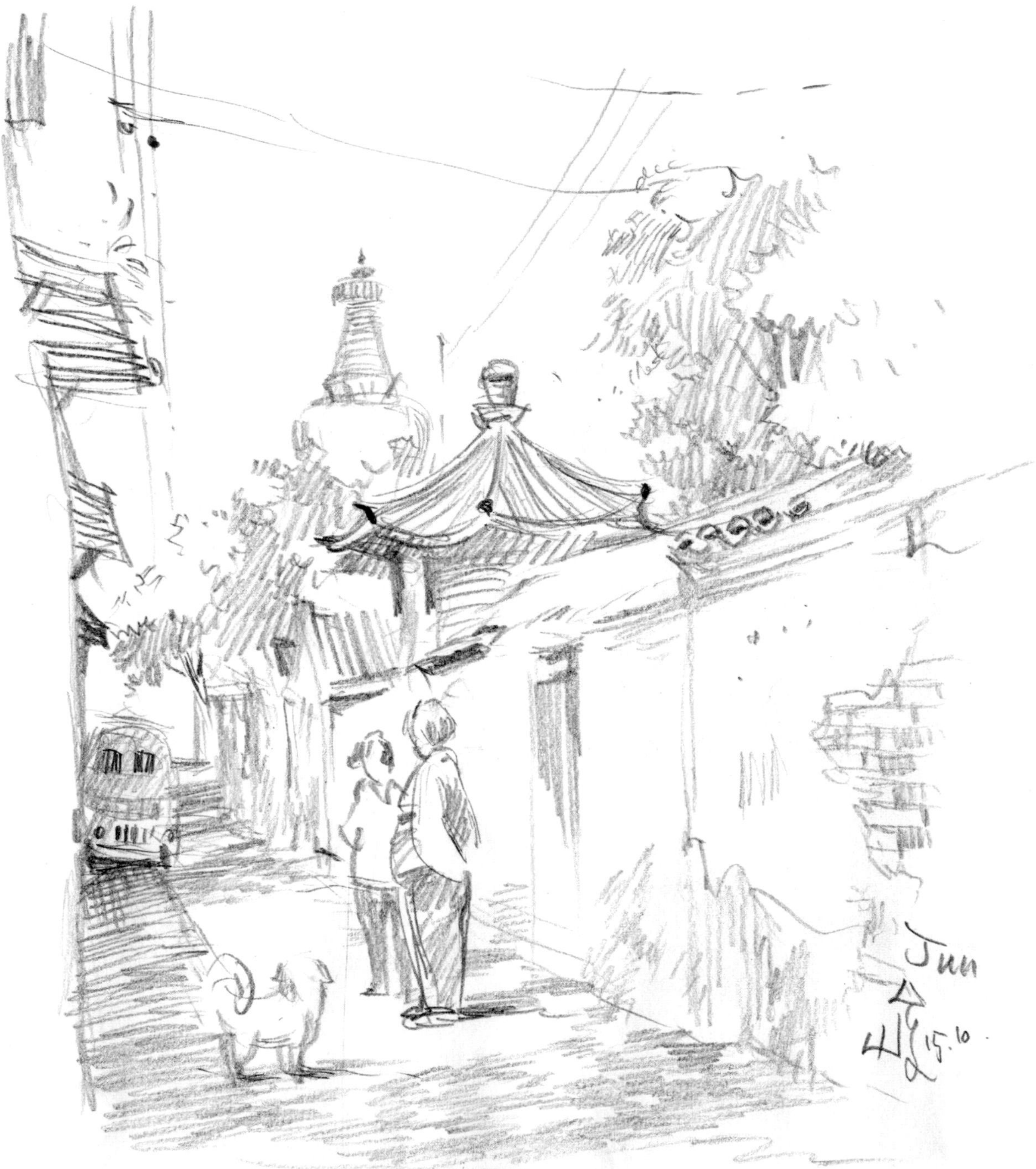
Jun
15.10

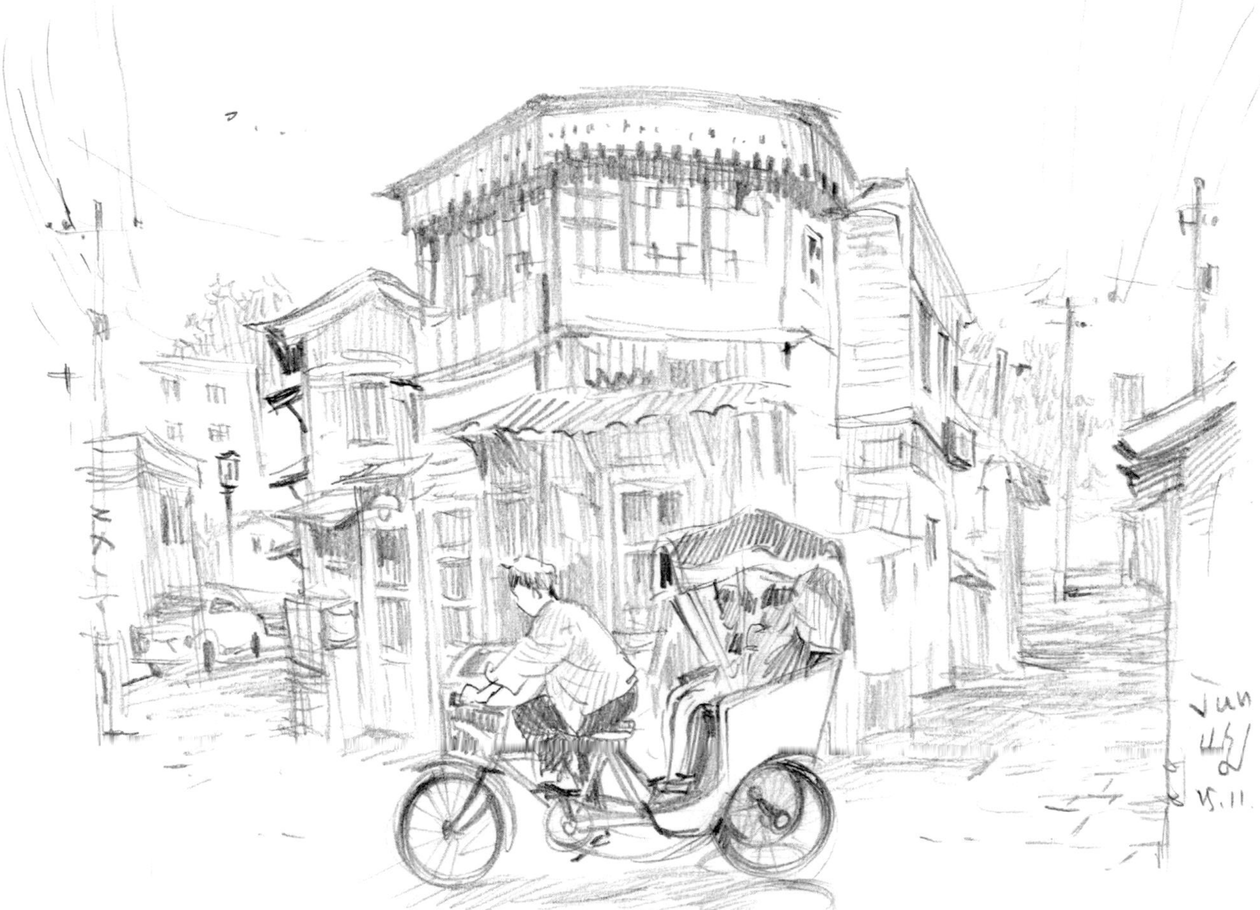
Jun
15.11

ABOUT THE AUTHOR

Nie Jun was born in 1975 in Xining, in the province of Qinghai, China. He began drawing at an early age by copying *lianhuanhua* (traditional Chinese palm-sized picture books of sequential art). He soon became a fan of Osamu Tezuka, Zhang Leping, and black-and-white pirated editions of Tintin. As a teenager, he won a contest sponsored by a comics magazine and had his drawings published for the first time. Later, he was deeply influenced by the range of works within the Chinese comics scene, as well as by Japanese artists Akira Toriyama and Katsuhiro Otomo, not to mention Moebius (the French cartoonist Jean Giraud). In 1995 he began to publish his art in magazines. He lives in Beijing and teaches drawing to university students.